TOM DELONGE PRESENTS

CATHEDRALS OF GLASS

A PLANET OF BLOOD AND ICE

BY NEW YORK TIMES BESTSELLING AUTHOR

A.J. HARTLEY

To The Stars, Inc.
1051 S. Coast Hwy 101 Suite B, Encinitas, CA 92024
ToTheStars.Media
To The Stars… is a trademark of *To The Stars, Inc.*

Editor: Elizabeth Law
Copy Editor: Tom Willkens
Managing Editor: Kari DeLonge
Consulting: Booktrix
Book Design by Lamp Post

Manufactured in the United States of America

ISBN 978-1-943272-26-6 (Hard Cover trade)
ISBN 978-1-943272-24-2 (Hard Cover Limited Edition)
978-1-943272-25-9 (eBook)

Distributed worldwide by Simon & Schuster

DEDICATION

*For Finie and Sebastian, and to all those who feel just
a little out of step with the world around them.*

ACKNOWLEDGEMENTS

Special thanks to those who gave me notes on early drafts of the book: Carrie Ryan, Lissa Price, Stacey Glick, Raven Wei, Lauren Nicholson, Finie Osako and Elizabeth Law, and to Tom DeLonge and all at To The Stars, without whose vision this would not have been published.

FOREWORD
by Tom DeLonge

THERE ARE MANY THINGS IN OUR LIVES THAT WE DON'T understand; for instance, how do our dogs know when we are about to arrive home? Or, how do some mothers feel pain when their children are hurt, even when they are far away? And how did a man bend a spoon with his mind, as witnessed by a powerful head of state?

We don't know the answers to these questions, but there is no disputing that these strange things do happen.

Did you know that scientists proved plants can feel human intent? They proved that the plants knew when they were threatened, cherished and even when their human owners were having sexual intercourse in the next room.

For every grain of sand on all the beaches in the world, there is a synapse in your brain, a connection organically formed to store information, solve problems, and *access the infinite*. Over time, humans are expected to achieve great things "if we put our minds to it," as the saying goes.

When I met AJ Hartley, I had him perfectly matched in my mind to write *Sekret Machines*, a story that spans as much space itself, as it does events connected to consciousness (coming in Book 3). But then AJ mentioned he had another story that he had just written that he called *Eyes in the Dark*. At first, the title seemed too cliché to me, but upon experiencing the story, I realized it made perfect sense. But still, I felt there was something else out there we could find that sounded more poetic, more ominous.

AJ has a gift for words and for imagination. These gifts are displayed in all of his novels. What caught me off-guard this time was something else completely: he was playing with the delicate and diverse perceptions of the human mind. Consciousness itself was a character. That resonated with me, and thus with what To The Stars is all about.

I have about fifty stories I want to tell, so there is not that much room in my kitchen. I'm like a pissed-off grandmother baking on Christmas morning. Don't dare enter! But then here comes this guy with a damned good recipe. And most of it is already cooked. It just needs a nice plate, and a party that is hungry. And here you have our collaboration.

We worked on a new title, and after a series of wordplay and thought clusters, we landed on *Cathedrals of Glass*, a play on the mountainous landscape within the story that is composed of a beautiful, but deadly mix of sharpened glass and ice.

What I love about the play on the word "cathedrals" is much of the esotericism behind the monuments themselves. Did you know that ancient cathedrals contain a long-forgotten science that is full of what the architects called "sacred geometry"? It was architecture that somehow managed to resonate certain (un)natural frequencies with human biology. Creating a resonate oscillator with the human mind. What a wild concept. There is a lot that we just don't fucking know! And that is why I started my company, To The Stars. Because we need to know more. And by sorting these mysterious concepts within a cohesive explanation, or story they all may just start to make sense to people. And in turn re-ignite that forgotten part of human experience from our distant past. (Atlantis anyone? Oh . . . wait . . . that is *Sekret Machines Book 2*! I keep getting ahead of myself here!)

When we evolve over the next few hundred years, I truly believe humanity will change profoundly. All the conspiratorial and esoteric concepts about religious rites, rituals, sacred geometry, remote viewing, ESP, telepathy and astral-travel will become "normal" science. And we will long forget our Texas Instruments calculators, because there will be a re-discovered APPLE supercomputer in the ether, one that we can access whenever we desire, and which is way more fun to use than the latest iPhone.

Cathedrals of Glass: A Planet of Blood and Ice, explores these questions: What are souls? Where do they go? What is consciousness and where does it live? What is the power of the human mind? And what is the threat of it unleashed? Are ghosts, consciousness and etheric apparitions all part of the same galactic operating system? Or, are we to blame for those incarnations ourselves, literally forming matter and physical holograms out of "mind-power," as if the human mind itself can assemble a tangible, organic property out of invisible waves of light? . . . Some call those "waves of probability."

Maybe an apparition is just a hologram your mind "believed" into existence. Because when you believe something truly and totally, well . . . maybe you actually *can* walk on water like Jesus. Hell, I bet you could walk on fire itself, like they do in those far-out Middle-Eastern rituals. Or, maybe you could commit to something more necessary, like changing the weather, as the Native Americans did during those legendary rain dances we heard so much about as kids.

Either way, we must not pretend we know how to contain the potential of the human mind. We must not try to predict it, ignore it, or worse, *not use it*.

Cathedrals of Glass: A Planet of Blood and Ice, will give you a violent tow up supernatural mountain, and then drop you into the dark forbidding abyss. The story is modern and cerebral, told through the eyes and ears of young adults along isolated and troubled paths. Here, life and death are at their doorstep, and the universe likes to play tricks. People can die from such nefarious games. After reading *Cathedrals*, you will think twice about what is real, and what is possible . . .

And then maybe you, yourself, can learn how to dance across that delicate boundary of human existence . . .

Like walking on water, fire, or making the sky rain.

Oh yeah, or, bending metal spoons with your mind.

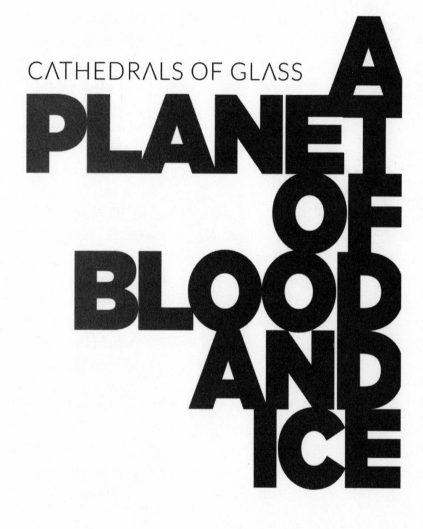

CATHEDRALS OF GLASS

A PLANET OF BLOOD AND ICE

CHAPTER

I WAS AWAKE WHEN THE SHIP STARTED TO DIVE. I shouldn't have been, but I was wandering the ship by myself before the others woke up. It was just the kind of minor rebelliousness that had gotten me shipped off to the reeducation facility in the first place. Ironically, it saved my life. Saved all of our lives, in fact.

For a while.

We were supposed to wake up after the journey was 95 percent done, giving us just a little time to come to so we weren't too groggy for our first lecture on how to be better citizens. But I'd been on these rust-buckets twice before. The transit agent had mouthed the numbers of her access code as she typed them in, and moments later my fingers had flashed unseen over the controls as I smiled into her glacial stare.

Vermin, said her eyes. *Deviant.*

I was used to that, and from people who mattered to me a good deal more than some stone-faced security drone.

●

ON WAKING, IT TOOK ME ABOUT FIVE MINUTES TO REALIZE that something was wrong.

As I waited for the nausea to pass, I disconnected the electrodes on my temples, pulled out the IV line, and took a sip of water from the bottle in my "Comfort Package." I cracked the lid of the pod, onto which I had stuck an ancient picture of an angel, and peered out. When I was satisfied that no one else was moving about, I climbed out into the dark hull of the ship.

It was called the *Phetteron*, one of a fleet of identical transports that had been in service at least fifty years. A pilotless drone, equipped with none of the comforts of home, it was little more than a subsectioned metal box with an engine. I sniffed. The air was cool and lifeless, edged with the muted tang of fuel and iron. It was a ship from another age, about as far from the sleek glass and plastic and chrome that had been the backdrop of my life to date as I could imagine. I'd had sixteen years of the polished, clean, and tech-dependent world that was Home. There you never saw the insides of things. Only the gleaming surface.

The *Phetteron*, by contrast, was a wheezing study of insides. It was bare and practical and almost embarrassingly exposed, a place of braces and cables and long, smeared seams made by welding equipment. It made me think of bones and sinews, like I was inside a living thing. You could almost sense the men who had once bolted it together in a former age, when people did things with their hands, muscles straining, sweat beading on their foreheads. It was an image most girls my age would find repellent, but bodily stuff didn't bother me as much as it should: part of the reason I had wound up on this miserable jaunt in the first place.

I found my way to the vision port beyond the other stasis pods—ten of them, one for each of us. On Home we lived in family units, each individual in his or her own subunits, and our communication with others—even our parents—was almost entirely virtual, regardless of how far apart we were in geographical space. We were private people—everyone on Home was—and being physically close to others, particularly to strangers, produced a discomfort close to panic.

Partly as a result, it was satisfying to walk again. Few people on Home would react to the confinement by wanting to move around, but the artificial gravity units on these old transports generated less than an entire g, so if you focused, you could sense your own lightness as you moved around. It wasn't much, and most people wouldn't notice it, but I took long, high strides, enjoying the fractional delay, the feeling of poise and gracefulness. It was, I imagined, a bit like being a dancer. Even here, effectively alone in space, the idea embarrassed me a little.

When I reached the vision port, I pulled the manual release lever and pushed up the blind.

Though I'd woken early, I should have been able to see Jerem—the moon where the reeducation facility was located—lining up with the ship, but there was no sign of it.

Weird.

I pressed my face to the cold glass of the port and gazed out at the blackness and silence of space, pushing away the memory of my parents seeing me off, the grief in my mother's face, the disappointment, the way my father kept fiddling with the cuffs of his jacket and looking around as if afraid someone would see . . . For a long moment I just sat there, listening to the creak and drone of the ship. It sounded like breathing.

Where the hell was that moon?

I made my way up to the flight deck over a narrow gantry made of perforated metal plates, past the steps down to the engine room and storage hold, and tried the door.

Locked.

But there was a monitor built into the adjacent bulk-head. I tried the transit agent's access code and, when it got me into the system, went straight to check the navigation log. The numbers were all wrong.

The journey from Home to Jerem took six days. We had only been put in stasis because there was nothing to do onboard a minimal transport like this, and because making sure we slept all the way meant there was no need for a crew. The whole flight was automated.

Six days.

But I scrolled back through entry after entry, days apart. Weeks. I stared, my heart hammering hard in my throat as I checked and double-checked.

What the hell?

We had been in space for over a month. There was no sign of Jerem ahead because we had flown right by it weeks ago. Now we were speeding through the black towards God-alone-knew-what. I switched the screen to display the forward view, and in the same instant the ship rolled hard to the left. A vast, pale planet slid into place, filling the screen. It was blue-gray and covered with what looked to be a swirling fog. I knew what it was instantly. Everyone on Home did. Its picture was on every educational interface unit in every authorized city.

It was Valkrys, the ice planet. Home's uninhabited, uninhabitable neighbor, a place so hostile that even unmanned ships did not attempt to navigate the asteroid field that surrounded it.

No.

We were already close enough to see that the dusty haze surrounding the planet was actually made up of a billion irregular rocks. It might as well have been a minefield. We weren't going to Jerem; we were going to Valkrys. Worse, we had arrived, and now we were going down. Which meant that we were dead.

No contrary position viable.

A Home phrase I had always despised but that had never seemed more apt.

7

The deck tilted under my feet, too fast for me to regain my balance. My hip slammed against the control panel as I fought to stay upright. We were rolling, the ship groaning as she began a slow, downward spiral, corkscrewing into the asteroid field. This wasn't a landing. It was a crash.

I stared at the cascading digits of the altimeter, then I felt the first shudder of the ship's hull as an asteroid cannoned off the side. The impact broke the spell, and I doubled back into the passenger hold, my feet pounding the metal decking. There was another asteroid bang, and our momentum seemed to stall for a moment—then a third, bigger this time, followed by the yawn of creaking metal. We were coming apart.

A looping siren began to shriek.

The ship kicked right, rolling now, out of control. I stumbled, then made my faltering way the final ten yards to where a faded red button sat under a clear protective housing. I mashed it with my palm.

Another cycling alarm began, honking like some foghorn from centuries ago, and then every stasis pod was hissing as their covers disengaged.

My companions for reeducation on this off-world death trap were, like me, delinquents, attitudinal subversives, and behavioral deviants. I had just woken them up.

CHAPTER

C OMING OUT OF STASIS IS ALWAYS NAUSEATING, BUT to wake up in a ship that is spinning from one asteroid collision to another was about as close to hell as I could imagine. A boy threw up. One of the girls started screaming.

"Shut up!" I yelled. "All of you. We're crashing. We have minutes, maybe less. Someone needs to take the helm and land this thing. Does anyone know anything about flying? Games, even? Simulators?"

For a moment they just stared at me, shocked and offended that I was talking directly to them like this. Most were dressed in their sleek, fashionable Home clothes, all buttons and zippers and glossy fabrics. They were what you wore in your booth for online chatting and virtual parties, and they made you look like an airnet model selling

9

synthezine. Trendy, clean, polished. Here, in the gloomy, stripped-down interior of the ancient transport, the group looked absurd. Out of their depth. A girl with short, black hair, dyed with patches of fiery orange, shot me a disbelieving, contemptuous look. But before anyone could say anything, there was a deafening clang as another asteroid struck the hull. The ship kicked to the side, and something mechanical in the vessel's guts let out a juddering whine. We weren't going to last much longer.

One of the other boys, tall, athletic, and wearing what looked like a uniform, shook his head as if to clear it and moved towards me. He was pale with shock, but nodded as he braced himself for another asteroid strike and said, "I'm an air force cadet. Let me look at the controls."

The Cadets were the youth training division of Home's security services. They were still divided into the old military classifications—army, air force, navy, intelligence—but since there was barely anyone left to fight, they were really just a branch of the government police. That someone on board might know his way around the ship was about as close to good news as seemed possible.

I ran clumsily back to the flight deck without a word, clinging to the girders as something somewhere snapped and the gantry started to swing.

"Hell of a way to wake a guy up," yelled the boy over the din.

He had a hard, angular face. Good looking, I supposed, but with a little too much of the skull about it, a feature emphasized by his close-cut hair. I got out of the way so he could see the flight deck access panel. The others were coming after him, some urgent, some hesitant, all scared. The girl who had been screaming started up again. She still hadn't left her stasis pod.

I punched the transit agent's code into the pad, but it flashed red. Locked. Having a pilot wasn't much use if we couldn't get to the controls. It was typical of Home Gov to pack us off in this can without trusting us to control it if something went wrong.

"Let me try," said the boy.

His face looked clammy from stasis, probably feeling the pitch and yaw of the ship even more than I was, but he was either playing it cool or clinging to some vestige of his cadet training. He swiped his ID through the lock mechanism, then tapped a half-dozen keystrokes into the pad. It turned green, and something disengaged with a heavy clunk.

He nodded, unsmiling, and twisted the release handle, wresting the twin doors apart just wide enough for us to squeeze through.

The cabin had a pair of empty seats and a bank of lifeless controls. With hurried taps of his fingers, the boy woke a set of sleeping screens as he slid into the left-hand chair. The nose of the ship was paneled with transparent viewers, and the gray planet filled our field of vision, clouded with the thousand floating rocks that shot past us as we dived. Another glimpse of hell.

"Well?" I demanded.

He glanced over his shoulder into the passenger hold, then returned his gaze to the *Phetteron*'s operational center.

11

Despite the veering ship and the terrible noise, he was eerily calm.

"I guess I'm our best hope," he said, flipping switches and studying the screens. "Now, if you could keep the others quiet so I can think . . ."

He turned a handle and punched three buttons in rapid succession. A display flickered into life and something beeped. The sirens died, and there was a sudden unnerving silence.

Through the windows ahead, the asteroids seemed to be getting thicker and larger. One direct hit on the nose, and that would be it.

I moved back to the door and addressed the black-haired girl. She was about my age, or near enough, with dark skin and wide eyes that had none of the sneering composure with which she had considered me moments before.

"Keep them quiet," I said. "He knows what he's doing. Just needs to concentrate."

And then I dragged the cabin door closed. In spite of everything, I found myself momentarily embarrassed to be alone with this strange boy. The ship shuddered, and the lightness I had felt when I first started moving around the hold suddenly increased, as if my stomach had floated out of my body. I grabbed hold of the wall and manhandled my way into the copilot's seat.

"We're losing artificial gravity," I said.

The boy said nothing. Without the echoing of the main hold, the quiet was unnerving. I turned to him, irritated, but saw that he had taken hold of the angled attitude control bars and was pulling them towards his chest, his teeth clenched. I checked the forward viewer. An asteroid lay dead ahead and closing fast. It was huge, filling the window like a wall of rock.

"Can you . . . ?" I began.

"Remember what I said about quiet?" he remarked, not taking his eyes off the windows in front of him. "And don't touch anything. These seats are equipped with an ejection system that will blow you straight out into the air. Since there isn't any out there right now, that would be bad."

With that, he twisted the control bars hard to the left, and the ship rolled and banked as the asteroid seemed to float up to the right. There was a thud and a squeal of metal, but instead of peeling the ship open and exposing us to the void of space, the asteroid drifted past.

"Close," I muttered.

"I got past one asteroid," he answered, not looking at me. "There are thousands. Where the hell are we?"

"Valkrys," I said.

He looked at me then, a quick, hard look full of raw emotion so powerful I could almost feel it, but he didn't dispute what I'd said.

"I've only got partial control," he said. "I can point the ship where I want it to go, which might get us through the asteroids if we're very lucky. But I can't fight the pull of the planet. We're going down. The only question is—"

"Whether we land or crash?"

"Oh no," he said, with a bleak smile. "The question is whether I can keep enough of the hull intact so that we don't all get roasted to a crisp as we enter the atmosphere. We're definitely going to crash."

I stared at him.

He shrugged.

"Maybe if we can find a nice open spot," he conceded, "we can crash . . . gently."

"Just get us down," I said, unamused.

He yanked hard on the controls, and the ship slewed to the right, out of the path of another hurtling asteroid.

"You're full of commands for someone whose contribution so far has been sitting," he added. "So long as I'm flying this thing, I'm in charge. Captain Sevin. And you are?"

"Sola," I replied, tartly. "And if I hadn't woken you, you wouldn't have had the opportunity to show what an ace pilot you are."

"Fine, and if we get out of this alive," he answered, "which right now doesn't seem that likely, we can discuss why you were awake before the rest of us and why we're halfway across the solar system instead of being bored to death by Home's finest reeducators."

I shot him a hard look.

"You think I had something to do with why we're here?" I demanded.

"No offense," he said, still unnervingly calm. "But none of us are what you might call model citizens, so ditch the righteous indignation. Put your energy into something useful, like sealing off aft quadrant four. Looks like we're on the point of a hull breach. That panel there. See? Where I'm pointing."

He did it without looking at me. I found the control and threw the switch.

"Better," he said. "Now, brace yourself. We're going down."

CHAPTER

THE ASTEROIDS WERE GONE, AND THE SHIP'S DESCENT was perhaps more controlled than it had been, but we were going down fast and hard, spearing through the atmosphere. The windows first fogged, then glowed amber. I could smell burning. The cabin was suddenly sweltering.

"We gonna make it?" I asked. I didn't want to, but the words just came out.

For a moment Sevin said nothing. I felt what I couldn't see in his sweating face: Doubt. Terror. Hopelessness. But then he forced a smile and replied almost casually, "Ask me again in five minutes. If we can talk about it, I'd say we did okay."

I had no response to that, and even if I had, my attention was suddenly seized by a noise unlike any we'd heard so far: a sharp crack followed by a rumble that shook the red-hot ship from nose to tail.

"What the hell was that?" I muttered, unstrapping myself from the copilot's seat.

"Nothing good," said Sevin, eyes locked unblinking on the glowing windshield.

As soon as I released the safety buckle, I felt myself floating out of the seat. The artificial grav unit was shot.

"I'd stay strapped in if I were you," said Sevin.

I ignored him, blundering back to the bulkhead door and hitting the release button, my feet no longer touching the metal decking. There was a dull clunk, and I pulled at the handle, bracing myself against the wall for leverage. The formed steel slid unevenly open, one side grinding and eventually sticking halfway shut. The hold beyond was full of thick brown smoke that smelled of electricity and burnt rubber.

"Sit down!" Sevin called after me, but I ignored him.

I squeezed through, grabbing the cabin's fire extinguisher as I went, and tried to see what was going on through the smog. The gantry still swung precariously. At the far end were the ranks of stasis pods, boys on the left, girls on the right. Below us the crippled engines whined and snarled. And directly ahead was a flickering orange light. The stern was on fire.

It was impossible to tell how much of the unbearable heat was coming from the exterior of the hull and how much was the blaze inside, but it didn't much matter. I cocked the extinguisher and made for the firelight, pulling myself along the gantry with one hand, shooting the extinguisher ahead of me with the other. Great plumes of carbon dioxide smoke came out, reducing visibility still further. I moved between the stasis pods, spraying wherever I saw flames, vaguely aware that there was no other sign of life. The others had taken refuge in their pods and closed them. Probably smart. They were at least restrained.

I, by contrast, was balancing on the ruined metal walkway, both hands on the extinguisher, when a piece of the ship's tail tore free. One moment I was peering into an impenetrable wall of smoke, the next there was a sudden blaze of light. The smoke vanished as a wind caught me up and threw me toward the ceiling where the rear bulkhead had been, but where there was now nothing at all: a wide expanse of freezing, empty air. No ceiling. No roof of any kind. Just a swirling, airless gale that felt like it might tear the ship to pieces. I seized the gantry, clinging with both hands as the fire extinguisher flew from my hands and into the abyss, feeling my legs floating free as the hole in the roof tried to suck me out into the sky.

The raging heat of reentry had gone entirely, which meant we were low, and through the horror of the moment I remember thinking quite clearly that Sevin had done as well as anyone could expect, that he might actually get us to the ground, that if I could just hold on for a few more seconds . . .

And then I felt the impact. The ship buckled as if it was made of card, tearing open like a gutted fish, and suddenly there was only brilliant light and searing, blinding pain. Then nothing.

CHAPTER

I DREAMED OF HOME. NOT THE SLEEK BOOTHS AND virtual gatherings, not the airnet commercials for the latest pads and gadgets, not the massive broadcast screens where smiling cybermodels read the news and briefed the populace on changes in behavioral law. Not the ever-present slogan "Home Looks After Its Own." I dreamed of the Home I only saw when I went roaming.

That was what they called it when you slipped out after curfew or strayed beyond your designated range. I'd been caught three times, which was why I was on this transport in the first place, bound for a week's reeducation. Again. There they would ask the question they always asked: why do you do it? You know it's against the law. You know it's dangerous to stray beyond the protection of your personal security zone. You know it risks interaction with people who live outside the law, that it might involve actual physical contact with other human beings in ways contrary to taste and safety. You know it means coming off the tech grid and leaving the Designated Sanitized Zone that the Home Governmental Agency created for your own good. You know that you're exposing yourself to the risk of bodily harm and emotional trauma, and you don't even try to do anything but walk around. You know no contrary position is viable. You know Home can't look after its own if you don't let us. So why? Why do you do it?

I couldn't answer. I didn't know why I did it. I just did.

And that was what I dreamed of. Slipping out of my room and out of our twenty-sixth floor apartment; reprograming the elevator so that it would take me down even after the curfew lockdown; rigging the service entrance so that I could shimmy through the delivery hatch, dirtying my immaculate pants on the oil as I did so. Smiling at the stain. Rubbing it with my fingers. Then rolling out across the gravel and up into a run. An actual run! Feet pounding, blood pumping, chest heaving, sweat pouring, hair streaming. Out through the empty streets of Sindrone where the towering halls of servers rose like the cathedrals of old. Alone in the world. Touching the walls with my fingers, my cheek. Lapping up the sensation of contact, of openness, of freedom . . .

I felt it in my body. Not my head. That I had left behind with my comm pad. I felt it in my thighs, my lips, my fingertips. I felt it stir in my gut. And as I was experiencing it, I felt only joy and exhilaration. No embarrassment. No shame. That was why I had to be reeducated.

Normally when I dreamed of roaming, I awoke to confusion and embarrassment as the exhilaration of the dream died. I'd lie still for twenty minutes or more, wondering what was wrong with me. Not today.

Today I woke quickly, and the first thing I registered was the cold. It was bitter, biting, unlike anything I had ever experienced. There was a hard, chill light that cast deep, black shadows through the belly of the ravaged ship.

The ship.

I was on a crippled transport, the *Phetteron*. I had never reached the facility on Jerem. I was struck by a sudden panic and tried to get up.

"Easy," said a voice. "You've had a bad fall, and there are lots of hard edges around you. Take a moment to wake up properly before you start jumping about."

He was so close. I felt my throat tighten with something just this side of revulsion at the proximity of the boy.

"Sevin?" I said. "We made it?"

"In a manner of speaking," he said. "We're down, and everyone is still alive, but we took some serious knocks."

"How serious?" I asked, sitting up.

"The people or the ship?"

"Both."

"The people are mostly fine, physically. A few cuts and bruises. One of the girls has a nasty gash on her head that needs attending to, and one of the boys has what looks like a broken arm."

"A broken arm?" I echoed. "How can you tell?"

His confidence flickered.

"Read about them in the cadet manual," he said. "Symptoms seem to fit."

"How are they doing mentally?"

He took a breath and shook his head.

"I don't know which is worse," he said, "the fact that we aren't where we were supposed to be, that we crashed, or that we're all stuck here together only a few feet apart . . ."

"And the ship?"

"Done," he said. "I'm amazed it held together as well as it did, but we lost an entire panel from the aft section and the engines are fried. We're not going anywhere."

Since landing he had put on the jacket from his cadet uniform, navy blue and trimmed with piping. There were a pair of brass studs on the collar. Insignia or rank, I supposed. He was probably just wearing the jacket for warmth, but it gave him an air of authority.

"Have you been outside?" I asked, trying to sound like it was an ordinary question.

"You remember where we are, right?" he said, eyebrows raised and voice lowered.

I started to say the name, but caught myself. No need to cause a panic just yet.

"Exactly," said Sevin. "So take a moment to come to, and then we'll talk properly."

I nodded, which made my head pound so badly that I stopped and squeezed my eyes shut. When I opened them, he had gone.

A PLANET OF BLOOD AND ICE

"Quite the commander," said a boy lying beside me. He was cradling his left arm across his chest. Apparently he was the one with the broken arm. His sleeve was almost touching mine.

"Sevin?" I said, fighting the impulse to cringe away. "We wouldn't be here without him."

"I meant you," said the boy. He was pale, dark haired, with blue-gray eyes. Handsome, but less angular than Sevin. It was a face you could trust—or at least one you wanted to. "Sevin just took the controls when you told him to," he said. "I'm Bryce, by the way. Strange, just saying it like that."

I gave him a sympathetic nod. I couldn't remember the last time I had met someone in person without being introduced via vidchat first. I wasn't sure I ever had. And even the closest friends and family kept further apart than the inches between me and this boy.

"Sola," I said, awkward. It felt like we should do something really old school, like shake hands or something, and I was momentarily glad his arm was broken so he wouldn't consider trying.

He smiled, but it was almost a wince, and when he shifted, trying to get comfortable, his shoulder touched mine. I sat up, trying to hide the way I shrank away from him, but he saw it anyway. I heard his flash of embarrassment and irritation, which was crazy, because you couldn't hear such things.

"What?" I asked.

"I didn't say anything," he answered.

"Right," I said, more uncomfortable still. I looked directly into his face, into his eyes, and for a moment it was like having vertigo, a wild sense of tumbling, as if the ship were still plunging through space and I were falling into his mind. For a fraction of a second, it was like we had changed places. I could feel the throbbing pain in his arm, his unease at being so close to me, his mounting outrage and panic when he felt the link between us . . .

It broke immediately. For a moment we just stared at each other, baffled and uncomfortable. Then I fled.

I scrambled to my feet and steadied myself. My vision swam as I looked around the battered, wreckage-strewn hull, then I made for where the others had gathered. I shrugged off whatever that had been with Bryce. I had, after all, had a hard fall.

"Can't believe I broke my arm," he said wonderingly. "Who does that? It's like something that happened hundreds of years ago. You think they can still fix it—when we get Home, I mean?"

"I'm sure," I said, more to keep his spirits up than because I really was. I had never heard of anyone actually breaking a bone.

"Our savior, I presume," said another boy. He was lean, not as tall as Bryce or Sevin, tanned with black hair, dark eyes the same slim shape as mine, and an open, smiling face. He'd wrapped the blanket from his stasis pod around his shoulders against the cold.

"Sola, right? My name's Trest. I know: stupid name. Normally I'd warn you in advance with a text; but here I guess I have to just say it, which is several kinds of weird. It was my father's—the name, I mean. I tried to give it back to him and call myself something sensible like Plantpot or Landfill, but no one was buying it. The problem with names is that it doesn't matter how cool they are if no one else will call you them. I'm babbling. Sorry. I deal with stress by throwing words at it. People get caught in the crossfire."

"It's cool," I said, smiling. "I'm kind of the opposite, but I know what you mean."

"Strong and silent," said Trest. "Excellent. Very commander-y. You and Brigadier General Sevin will have us back in the sky in time for tea. Not actual tea, of course. Figure of speech."

"Not so sure about that," I said, eying the sky showing through the roof at the far end of the hold.

"Right," said Trest, following my gaze. "Because the ship is, sort of, broken."

"You could say that."

"What with the massive hole and all," Trest agreed. "Right. Could make it tough to breathe in space."

"A little bit," I said, smiling again. "I'm looking for a girl with a head wound."

"Now there's a sentence you don't often hear," said Trest. "Amazingly, I don't have one. A head wound, I mean. Or a girl, for that matter."

I nodded.

"You know where she is?" I asked.

"Over there," said Trest, nodding. "Her name is Carlann."

"Okay. Thanks," I said, biting down the unease I felt at having so many people so close to me.

"Well, I'll leave you to figure out our salvation," said Trest, smiling back and bobbing his head in a self-deprecating nod, "without being subjected to a string of verbal idiocy."

"It's nice to meet you," I said.

"Yeah?" said Trest, clearly surprised and pleased, though the remark seemed to fluster him still further. "Right. You're nice to meet, too."

I grinned, and he flushed.

"Oh, and I like the hair," he said, nodding at the patch I had dyed over my right eye. "Very . . . blue."

"Thanks," I said. "My mom isn't a fan."

I said it lightly, like it didn't really matter.

"I got this ear chain," he said, fingering a loop of tiny silver links that ran from the top of his ear round the edge to the lobe. "Makes people think I have a personality," he added, grinning.

"I think they'd get that anyway," I answered.

"I'm going to go now," he said, nodding over to a corner where some of the others had gathered. "Over there. Safely out of earshot so you can recover. But you should prepare yourself for more babbling later."

"I'll count on it," I said, still smiling, though it took an effort. All these people so close together, talking like we knew each other: it was more than unsettling. I was relieved to note that the others seemed a lot less comfortable talking than Trest. The black-and-orange-haired girl was sitting by herself, watching everyone in silence, and there was a blond boy who had his hands over his eyes as if trying to shut the whole situation out.

Carlann, the girl with the head wound, was the one who had been screaming. She had been too scared to move when everyone else had returned to their stasis pods during the crash, and one of the guidance struts had lashed across the top of her head when the tail section came free. She wasn't screaming now. She was quite still and silent, her face white with fear beneath a slick, crimson mask of blood. Red spattered the front of her fashionable gray clothes and the beaded necklace she wore around her throat. She was about fifteen. Maybe less. Sevin was examining her, but he looked like he'd rather be flying through asteroids.

"Let me see," I said. Sevin backed off, relieved to turn the injured girl over to someone else. No one else was close enough to touch her, but that was Home people for you. We don't like bodies, and we *really* don't like to see them damaged and oozing. Reminds us we aren't just minds.

I squatted down and took her face in my hands. Even in her terror, she flinched at the intimacy of the intrusion.

"Sorry," I said. "I just need to see. Your name's Carlann?"

"Yes," whispered the girl. "Don't touch me."

"I just want to look."

"Am I going to die?"

"No, Carlann," I said. "Just tip your head forward."

She did so, and the blood flowing down her face increased. One of the other girls gasped and shifted back, as if Carlann might be contagious.

"I'm going to need some scissors," I said, shooting them a hard look. "See what you can find."

They scattered, glad of a reason to be elsewhere and apart. Sevin looked at me, then nodded.

"Even on an automated ship like this, there should be an emergency locker," he said, rising. "I'll see if I can locate it below decks."

"What are you going to do?" asked Carlann. "I want to talk to my parents."

"I just want to get a look at the wound," I said. "That means I need to cut your hair."

"My hair?" said Carlann, despairing.

"Sorry. But it will grow back."

"Can't it wait till we get Home?"

"Just need to be sure nothing needs doing now," I said, glad that Sevin was out of earshot.

"Will it hurt?" she asked.

"No," I said, smiling again. My fingers were slick with blood. It was amazing the girl was still conscious. I tested her skull gently, feeling for indentations or soft patches, but it felt whole and hard. With luck, the gash would turn out to be a superficial wound, though it needed to be closed.

"I like your necklace," I said.

"It's a choker," she answered in a tone that suggested she was used to correcting people on this point.

One of the girls came running back to me holding something in the air. A transparent plastic box. She was black and, at about eleven years old, was the youngest on board. Her triumph was mingled with embarrassment.

"Sewing kit," she explained, thrusting it at me.

"Where on earth did you find that?" I asked, opening it and taking out a pair of silver scissors. "Clever girl."

She looked away.

"It's yours?" I said, trying to sound merely curious.

"I'm not supposed to have it," said the girl. "But I wanted something to do at the facility. I love real games, of course," she added hastily, "on the pads and screens, but sometimes I like to . . ." Her enthusiasm dried up as her embarrassment won out.

"Sometimes you like to do things with your hands," I completed for her.

The girl just nodded, so I smiled to show I wasn't judging her. Sewing made no less sense than roaming, I supposed.

"Okay," I said to Carlann. "I'm going to cut some of the hair from the back. I'll take as little as I can and make it so you'll be able to brush the rest over the spot. You ready?"

Carlann tensed, then nodded.

"I'm cold," she said.

She had been clinging to her blanket like a toddler, more for security than warmth, but she released it to me when I tugged at it. I wrapped it around her shoulders and tucked it in.

"Better?" I said.

"No," she said. "But it will be. Thanks."

"I'm going to start now," I said.

"Okay," said the girl. "Don't tell me about it."

I began to cut, slipping the scissor blades as close to the scalp as I could get them, feeling gingerly with my fingers before shearing off Carlann's rich, chestnut hair. The younger girl who had supplied the sewing kit watched, fascinated. When the first locks fell away, she pushed them out of sight with her shoe so that Carlann wouldn't be upset at how much I had cut. I gave her a grateful look, and she smiled briefly, eyes fastened on the blood-flecked scissors.

"I'm Muce," she volunteered, pronouncing it like there was a "y" after the "M." "I'm disobedient."

I grinned at her.

"I think you're in good company," I said.

I turned Carlann's head into the light and froze.

The wound was perhaps three inches long and bleeding freely. But that wasn't what had made the breath catch in my throat. Just beneath the cut, right in the center of her head, was a tattoo of a triangle, its sides lined with deep-red ink. Muce gaped, but she read my look and hurriedly turned away.

"What?" asked Carlann. "Is it bad?"

"It's fine," I said. "But we need to close it."

Carlann shrank away. "I'll wait till we get Home," she said.

I hesitated at that, suddenly aware that the others had grown quiet and watchful. I sensed them looking at us, waiting to see what I would say.

"We're not going Home," said Sevin, coming up the aft stairs and onto the metal gangway lugging a plastic crate. "Not anytime soon."

30

Carlann gasped, and, as she began to sob, I shot him a hard look.

"No point lying about it," said Sevin, brash as ever. "The ship is crippled. There's a hole in it as big as a Skyball table, or hadn't you noticed? And the closest moon or planet is weeks away."

"The F950 is five times as fast as this piece of junk," said the boy with the shock of blond hair.

"And has a range of 250 peks," said Sevin with a steely grin. "Anything that can reach us out here will do twice our speed at most."

"But . . . Home looks after its own," said Carlann. "No contrary position is viable. They'll come for us."

She said it lightly, reassured by the familiarity of the idea. No one pulled a face or rolled their eyes. We might have been, in small ways, rebels, but there were some things we just accepted, knew in our innermost being. Home might be a bit dull, synthetic, and restrictive, but it was also essentially benevolent.

"Of course they'll come for us," said Sevin, as if nothing could be more obvious. "And maybe rescue is already en route. But it's going to take a while, so you'd better get used to the idea of waiting here on this rock."

They stared at him. The blond boy frowned at the comm pad he had been playing with and then looked up with desperate eyes.

"Where can I charge this?" he said.

"Main power is offline," said Sevin, "and won't be coming back on. There's a backup generator that will give us a little energy for essentials—which doesn't include playing Narl Herder on your pad—and there's a solar panel we might be able to hook up to give it a boost. But whatever power we can scrape together should be used for light and heat. If we don't get some warmth in here, we'll freeze to death."

It might have been just a figure of speech, but it might not. On Home, where practically no one had to actually go outside, the temperature of life was constant and stable regardless of season. The air in the ship was cold in ways I had never known before, a cold that made you feel as if your bones were made of metal. And the temperature was, I suspected, falling. Carlann's pale face now had a bluish tinge, and her lips had turned a thin lilac color that I didn't like.

"Wasn't going to play Narl Herder," said the blond boy. "Was going to send a pulse to my parents."

"There's no signal out here," said Sevin. "You won't be able to do much with your comm pad, and you certainly can't send a pulse."

Everyone looked up then, their faces blank as if Sevin were speaking a strange language. One of them put a hand to her mouth, her eyes brimming.

"I don't understand," said the boy.

He did. He just couldn't deal with the idea.

"There's no signal," said Sevin again, ignoring the frightened looks around him and keeping his face impassive. "We're on our own. Not that tough to grasp."

But it was, however lightly he tossed the phrase off. I doubted any of them had ever been without a signal before.

It was like losing a limb. Worse, even, because limbs were just body parts. This was like losing the world.

The others were all standing apart or sitting with their arms and legs tight to their bodies, putting as much distance from each other as the cramped ship would allow. Several of them held their blank and silent comm pads and stared at them as if willing them to come to life, pointedly not looking at each other. If I closed my eyes, I thought with a shudder, I could probably smell them. For a moment, it was all I could do not to climb back into my stasis pod and close the lid.

"What's in the emergency store?" asked the boy with the broken arm, Bryce. I think he said it just to break the awful silence.

"Not enough," said Sevin. "A couple of flashlights, some emergency medical supplies, a battery-powered space heater, some blankets, a crate of bottled water, and some protein bars. Food for a few days if we're careful. There's no dermo-bond or anything like that," he added, looking at me.

"The wound needs closing," I said with careful emphasis. We didn't have time to debate the matter.

"How?" asked Sevin.

"The old-fashioned way," I said, managing a smile.

Muce looked anxious.

"What's that?" she asked.

"Just a few stitches should do it," I said. "Muce, can I see that sewing kit again, please?"

Carlann's eyes went very wide as she fixed her gaze on the sewing kit. When I removed the needle, she started to shake her head.

"No," she said. "I'll be fine."

"No," I said firmly. "You won't. I have to close it, and I have to do it now."

"I don't understand," said one of the girls. "We were supposed to be on Jerem. We were supposed to only be on the ship for five days. Where are we? Why is it so cold?"

"What we need to focus on," I said, "is keeping calm and safe while I take care of Carlann here—"

"Valkrys," said Sevin. "We're on Valkrys."

Even without the gasps, the groans of horror, you could feel the effect of the word on the huddled kids. The already frigid ship seemed to dip well below freezing.

"It can't be," said Muce. "He's not right, is he?"

I frowned at Sevin, but there was no point dodging the truth.

"He's right," I said.

They all started talking at once, venting expletives, demanding explanations, crying, apologizing out loud to their parents for the indiscretions that had put them on this nightmare trip. Some punched desperately at their comm pads, determined to find a signal they knew couldn't possibly be there. Others put their heads in their hands. Trest, as he had promised, babbled, though there was none of the self-conscious and quirky humor about him now. He was genuinely frightened. Carlann twisted away from me to stare at him. Blood was running in a slow trickle down her neck, but she seemed to have forgotten about her injury.

The noise they made was deafening, and covering my ears didn't help. It wasn't just the sound of their despair that got to me; it was the feelings that generated the sound. I knew that made no sense—the idea that I was hearing feelings, not words—but that was what it felt like. I sensed it all, the dread, the terror, the outrage . . . and, from Sevin, a kind of gleeful delight at what his words had produced. I stared at him, aghast at the unsettling awareness of what was in his head, his heart. But there was no trace of it on his face, and when he turned quickly to face me, it—whatever it had been—had vanished.

"Here," said Muce, taking the sewing kit from me. "I'm good at threading needles."

I hesitated, refocusing.

"Sure," I said, tearing open a sterile package of wipes.

As if the action calmed her, Muce sucked on the end of the thread for a second, then closed one eye and threaded the needle on her first attempt. Apparently oblivious to the shouting and crying around her, she deftly knotted one end of the thread and offered it to me. Her composure inspired me. I took the needle and turned my attention back to Carlann.

"Bend your head," I said.

The girl looked terrified, but her sobs abated, and she did as she was told. Somehow the action seemed to quiet the others, too, if only because they had some new fiasco to focus on. I swallowed hard, pushing down my apprehension, and got to work, using the wipe to mop up the worst of the blood till I could see the edges of the wound. Then, feeling the eyes of the others on me, I pushed the needle into the skin—not too deep—and threaded it through to the other side. I heard Carlann's gasp of shock and pain, but Sevin held her still. I took a breath, then drew the flap closed as best I could, all the time trying to ignore the red triangle tattoo and what—if anything—it could mean.

There was a long, tense silence.

"How did you learn to do that?" asked Sevin at last. I could hear the distaste in his voice.

"Old screeners," I breathed, not taking my eyes from the wound. "History. Used to watch them with my mom when I was little."

"History?" Sevin repeated, baffled. "Why?"

I shrugged and said nothing, staying focused on my work. It had been generations since kids on Home were taught history. We were taught to always look forward.

But here I was, needle in hand.

It took ten long minutes to finish the stitches, Muce dabbing at the edges of the cut with the bloody wipe, and in that time I said nothing. The day before boarding this ship—which, since I had been asleep, felt like yesterday—I would have been horrified to be so close to another person, even if my hands weren't tacky with their blood. Now I pushed my revulsion down and got on with it because I couldn't think of what else to do. As I worked, my mind strayed over what had happened since waking up on Valkrys, and one thing stood out over everything else.

I had always been what you might call an intuitive kid. On those rare occasions when I was physically close to people, I got strong impressions of their feelings even when they didn't express them. It bothered my parents sometimes, who linked it to my impulse to roam, so I had learned to keep my instincts to myself. But since waking on the ship, since crashing, those instincts had been heightened to an alarming degree. Where I used to have the occasional dull instinct about someone's mood, it was now something sharper and more distinct, and it was almost constant, like background noise from another room. I had felt it with Bryce and with Sevin. I could even feel something from Carlann and Muce as I worked, the former's barely contained horror and outrage, the latter's genuine interest in what I was doing. It wasn't mind reading; I didn't get words or images. Just impressions, a wash of moods that got sharper as the feelings intensified. I had never experienced anything like it before. It scared me.

CHAPTER 5

THEY CLAPPED FOR CARLANN WHEN WE WERE DONE, and she smiled; it was a little wan, but a smile nonetheless. I was pleased to note that her face had lost some of its frozen look. Everyone was huddled together at the front end of the hold, as far from the gaping hole in the rear hull roof as they could get. We were wrapped in blankets and whatever else we could find, but it was still bitterly cold. Sevin had handed everyone half a protein bar, which didn't begin to fill them up after weeks in stasis, but they had taken their portions meekly, still in a collective state of shock. Predictably, no one wanted to share water bottles, so they were each given one and told to make it last.

"How long?" said the blond boy, whose name was Dren.

Momentarily caught off guard, Sevin shrugged.

"As long as possible," he said.

Dren looked down, radiating misery and resentment.

"We need to find a water source."

That was Bryce. His arm had been strapped with a piece of pipe and some duct tape, and he had fashioned a canvas sling from a restraining tie he had found in the cargo hold. Everyone stared at him.

"You mean go outside?" asked a tall, slim girl with long hair so pale it was almost silver. "This is Valkrys."

"Might not be as bad as we think," said Trest. "I know what we've been taught—that Home looks after its own, and no contrary positions are viable—but you never know."

"Meaning what?" asked Sevin.

"We get our information from the tech grid, same as our teachers and our parents," he said. He held up his hands in a defensive gesture, knowing that what he was about to say would be unpopular. "All of that stuff is maintained by the government. I spend a lot of time surfing the grid—"

"Everyone does," said Dren.

"Maybe," Trest persisted, fingering the loop of fine chain around his ear. "I'm just saying that not everyone thinks everything in the tech grid can be trusted, that the government suppresses anything it doesn't want us to know. There have been terrorist attacks—"

"Oh, please," sneered Sevin. "I think we have enough actual problems without dredging up every half-baked conspiracy theory hidden in the corners of the infonet."

Trest shrugged, smiling in a way that said he had expected no less and didn't much care.

"Thanks for that, *cadet*," he said, emphasizing the last word.

"What's that supposed to mean?" Sevin demanded, bristling.

"Well, let's just say," said Trest, "that if I wanted an alternate view on how the Home government regulates information, I wouldn't seek out the opinion of someone being trained to fight for them."

"I'm a pilot," said Sevin.

"Someone being trained to fly for them then," Trest clarified. "All I'm saying," he said, "and with due respect to Brigadier General Sevin—"

"Don't call me that," Sevin cut in.

"—is that it might not be as bad out there as we've been told," Trest persisted. "I mean, we're alive now, aren't we? Who would have thought that was possible?"

"This is hardly the time to start questioning everything we believe . . ." Sevin began, stiffly.

"The point," Bryce inserted reasonably, "is that we don't have enough food or water to last more than a few days. Not nearly enough time to last till we're rescued. And this place isn't getting any warmer, is it?"

"I'm working on getting that secondary power generator up and running," said Sevin, defensive.

"And that's good," said Bryce. "But we don't know that we *can* get it working. We're all kind of out of our depth here. Looking for another source of shelter makes sense, even if it's just a backup. According to the environmental gauge, the air is breathable. Slightly less oxygen than we're used to, perhaps, but breathable. And since there's a huge hole in the ship, outside is really no different from in. Maybe if we went out, we could find water . . ."

"We're not opening that hatch," said Sevin. He spoke with such certainty that, for a second, everyone acted like that was the end of the discussion.

"Who put you in charge?" I asked.

I said it lightly, with a half-smile, hoping he wouldn't get confrontational, but at the same time, I made my way along the frozen gangway towards the tail, where the roof had been torn away. I looked for some usable wreckage and found a piece of the girder that had hit Carlann as it came free. I braced it against part of the inner frame and used it to hoist my way up.

"What are you doing?" Sevin demanded.

"Taking a look," I said, reaching up as high as I could and grasping a length of heavy pipe that ran along the inside of the roof. It was buckled but unbroken and did not yield as I grabbed it and transferred my weight.

I could feel the others staring at me. People back on Home had spent centuries finding ways to avoid any kind of physical exertion. Back in the day, our ancestors had worked outdoors, played sports, exercised. But we had evolved away from such things, and they had become faintly embarrassing. We stayed indoors. We used our brains, and our gadgets did most of the rest. We still had sport of a kind, but it was all virtual. Exercise, which had become unimportant once we had mastered nutritional intake, was kept to a minimum, and anyone who overdid it was considered an embarrassing throwback. I felt their eyes on me as I clambered and swung about, apelike.

We had seen nothing of Valkrys but the pale sky through the tear in the hull roof. Even the cabin windows were too scarred by rubble and scorching to see through. I hauled myself up, the edge of the torn metal cutting into my fingers until I could shift my grip and push up onto my elbows. The wind hit me hard in the face, freezing but dry. I took a breath and levered myself out completely, then stood up on the battered roof, hugging my coat to my chest in the icy gale, and stared.

It was extraordinarily beautiful.

Hostile, yes. Empty, bleak, and surely impossible to live in, but still beautiful. The ground was a pure, dazzling white, a great undulating sheet that spread out in all directions. Snow. The ship was half buried in a great bank of it, but the crust looked hard, and the air was clear. Most startling of all were the jagged ridges of blue that rose up from the snowfield, some mere ripples like shark fins frozen in the act of breaking the surface, others towering mountains with crisp, jagged lines that sparkled like sapphires in the sun.

"What do you see?" asked Bryce.

"Come look," I called, not looking down. "For one thing, I think we've found our water supply. Snow. What we need now is food."

I heard movement below and turned to find nine upturned faces gazing at me from the crippled ship. Several were dragging boxes over to make their ascent easier. Then they were coming up, cautiously, anxious and surprised by their own bravery. I took a few steps along the roof to give them room.

They clambered out, clustering together and gazing about them. For a few seconds, we forgot the cold, we forgot that we were abandoned on a distant planet where we would have to coexist for weeks or more. We saw only the splendor of the view, the distant pinnacles shimmering from turquoise to deep violet, the sweep of the snow, the sense that this was our secret place, a world no one had seen and that we had claimed as our own.

Meanwhile, Sevin said nothing, a sour look on his face.

While they stared and giggled, I climbed down one of the engine nacelles and dropped softly to the ground. No one noticed at first, but then they were watching me again, gaping, caught between horror and admiration. I felt it without looking at them.

The snow was frozen hard, with only the lightest dusting of powder on the surface. I swept some aside to see how deep it went and snatched my hand away with a hot thrill of pain. A bloody line, fine as a paper cut. Something had slashed my fingers.

I peered at the spot I had touched and saw, just breaking the white surface, a fine vein of blue. The same material, I guessed as the distant mountains. It looked like obsidian or glass, a deep cobalt color, translucent and sparkling. Its ridges narrowed to a razor's edge, flaked and splintered in places. A bead of my blood fell into the snow and blossomed briefly. Walking around out here was going to take real care. Put all your weight on a spot where one of those ridges crested, and you could slice your foot in half.

"Be careful," I said. The others were watching me. Some of them were spilling slowly, uncertainly out. The prospect of seeing snow, of walking on it, touching it, had overpowered all their cautious Home instincts.

I felt the pain in my finger, both hot and cold, terrifying and thrilling at the same time.

And I tasted the snow, squeezing it in my frozen fingers till it dropped into my mouth, cold and pure.

"Water," I said aloud.

I circled the ship slowly, studying the scrapes, dents, and burns of our descent and impact. Sevin was right. We were lucky to have made it down at all. When I saw the port viewer, I hoisted myself onto the twisted remains of the other nacelle, reached up and rubbed the ice and grit away. Maybe if we could look out, the ship would feel less claustrophobic.

I rubbed it with my sleeve, then moved on to the next and the next, brushing away the snow crystals and polishing out the dirt till my fingers turned red and numb from the cold. I had never felt anything like it in my life, and the sensation was both scary and invigorating. I would never have admitted any of it to the others, but I didn't need to. They felt the same. I was sure of it.

Which was enough for now. I climbed back onboard and made my way gingerly back to the hole in the roof. The others parted before me as if I had done something magical, and no one touched me as I returned to the hull, out of the wind.

It was, I thought, not much warmer inside than it had been out, but my fingers slowly thawed. As light seeped in through the scratched windows I had cleared, I looked at my hands, marveling as they returned to their usual color. I felt a confounding pride, almost awe, at my own body, in spite of its fragility.

"So now what?" said the girl with silvery hair once the others had followed me back inside. There was a new buzz of excitement in the air, as if this were some kind of jaunt or adventure, and several of the younger kids gleefully exclaimed how much better this was than being stuck at the boring old reeducation facility and watching endless docufeeds about how to be better citizens. Some of them had collected little mounds of snow in their plastic supplement pails, which they studied, rapt, as they slowly melted. It was amazing how quickly they had forgotten their sadness and panic, but I knew this was only a momentary respite.

Only Sevin seemed immune to the thrill of our situation. He avoided my eyes, but I felt it: a dull glow of resentment, as if I had taken his place or embarrassed him in front of the others.

At the silver-haired girl's question, everyone looked at me.

"Well," I said, "I guess we need to find a way to close that hole. We're going to need to keep in as much heat as we can, especially when the sun goes down—assuming it does. Does anyone know how long the days are on Valkrys?"

No one did.

"Then I guess we'll find out for ourselves," I said. "But our priorities are food and heat. The sun looks fairly low now, so I'd say we monitor it for an hour or so, see if it gets significantly lower. A day here might be fifteen hours, fifty, or five hundred. If it starts to get dark, we wait till morning, then send out an exploratory team for a few hours. They'll need to borrow extra coats—"

"Are you insane?" said Sevin. "It's Valkrys! No one lives here because they can't. Every kid on Home knows that. There's nothing out there."

"Part of the reason no one comes here," Bryce retorted, "is the asteroid field. We navigated that—thanks to you—so we've already beaten one set of odds. Who's to say we can't do it again down here?"

"I'm not going out there," said Sevin. "And you aren't exactly cut out to be the man of action right now, are you?"

Bryce frowned and looked at his broken arm. For a moment there was silence.

"I'll go," I said.

Sevin stared at me, disbelieving, and I felt it again: anger that I had disagreed with him.

"That's crazy," he said. "We don't know what's out there."

"I thought there was nothing out there," I said. "But I'd like to be sure. Anyone coming with me?"

"No," said Sevin, speaking on everyone else's behalf. I chose to misunderstand.

46

"So Sevin's out," I said. "Anyone else in?"

"I'll come," said Bryce. "I might not be much use, but I'm going nuts in here."

"Me too," said the willowy girl with the silver hair.

"And me," said Muce.

I smiled at her. She only came up to my armpit.

"Why don't you stay here and keep an eye on Carlann?" I said.

She considered this seriously, then nodded.

"Three is enough," I said. "For now, we monitor the sun."

It felt like an achievement, even if it didn't produce real action, and with the decision made, everyone relaxed a little. They relaxed even more when Teada, the girl with the patchily vibrant orange hair who had taken it upon herself to keep watch from the hole in the roof, announced that the sun was definitely going down. Our reconnaissance mission, if that was what it was, would have to wait till morning. I found myself disappointed, though that was probably just the old impulse to be out in the air, not cooped up with the others in the ship.

We used the plastic lids off the storage bins to fashion a panel, which we lashed across the hole in the roof with twine. Muce—bizarrely—was the only one who knew how to tie knots, and she instructed us how to do so. The panel didn't make much difference in terms of keeping the cold out, but it would do for now. It gave the illusion of no longer being open to the elements, and that lifted everyone's spirits.

We sat around the ship's only real lantern when the daylight started to fail. On Home, the soft electric glow of appliances and terminals never really went away, so we were unused to real darkness. It began in the stairwells, pooling as if the blackness were being poured in from above, filling the underdeck hold. Everyone instinctively moved away, huddling together and turning their backs on the shafts of shadow. When the metal down there groaned or creaked as the ship continued to settle or freeze, someone would glance over, stare uneasily down to where the handrail dipped into the blackness, and then look hurriedly away.

So we sat around the lantern, staring at it as if it held back some of the unease oozing from the darkness below. Sevin had managed to connect the solar panel to the generator, and that promised an extra hour or two of usable power tomorrow. We'd have to ration how we used it because the panel was damaged and working at only about 40 percent effectiveness, but it promised a renewable source of energy that should last till we were rescued. Again, the mood lightened, and even Sevin, proud of his work, seemed to unwind a little. As he handed out water bottles, he met my eyes for the first time since I planned the scouting mission, and he gave me a nod of acknowledgment and a half-smile. If there was any duplicity there, I didn't feel it.

"What about our meds?" asked Muce when the water bottles reached her.

Sevin frowned.

"I guess we'll just have to go without," he said. "There are painkillers in the med kit and some antibiotics."

"No," said Muce. "Our regular nighttime meds."

Sevin hesitated.

"I normally take two green ones and a white one that looks like a candytorp but isn't," said Muce.

Several people nodded their agreement.

"I take two green ones, too," said Dren, "and two orange ones."

"Me too," said Teada.

"Anyone used to take the little purple ones?" asked Trest.

"Me," I said.

"Those things were nasty. I'm on the diamond-shaped lozenge things now. You?"

I nodded. Most people on Home didn't take meds, so it struck me as odd that everyone onboard did. I was going to say as much, but Sevin cut me off.

"We don't have any of those."

"Not even the little orange ones?" asked Dren.

"No," said Sevin. "None of them."

"Great," said Dren, beaming. "They are horrible."

More good news. The atmosphere of festivity spread once more, and soon we were going round the circle and playing name games to remember who we all were. There was a thin, gangly boy called Herse. The girl with the silvery hair who had agreed to come with Bryce and me in the morning was Yasmine. She was graceful and elegant. Unsettlingly so.

The sky completed its turn from russet to purple, then black, and we fastened our eyes and minds on the lantern, sitting under our blankets and chattering happily about all the things we had done to get us here in the first place. Normally such matters would be secret, shameful, but here they connected us. At the reeducation facility, we would have been kept isolated, brought together only for group exercises in which our interaction would have been limited at best. Here, we were a community.

"One time," said Dren, "I pulled the cover off the transerver in my building and yanked all the cables out. Killed every monitor on the block. You'd think the world had ended! All these people wandering out into the hallways, staring at each other. Helpless. Like fish tossed out onto the beach. It was hilarious."

He puckered his mouth like a stranded fish, and everyone laughed—not just at him, but at the illicit thrill of it all.

"I light fires," said Teada. "Nothing big. Nothing dangerous or too destructive, though I did accidentally burn down our kitchen one time."

She flushed at the memory, but when everyone laughed, she grinned shyly.

"It wasn't a very nice kitchen," she added.

"I'm a hacker," said Trest, raising a confessional hand, and getting murmurs of understanding from several of the others. "Uninspired, I know, but I like to think of myself as pursuing a proud and noble tradition: creating chaos and absurdity through the implosion of other people's digital order."

"I flushed my comm pad down the sanitation system," said Muce.

"Or there's that," said Trest, grinning. "Terse and to the point."

There was a ripple of amusement.

"What about you, Sola?" Muce asked.

"Oh, nothing so dramatic," I said. "I just break out from time to time. Rig the doors and elevators so I can get down to the street and wander Sindrone. I like to have the city to myself."

"At night?" Muce prompted.

"Uh huh," I nodded.

"I'd never do that," said Muce, risking a glance towards the nearest stairwell. "I don't like the dark."

She wasn't the only one. Herse shifted in his huddled crouch and briefly, uneasily, looked past me to the shaft of blackness that led below to the underdeck. When his eyes returned to me, he looked wary.

"You don't steal stuff though," said Dren. It wasn't a question.

Several of the younger kids looked bemused. I just shook my head.

"You two know each other?" asked Teada.

It was Dren's turn to shake his head, but he looked smug.

"I'm just a good guesser," he said.

I gave him a look, and he smiled a private smile and winked at me, like we were old friends or more. I turned quickly away.

"So why do you break curfew if you don't steal anything?" asked Teada.

"I just like to be outside and alone."

More glances into the dark. More appraising looks. Some of their former unease was returning.

"Cool," said Teada. "Weird, but cool."

I considered the girl with the orange hair. I wasn't sure she really meant what she'd said, but I gave her a nod of acknowledgement.

"A roamer, huh?" said Yasmine. "Hence the shoes."

While everyone else wore soft, slipper like shoes, I wore walking boots with thick soles and laces. Not so much old-fashioned as antique.

"I guess," I said, bristling. Yasmine was easily the most beautiful girl on the ship. I don't know why that mattered, but it did. I felt momentarily humiliated, and that always makes me aggressive. I stared at her, daring her to say something else.

She nodded and smiled, seeming oblivious to my challenge. "I like them," she said, apparently meaning it. "Very retro."

My turn to nod and smile, with something like gratitude.

"I guess retro is another word for deviant," I said. "And you know what they say about deviance."

"*Deviance is unattractive . . .*" Trest intoned.

"*And jeopardizes all we hold dear*," the others completed in one voice. We'd all been hearing that phrase all our lives—and would likely have heard it a lot more if we'd made it to Jerem. A couple of them grinned sheepishly, but the familiar words gave them pause. Something

52

of the group's high spirits had leached out into the frozen night.

"I heard," said Yasmine, "that they ignore us most of the time—the city government, I mean. Turn a blind eye to our little misdeeds. Until something really bad happens."

"Like what?" asked Muce.

Yasmine shrugged.

"Murder," said Sevin.

That killed the laughter. Everyone stared at him.

"People don't get killed on Home," said Teada.

"Not usually, no," said Sevin. "But once in a while, it happens. Then they round up all the deviants—us—and pack them off to reeducation."

"Are you saying there was a murder recently?" I asked. "In an authorized city?"

"A week before they sentenced us to this little jaunt," said Sevin. "In Sindrone. The cadets were talking about it. Some guy who got locked out of his building by mistake in Sector Four. Someone took a knife and—"

He motioned a swift slash across his throat.

"Blood everywhere," he concluded, wolfishly.

There was an uneasy silence.

"You're making it up," said Muce.

"Perhaps," said Sevin, grinning. "But now that we know Sola likes to wander Sindrone at night, I think we should keep an eye on her." He paused for effect, and then, as every eye flicked uneasily my way, he threw his head back and laughed. The others relaxed slowly, but I glared at him. He just shrugged and grinned.

"What about you, Bryce?" said Trest. "What punched your ticket for this voyage of the damned?"

"Oh," said Bryce, "nothing exciting. Hacked my eduserver to change my grade on a test. Busted, obviously."

He smiled self-deprecatingly, but I felt a sudden certainty that he was lying. When I looked at him, his face went blank, like a comm screen when the power cuts off.

"Well," said Trest getting to his feet. "I'm tired. It's been a long, death-defying day, and I need my beauty sleep. Or rather, my mental balance sleep. Beauty is a lost cause."

He glanced back towards the stasis pods, and I felt his unease at the prospect of walking away from the lantern and past the darkened stairwells.

"And I have a walk across alien terrain tomorrow," said Yasmine, "so I think I'll turn in."

I nodded and managed not to say anything about her not needing her beauty sleep.

"We're just going to sleep in our pods?" asked Carlann.

"As opposed to?" said Sevin.

Carlann looked blank. She shrugged.

"But," she began, eyes wide, "at Home we have our own rooms, our own music, and . . . I don't know."

She finished lamely, looking down at her fidgeting hands. Though what she was saying made her sound young and unreasonable—what, after all, did it matter what we usually did on Home?—no one sneered or made jokes at her expense because we all felt the same thing. Sleep was private.

"Might be fun," said Trest. "All of us here together. Like camping, the way people used to."

"I don't want to *camp*," said Carlann simply. "I want to be by myself at Home."

"You'll be by yourself in your pod," Trest tried, with an encouraging smile. "All sealed up and safe."

"I'll still know you're there," she said.

"I think it's kind of exciting," said Yasmine, with a nod of encouragement to Trest. "All explorers together."

"We're not explorers," said Carlann, doggedly. "We're deviants who crashed on a hostile planet. No contrary position is viable."

"I'm going to suggest we stop saying that," said Trest.

"And I'm going to suggest we go to bed," said Sevin. "In our pods. Unless you'd rather sleep right here. Or in the underdeck?"

Put like that, even Carlann didn't argue the point.

Sevin picked up the lantern and took a few steps towards the pods, then held it up and waited for everyone to find theirs.

"I need to shut this off to conserve battery life," he said, "so you'll want to put your pod lights on till you get settled. It's going to be darker than you're used to."

Herse gave him a look of silent apprehension, then busied himself with the few bits of things in his stasis pod. I watched Sevin for a moment by the unearthly light of the pale lantern, wondering whether his crack about someone being murdered in Sindrone was just a joke, or if it had some basis in truth. The possibility bothered me, which was strange. We were, after all, about as far from Sindrone as we could possibly be.

As if to make the point, Sevin set the lantern down so that the shadows leapt strangely, then shut it off. It was as if the dark from the underdeck rose like a tide, engulfing the ship and plunging us all into blackness.

CHAPTER 6

THERE WAS ONLY ONE WASHROOM, AN ANCIENT, BARE
metal affair with a toilet, sink, and miniscule shower
stall, though we had decided not to use that until we
knew we could replenish the water supply. That meant getting access to the cistern and filling it with snow sometime
the next day. It was cold enough that body odor wouldn't
get bad for a day or two, so Sevin had suggested that
everyone sleep in the same things they came in. He looked
embarrassed when he said it, and almost everyone lowered
their eyes, alarmed—even ashamed—that this was our new
reality. Carlann pulled a disgusted face, but he was right.

We all had a week's supply of clothes in the hold, but we
would stay out of them as long as we could, which meant
we wouldn't have to brave the impenetrable darkness of
the windowless underdeck. Even back on Home, when the

57

lights had been on and we had been loading our luggage, I hadn't liked it down there in the twisting bowels of the ship. I could manage in what I was wearing for another day, though I suspected that the decision suited Sevin because it meant continuing to wear his uniform.

I stayed in the bathroom longer than I needed to, trying to pretend I was alone, but I could hear them just outside the door, their voices, the groaning of metal as they moved around. For a long moment, I stared at the streak of rust where the hot tap had been dripping on the dull steel of the basin, listening. I tried to recall the details of my sleek, warm bathroom back on Home with its music and soft lighting, but I caught my reflection in the streaked mirror and the memories fell away. I looked somehow young, and the blue streak in my hair that had seemed so important, so rebellious, just made that clearer.

To compensate, I tried to see where the pipes to the shower went, studying the panel lines to see where someone might crawl in to refill the water tank. I had thought the lack of power would be the hardest thing to endure, but not being able to wash properly suddenly seemed much worse. I was filled with the terrible certainty that we were only a couple of days of hot running water away from chaos and barbarism.

By the time I was done, everyone had already gone to bed, except Bryce. The only light came from the soft glow of a few stasis pods, whose shifting occupants caused uncanny shadows to ripple around the joists, cables, and ductwork of the ship. Bryce was standing by the side viewer, peering out into the night, his long chin resting on one fist. When he saw me, he gave me a nod that may or may not have been an invitation. I hesitated a fraction too long, then added to the awkwardness by saying, "The others have already turned in?"

Obviously they had.

Bryce nodded, nonchalant, and returned his gaze to the window. I dithered again, feeling the blood rise in my cheeks, and half-turned to my stasis pod with the little picture of the angel.

"Not the way I thought this would go," he mused, as if to himself.

"This?" I said.

"The trip. My reeducation. I'd been dreading it," he added. "But this . . ."

He gazed out into the night, and I felt the ripple of his emotions from weariness, worry, and even sadness to something simpler and far less negative.

"It's kind of amazing," he said, still staring at the snowscape outside. "I'm on Valkrys! I'm alive. There's no light, and I'm not sure when I'll bathe properly again, but I'm not being lectured about the evils of . . . everything. And the place itself, apart from being cold enough to freeze your fingers off, isn't so bad." He turned and gave me a smile. "Who'd have thought it, right?"

I smiled back and, since the invitation was now clear, made my slow way towards him.

"I mean," he continued in a distant, dreamy tone, "look at this place!"

I stood behind him, close enough to hear the sound of his breathing, close enough to catch the faint, musky aroma of his hair, trying to focus on what I could see through the window, not on him or the thudding of my heart.

"Beautiful, isn't it?" he said. "I mean, wild and terrifying and deadly, but yeah. Beautiful."

"I thought the exact same thing the first time I looked out," I said, pleased. "I guess we really are deviants."

"That's unattractive, you know," he added with dry humor.

"*And jeopardizes all we hold dear,*" I agreed.

He laughed, a little uncertainly, and looked back out of the window.

"If you can believe it, I always wanted to paint," he said. "Not on the pads, I mean. With actual paints. Stupid, I know, but if I could, if I had the stuff to do it . . . I'd love to try and paint this place. I know I could just snap a shot with my pad, but I want to build it, you know? Color by color, stroke by tiny stroke . . ."

He turned to smile at me, realized how close we were, and turned shyly back to the window, surveying the landscape with contented relish. I felt his curiosity, his uncertainty, and a different kind of fear that was almost excitement. I edged a fraction closer, suddenly wanting him to look at me with those blue-gray eyes in the same way. As he shifted, the pale light reflecting off the snow caught his hair. He ruffled it, to give his hands something to do, and I caught a glimpse of something on his scalp.

"Do that again," I said.

He hesitated, baffled, then did so.

"What?" he asked.

"There's some kind of mark under your hair," I said. "May I?"

I raised my hand to the back of his head and paused, till he gave me the fractional nod I needed. My mouth felt dry. So, I thought, was his.

His hair was black and short. I moved it carefully.

"Oh," he said. "The triangle."

I stared at him.

"Had it as long as I can remember," he said, reaching up and gently pushing my hand away.

Even though his fingers had touched mine, the intimacy of the moment had vanished. I felt his annoyance and something else. Humiliation.

"What does it mean?" I asked.

"Nothing," he said. "Doesn't need to mean anything, right?"

"Right," I said, not believing it, feeling him pull away, his mind becoming distant, brushing mine away as he had my hand.

I turned quickly.

"See what I have," I said, trying to sound playful.

"What do you mean?"

"Look in my hair," I said. "You have a triangle. Maybe I have a comm pad or a map of all the best vapo joints in Sindrone."

He hesitated, then decided to play along. The glow from the stasis pods lessened as someone else tried to sleep.

There was only one still on now, and it was open. Bryce's, I guessed.

"Okay," he said, "bend your neck."

I did so, feeling my hair fall around my face, feeling his fingertips pushing through to my scalp, strong, gentle fingers gathering and parting . . .

"Nothing," he said. "Wait: there's a recipe. How to make protein bars out of air and snow."

"Funny," I said, intoxicated by his closeness. "Anything else?"

He started to say something, then stopped.

"Yes," he said, and now his tone was quite different. It was low and serious, and his mind was full of confusion.

So was mine.

"Seriously?" I said. "What is it?"

"It's a triangle," he said. "Like mine. Exactly like it."

I struggled, but his grip tightened.

"Hold still," he said. "I can't believe it. It's the same."

"You'd better not be kidding," I said, suddenly uneasy.

"You know I'm not," he said, releasing me and moving so he could look into my face, his gaze penetrating. "Who are you?"

"I told you," I said. "My name is Sola. I'm a roamer en route to reeducation like you."

"What about your family? Your parents?"

"My father's a programmer," I said, unnerved by the intensity of his stare. "My mother works in local government. Waste management systems. Why?"

"Good middle-class jobs," said Bryce, thoughtfully.

"Everyone on Home is middle class," I said. "Near enough."

He smiled a hard, bitter smile.

"So they say," he said. "Home looks after its own."

"Carlann has the same tattoo," I said. "I saw it when I was stitching her head. It looks old, but it's quite clear."

He frowned again.

"That makes no sense," he said. He sat back, considering me, then came to a decision and got to his feet. "I'd better be turning in," he said.

"This doesn't disturb you?" I said, amazed.

"The tattoo?" he replied. "More than everything else on this trip, you mean?"

"But it suggests . . ." I began, but faltered. I had no idea how to end the sentence.

"Exactly," he said.

I looked down, but I couldn't let it end like this.

"Bryce," I said after him. He turned. "Did I say something to offend you?"

He stood there for a moment, as if trying to frame an answer, but finally just shook his head.

"Don't worry about it," he said. "Good night."

●

I RETURNED CAREFULLY TO MY STASIS POD—AVOIDING looking at the stairwells below, the darkness in which was now complete and liquid—popped open the acrylic sleeve, and slid in, adjusting the sheet as best I could and wrapping a blanket around me before closing the lid. After a few minutes in the private glow, I shut the light off and lay alone and silent in the dark, thinking about Bryce and the strange mark on his head. A mark we apparently shared.

To take my mind off it, I got out my comm pad and powered it on. Background operations and stored items came up on the screen, but that was all. No signal. I scrolled through a few images of friends and family, but they didn't make me feel either happy or sad, though the absence of the grid link icon disconcerted me more than I would have expected.

I found a copy of the same angel picture I had printed and stuck to the lid of the pod when I first boarded. It was taken from an antique painting in what had once been a cathedral in Sindrone, from the days when people still believed in gathering together to look for God. The image showed a beautiful, if slightly stiff, woman with wings hovering over a tiny little town.

I had stumbled on the picture years ago and kept it, for reasons I couldn't really explain. It made me feel safe, like someone was watching over me. But it wasn't just for comfort. I liked it, but it triggered something else inside me: a yearning desire not to be looked after by the angel, but to *be* her—up there, free and gazing down on the world. When I stared at it, fixing the picture with a focused, unblinking gaze until everything around me fell away completely, it felt both thrilling and a little sad. There were, after all, no such things as angels, as there were no longer any such things as cathedrals.

I powered the comm pad down and put it in my pocket.

For a moment, I thought I had tricked my brain into forgetting about Bryce, but his image floated up in my head however much I shifted and rolled, trying to get comfortable enough to sleep. Even inside the pod, it was cold enough that my breath fogged, and I wrapped my blanket tight around me. I didn't like the way it bound me, cocoon-like, but I needed to hold what little body heat I had.

It took me at least an hour to drop off, and my slumber, when it came, was uneasy, troubled by strange dreams. Once I woke, convinced someone had been peering through the clear plastic hood of my stasis pod as I slept, but there was no one there. I lay very still, listening, hearing only the muffled sound of the wind forcing its way through the patched-up hole in the roof, staring fixedly into the blackness of the ship.

Nothing.

I closed my eyes again tight, but a moment later, opened them again quickly. I had felt sure a light had passed over me. Not a flashlight beam. Something yellower and more diffuse. I stared through the clear cover of the pod, and I was sure of it. A shifting golden glow was coming from somewhere in the rear of the ship. It blossomed for a moment, creating hard, leaping shadows, then dimmed, though it did not disappear completely.

I rolled over, closing my eyes, and tried to shrug off my overactive imagination. But I could still feel it. A presence in the ship. Someone who wasn't supposed to be there, crouched in the blackness. Watching.

I was being ridiculous.

I forced myself to push the release button on the hood, feeling it slide open almost soundlessly. I rolled onto my belly and craned my neck, looking out into the ship.

It was truly dark now, as if the blackness of the under-deck had risen like a tide and drowned the rest of the ship. The air was cold and smelled faintly of oil and metal, but there was no sign of movement. So far as I could tell, all the stasis pods were closed. Another night, part of me might have wanted to get out and walk around—my old roaming instinct—but not tonight.

I was afraid of the dark, of its uncanny completeness.

There were no reassuring digiscreens. No glowing lamps. No comm pad linking me to the rest of the world. No world at all.

I was disconnected, unplugged for the first time in my life. Though I sometimes craved isolation, now I felt merely alone and lost in the night, scared of the blackness, of the wind, of the empty planet outside. I felt raw, stripped naked; all those layers of civilization I usually resented but took for granted had been peeled away until I felt like a baby, clueless and vulnerable . . .

Then I saw the glow again, amber now. It was coming from one of the stasis pods down the gangway. I craned my neck to see which one and counted them off. It was on the boys' side. But it wasn't Bryce, Trest, or Sevin. I knew where those were. There was that other boy—the thin, quiet kid,

Herse—but for some reason, he had been given a pod on the other side.

So it was Dren. The blond boy who had suggested he knew more about me than I had revealed.

I stared, disconcerted, and the glow flickered from inside the pod, then went out. I waited, but the darkness was sudden and complete. The light stayed off.

Probably the boy was just messing with his comm pad, playing a game or trying to get a signal.

So why had I sensed it so close to my own pod, as if he had been looking in?

I must have imagined that part. Dreamed it.

Yes, that was it. I was being childish, spooked by nothing more than the darkness—which had, until now, always been my friend, my thrill. With that in mind, I took hold of the edge of the stasis pod and pushed a cautious foot out onto the cold deck. Then the other. As I stood up, I felt the unease, the panic, the rootlessness and dread all fall away. This was my ship now. There was nothing in the darkness but me.

I moved softly along the gantry to the side window I had rubbed clear earlier, feeling pleased with myself, though I still steered clear of the steps to the underdeck. Even as my eyes got used to the lightlessness, the stairs stayed wells of blackness, as if by some inversion of gravity the darkness in the ship was actually pouring up from below. I moved quickly past the shaft and up to the window. It was still smeared and blurry, but I could just make out the pallor of the icy ground in the night. And on it . . .

I gasped, pressing my face to the window and staring.

Standing out in the snow, no more than thirty yards from the ship and half obscured by strange shadows, but still clear and undeniable, was a girl.

CHAPTER

SHE LOOKED ABOUT MY AGE OR A LITTLE LESS. SHE was small and frail and wore no outer jacket, over a thin, old-fashioned dress that billowed in the breeze with her hair. She was motionless. Just standing, looking at the ship, her head cocked slightly to one side, and I was as sure as I could be, even at this distance, that I had never seen her before. She was not one of ours.

It couldn't be, but there she was.

I stared, aghast, not sure what to do or think. I should wake Sevin or the others. I should go outside.

But.

It felt wrong. Impossible.

A girl on Valkrys? A girl we had not brought with us, out there in the freezing night, just looking? It made no sense, but the strangeness of it, the dreamlike and uncanny quality of the thing, acted on my mind like adrenaline.

I had to get closer.

I didn't wake the others. I put my boots and jacket on and walked to the plastic hatchway in the ceiling, releasing the rope ties with unsteady fingers, and climbed up and out.

It was savagely cold. No one could be out in this without protective gear. It just wasn't possible.

I slid down the fuselage and onto the packed snow, then picked my way round the *Phetteron*. Normally this would be bracing, a secret thrill, out in the night, wandering alone. But tonight I felt only tension and dread. Pressing myself against the frigid hull of the ship, I inched my way to the battered nose, certain beyond all else that if the girl was still out there, I did not want her to see me.

My breathing was rushed and shallow, my heart racing. As my eyes got used to the dark, my surroundings developed a curious, bluish hue unlike anything I had ever seen, and I thought the distant mountains were visible in ways they shouldn't be, as if they were glowing unevenly from within. A pair of small, pale moons rode high in the sky, but the light seemed to be coming as much from the rock itself as from above, and the shadows were uncanny and shifting, as if seen through water.

I shouldn't be out here, I thought.

The wind gusted, blowing a fine swirl of snow dust into my face, and—thinking of hair or fabric brushing against my skin—I shuddered with more than cold.

Go back, I thought. *Wake the others. Or just crawl into your stasis tube and close it and stay there till morning . . .*

I couldn't. I had to know. To see.

I rounded the nose of the ship with infinite care, still hugging the scored and dented metal as if it were a lifeline, an anchor on some rational version of the world. And then, without warning, I was round and out and staring at the spot where the girl had been.

Even in the odd and uneven light, it was clear. She was not there.

Perhaps she never had been. I stood there considering the possibility, hugging my jacket around me till I could stand the biting wind no longer and began working my way back to the tear in the hull roof. No. I decided. Unlikely as it may be, the girl had been no trick of the strange light, no delusion of my anxious, confused, half-sleeping brain. I just didn't believe that. She had been real. She was gone now. But she had been there.

Back on board I checked the viewer once more, but there was nothing to see except the cold, empty planet. So I returned to my stasis tube, lay down, and closed the hood.

Going out should have made me feel better. So should the fact that the girl was no longer visible. They didn't. I still felt like we were being watched and that parts of the ship were unnaturally dark. I lay motionless for a long time, and if I slept at all, it was in such brief snatches that I was unaware of losing even a moment's consciousness.

CHAPTER

I GOT UP THE MOMENT DAWN GRAYED THE DARKNESS, and was not the first to do so, but the previous evening's cheerful atmosphere had utterly gone. Everyone had a hunted, haunted look about them that suggested more than tiredness. No one said anything about the previous night, but they were jittery, constantly glancing about, and the line for the toilet was both subdued and irritable.

Maybe the sense of adventure had worn off some. Maybe it was the bitter cold. Maybe it was the humiliation of waiting patiently to use a toilet used moments before by someone else, a toilet that retained their warmth, their smell. And maybe I hadn't been the only one to see something inexplicable last night.

Inexplicable, I thought, like it was just a mystery, a puzzle. Like I wasn't scared.

"You guys need to get used to not using your comm pads," Sevin said. "We'll need to use the power we have for recharging very carefully."

I gave Dren a significant look, but he didn't react. He just looked at me a little too fixedly, his head tipped onto one shoulder. It was an odd look, empty in the way animals' gazes in pictures sometimes are. A moment later, it was gone, and he was just Dren, giving me his smug stare. I turned away, keen to get out of there, if only for a couple of hours. I said nothing about the girl I had seen through the viewer, partly because I didn't want to scare the others and partly because saying it would make it real.

"Sola."

I turned and found Teada waving to me from the rear of the ship. She was standing on a crate beneath the panel we had fitted across the hole in the roof, which was rattling and whistling. I made my way along the narrow gangway past the others, who sat in subdued huddles. When they were all in their stasis pods, it wasn't so bad; but when everyone was up, the ship instantly became crowded and claustrophobic. This was not a vessel designed for its passengers to be conscious.

"What?" I asked when I reached Teada.

"I don't think you're gonna be going out today," she said. "Not for a while, at least. Look."

She offered a hand to help me up onto the crate, but I hesitated before I took it, swallowing back the discomfort such contact inevitably produced. Teada read the reluctance in my eyes and gave me a knowing sideways grin.

"Feels like we're a long way from Home, doesn't it?" she said.

She wasn't talking about physical distance. I gave her a rueful smile and nodded.

"My parents would have seven types of fits if they could see how we were living," I said. Part of them would blame me for it, too, I thought, but I kept that to myself. Whether Teada guessed what I was thinking or not, her grin became a little worn, and her eyes held something like sadness.

"So what's the problem?" I asked, keen to change the subject. I was standing on the crate next to her now, almost close enough to feel the warmth of her body.

Teada nudged one corner of the plastic up, and the entire panel bucked and rippled in the wind. Cold air washed over us in a jet as a handful of snowflakes blew into the *Phetteron* and settled on our faces.

"Storm," said Teada. "It's been building for an hour. Can't see much of anything out there, and it's getting worse."

"Surely we can slip out for a little while," I said, frustrated. I pushed the panel up as far as the rope would permit and stood on my tiptoes so that I could look out. The frigid wind made my eyes water, but there was nothing to see anyway. The blizzard was impenetrable.

I cursed.

"What the hell are you doing?" called Sevin.

I turned angrily and saw him standing below me, wreathed in stray snowflakes. He was carrying a box of protein bars.

"We're trying to keep what little warmth we have inside," he roared. "Get down from there."

"I was trying to see what conditions were like before we went out," I shot back, hopping down from the crate and staring him down.

"Well, I would have thought it was pretty obvious," he replied. "You can't go out in this."

"Says who?" I shouted. "You might have landed the ship, Sevin, but that doesn't make you our commander."

"Then who is? You?" he sneered.

"Maybe we don't need a commander," I returned. "Maybe we can make decisions for ourselves."

"Like the decision to go exploring in zero visibility? Fine. Knock yourself out. We could do with one less mouth to feed."

"Maybe I'll find food of my own," I said, not believing it. Food came in sealed wrappers and tamperproof bottles. If there was some form of naturally occurring food here, I probably wouldn't even recognize it, let alone have the courage to try it.

"Sure," Sevin answered. "And maybe you'll fall down a ravine. Either way."

He shrugged like he didn't much care what happened to me, but his face was flushed with anger. Everyone had stopped what they were doing to watch and listen. I felt their eyes on me—Bryce, Trest, little Muce—and suddenly the pressure was almost unbearable. I wanted to storm out noisily, but the little ship gave me nowhere to go.

Outside, I was ashamed to admit to myself, wasn't an option, and even in daylight the stairs to the underdeck had an aura of menace.

I snatched one of the protein bars from his box, stormed past him, and flipped the lid of my stasis pod. Everyone watched in silence as I climbed in and closed it, rolling onto my stomach and pulling the blind so that no one could see in.

I tried to think of the angel picture on my comm pad, serene and watchful and free; but I was furious, far too furious to actually sleep, though I suddenly felt quite exhausted. I knew Sevin was right, but he had backed me into a corner. Or maybe I had done that all by myself. That just made me feel worse. I should have swallowed my childish unease and gone downstairs. There I could have wandered beyond the gaze of the others. As it was, I was trapped in my pod till I decided to slink out, watched by everybody . . .

It was colder than it had been overnight, but in my anger I had left my blanket outside, so I just lay huddled there, knees drawn up to my chest, teeth chattering. After a few minutes, I opened the protein bar with the smallest movements I could manage, hoping vaguely that everyone would think I was asleep. I munched quietly, still face-down, wishing I was outside, wishing I was Home, wishing I was anywhere but here.

●

I WAS ELEVEN WHEN I FIRST WENT ROAMING. BEFORE THEN, I had sort of wandered off by accident while out with my family, but that was the first time I deliberately broke curfew. The lockdown system on the floor of our apartment building had been malfunctioning for two days. The first night I had been afraid, but nothing happened. On the second, my faith in the essential safety of Sindrone trumped the hazy paranoia that was the paradoxical flipside of that safety.

"We're perfectly safe because we have security," my father used to say.

"Safe from what?" I asked.

"Everything. Nothing can harm us. Nothing wants to."

"So why do we need security?"

He gave me his knowing smile that felt like a pat on the head.

"It's because there is such good security in places like Sindrone that there is no crime," said my father. "That's true of all affiliated cities. We're so well protected that bad people know there's no point in trying anything. So they either become law-abiding citizens like the rest of us, or they go somewhere else."

"Like where?"

"I believe there are outlying settlements on Jerem and Kaylix where things are a little less orderly," he said, vaguely, his eyes on his comm pad, "but we don't need to worry too much about them."

Kaylix was another of Home's moons.

"Sindrone is the safest pace in the universe," he added. "The lockdown system will be up and running in a day or two, but till then there's absolutely nothing to worry about."

I was so convinced by what he told me that I decided right then that I would slip out that night. I lay awake in my clothes till just after midnight, then got up. My parents were asleep in their respective rooms, and though I was inordinately careful not to make a noise, getting out was easy. With the lockdown system out of order, I rode the elevator to the ground floor and slipped out the back door because I knew the front was being monitored.

I was only outside for eighteen minutes. That was how long it took the security services to respond to the exit alarm I had unknowingly triggered, spot me on the surveillance cameras mounted on every street corner, and come get me. Eighteen minutes. It would have been less, but I had started running as soon as I got to the street and was much further away from the apartment than anyone expected.

I loved it. The night. The silence. The lights of the great glass towers against the sky. The feeling of being alone in the world, unhitched from the tech grid into which I was wired all my waking hours. At first I was anxious, and being without my comm pad made me feel like I had forgotten something important; but as the thrill of the experience itself swept over me, I became someone entirely new. I felt the ground through the soles of my shoes as if I had never taken a step before, aware of my own weight and the way my bones and muscles moved me. I was—and this I would never admit to anyone—like an animal, at home in the darkness, living on instincts, on smell and sight and touch and hearing . . .

Eighteen minutes.

My father seemed merely baffled, assuming I had wound up outside by some kind of accident, but my mother's shock and disappointment were deeper and more acute. When the security services brought me home, she was so angry she couldn't speak. She hid her trembling hands behind her back so the others wouldn't see. When the officers had gone, my father sat me down and told me how I should be more careful—never ever go out after nightfall, and never go anywhere without my comm pad—but my mother just watched me sideways, saying nothing, gripped by some deep-seated alarm or fear.

The night before, she had come into my room and kissed me, an old-fashioned habit of hers I was sure none of my friends' parents did and I never spoke of. After that night, she never did it again. Not when I was sad or confused or angry. Not casually or when she sensed I might need it most. Never.

It was almost a year before I went roaming again. This time, the lockdown collapse was the result of power failure affecting the whole block, so I had almost an hour to myself before the security services were alerted. I made it back to the apartment before they could track me. When I said I'd been at home the whole time, my mother stared at me knowingly, as furious as before. Later, though, I wondered if there was something else under her anger, something like fear.

When I was younger, we used to spend time together in ways few parents on Home did. She would walk me through things on the techgrid that she liked, share old screenbooks with me, actually sit beside me and share a device so that I would feel her shoulder warm against mine. That all stopped after that first night's roaming, as if she thought that being more like a regular family would curb my wayward instincts.

It didn't.

I went out twice more before I got caught, and every time the thing that worried me most, that very nearly prevented me from roaming, wasn't the fear of breaking the law. It wasn't getting in trouble with the security services or risking some indelible mark on my government record or the consequences for my adult future. It wasn't the shame of being discovered or the baffled anger of my father as he begged me to explain why I was doing something so pointless and irrational. It was that look on my mother's face.

I had never seen anything like it before, certainly not on someone who had always been as nurturing and attentive a parent as anyone on Home could hope to have. But after that year, my relationship with her changed forever. She rarely spoke to me and never about anything personal. She avoided being alone with me, and on those rare occasions where we would eat at the same time or sit together in the shared room on our comm pads, I would catch her watching me unreadably.

For over a year I stayed in, resisting every urge and opportunity to roam, sure that if I proved myself good and obedient, her attitude would change and I would get my mother back.

But the damage, it seemed, was done.

She kept her distance, and as I got used to it, as habit slowly convinced me that it was normal, I abandoned the idea of winning her back. What did I care if she showed me neither love nor even affection? I started sneaking out again, for longer now, staying out till dawn and wandering for miles, not even bothering to make it home undetected. By the time I was sentenced to reeducation for the second time, my mother had become a stranger to me, someone who went through the motions of parental responsibility out of a sense of obligation. She did not know me, or attempt to, and the feeling was mutual.

Two days after my fifteenth birthday, she was diagnosed with cancer. She went through a course of exhausting and humiliating treatments that reduced her to a wizened, hairless wretch. She looked at least a hundred years old in the absurd knitted cap she insisted on wearing over her bald scalp, her last, failed attempt at dignity. I sat with her. I told her I was sorry for making her life so stressful and that I would make it up to her, but she just looked at me as if I were someone she had never met before.

The doctors said she beat the cancer, like it was a war she had won on her own; but if so, it was the kind of war after which even the victors are so crippled and weary that they might as well have lost. She retreated into herself, barely speaking to anyone, staying in her room and reading old screenbooks. When word came of my latest reeducation sentence, she just nodded to show she'd heard but did not look at me. My father gave her a long, anguished look.

When he turned to me, his eyes said, quite plainly, *This is Your Fault*.

I resolved to get through reeducation and then never roam again. Because however angry I was at my father for daring to imply I was responsible for my mother's collapse, for our collapse as a family, I knew he was right. I would get through my stint on Jerem and then I would go home, finish my studies, enter a government training program, be a good citizen. No contrary position was viable.

Except, of course, that I had never made it to Jerem, and the escape I had promised myself, an escape I probably lacked the courage to actually try even if I could pull it off, had been forced on me. I had left my family further behind than I could ever have planned, and I was—perhaps predictably—miserable and alone for all the closeness of my fellow deviants.

Deviance is unattractive, I thought, *and jeopardizes all we hold dear*.

But losing what I held dear was the least of my problems. I had seen a girl I did not know out there in the snow, and some long-forgotten instinct had woken. It told me to be afraid. There was something terrible out there. Something that wanted to come in.

CHAPTER

AMAZINGLY, I DID SLEEP. EVENTUALLY. JUST FOR AN hour. But I woke slowly, and that was good. The pod had warmed up a little, and rest had drained some of my fury and embarrassment. The stasis pods weren't completely airtight, and some of the sound from the main hold seeped in: the clanking of feet on the metal gangway, creaking cables, occasional shouts of muffled laughter. I lay there, listening, enjoying my isolation until I felt I could rejoin the others. If I timed it right, they'd be busy doing something, or talking as a group, and I could slip out unnoticed.

I opened the pod and climbed out in a single decisive motion.

The nine others were all sitting together in a rough horseshoe down by the doors that led into the flight deck.

Sevin was the focus of the group. Most of the rest had their backs to me, though a few turned when they heard the hiss of my pod opening. Muce gave me a wave that I, falteringly, returned. Sevin's eyes found me in the gloom, but he kept talking, like a teacher in one of those schools they used to have before the infonet.

I stood up and stretched pointedly, rolling my head and extending my arms till I felt sinews pop and ease. It was still very cold in the main hold, and I found my blanket, wrapping it around my shoulders. The jerry-rigged hatch was still straining and fluttering in the storm, though someone had lashed it more firmly into place.

"Sola," said Sevin, at last. "Please join us."

He said it carefully, neither welcoming nor commanding, an attempt at neutrality that suggested we could move beyond our last exchange as if it never happened.

"What's this?" I said, approaching the group, but unable to keep the defiance out of my voice.

"*Phetteron* Council," said Sevin, and now he smiled slightly self-consciously.

"Glad it's nothing pompous," I said.

Teada grinned at me and ran one hand through her unevenly orange hair.

"We've decided to meet as a group twice a day," said Sevin, breezing right past my remark. "Update our situation, share ideas, make plans. Everyone gets to talk. Come sit down. We'd appreciate your input."

I hesitated and looked away, then shrugged and joined them, trying to look like I was only doing so because I had no better way of using my time. I sat next to Muce, who beamed at me. Yasmine gave me a cool smile and a nod. Bryce, sitting opposite her, smiled too, if a little too carefully. I looked down, self-conscious.

I had behaved badly, stupidly, and the fact that everyone was pretending I hadn't made it feel worse. I resolved to sit still and silent while the *Phetteron* Council went through whatever absurd business it had to discuss.

Except that it wasn't absurd. They talked about bathroom rotations, food rations, and how they would trap the snow and melt it into drinking water. They talked about going through the care packages they had all brought from Home, the little luxuries set aside for them by their parents to make reeducation a little more bearable, and pooling all resources that weren't too personal to share. Everyone had candy and zip pops, and several of them had specially flavored protein packs. What had been private luxuries would now be carefully and evenly distributed. Dren frowned at this, but Sevin talked about how much stronger we were as a unit, watching out for each other, and the blond boy eventually nodded his agreement. Muce said she didn't want to go get her care package from the underdeck because it was "deeply creepy," and though several people smiled indulgently, there was a ripple of agreement around the horseshoe that made me feel better.

Next, Sevin went around the circle inventorying their hobbies and abilities: anything that might prove useful in the days to come. The most common skills were tech-related, which weren't much use out here. Trest suggested they poke around in the ship's comm system and see if there was some way of boosting an emergency signal, but he didn't sound hopeful. Muce volunteered to mend any clothing that had been damaged in the crash and said she would try making jackets out of some coarse fabric that had been used as a grease cover for the luggage.

"Can't promise anything cool-looking," she said, remarkably composed for her age, "but maybe I can turn that stuff into an extra outer layer."

"Be thankful for deviant skills," said Trest, smiling.

"Deviance is unattractive," said Carlann, reflexively. This time no one joined in to finish the refrain (*and jeopardizes all we hold dear*), and she wilted a little under Dren's critical stare.

"Sola?" said Sevin. "That seems to bring us to you."

I felt myself grow tense and defensive. Everyone was looking at me again, and it was clear no one had forgotten our earlier exchange.

"Not sure," I said. "My tech skills are nothing like these guys'."

"I was thinking of you for more . . ." he sought for the word, "physical stuff."

I bristled.

"Outdoors," he said, hurriedly. "Seems you can look after yourself."

It was his turn to be embarrassed. I relaxed a little and shrugged.

"Maybe you can lead that reconnaissance mission as soon as the storm has passed," he added. He was trying to be conciliatory, but it was tough not to feel like the group's

pet monkey, the degenerate who was comfortable clambering about, grunting and sweating, while everyone else continued to live a life as close to Home as they could manage.
I frowned and considered returning to my stasis pod. From
where I sat, I could just make out the little square picture
of the angel.

"Compared with Sola," said Bryce, agreeing with Sevin
conspicuously, "I'm afraid I'm pretty useless. Especially
with this arm. But I'll do what I can, of course."

He looked at me pointedly. He was saying he'd follow
my lead, and everyone knew it. I looked at Sevin, but he
was studying Bryce. He nodded once, then, without looking at me, turned back to the group.

"Carlann," he said. "What about you?"

And the moment passed.

●

WHEN WE WERE DONE, BRYCE MEANDERED HIS WAY TOWARD
me, as if he were stumbling upon me by chance.

"Hey," I said, cautious.

"About last night," he said. He paused, then blurted it
out. "I'm sorry if I was weird about, you know, the tattoo
thing."

"It's fine," I said. "It *is* weird."

"Weirder than you realize," he said.

"What do you mean?" I asked.

"We're not the only ones." He had lowered his voice
and was looking around at the others. "Muce has it. And

Dren, and I think maybe Herse, though I didn't get a good look."

"The same tattoo?"

"Exactly," Bryce answered, thoroughly perplexed.

"Who doesn't have it?"

"Those are the only ones I've been able to check," he said. "Muce's is hard to see because her skin is so dark, but her hair is short so you just need to look closely. Herse was toweling off after his morning wash, and I saw it."

"And Dren?"

Bryce's eyes flickered away, and I felt a tension in his mind.

"I saw it before," he said, not meeting my gaze. "He wears his hair pretty short in the back."

He was being evasive. I had been behind Dren twice earlier and was unable to see anything through his thatch of blond hair. I decided to let it go.

"So everyone on board who you have looked at so far has it?" I said.

This was beyond coincidence.

He nodded.

"Why did you ask me what my parents did?" I said.

"Oh," he said with a shrug meant to suggest casualness. "I wondered if it was some kind of professional thing. Or religious, maybe."

"My parents aren't religious," I said. "Are yours?"

On Home that would be very unusual. He hesitated again, and I sensed his evasion.

"No," he said. "Not really."

I was still looking at him, unable to keep the skepticism out of my face, when Yasmine called. He went to join her after giving me the smallest nod of apology. I watched them for a second but looked away when Teada joined me.

"You think little baby Sevin popped out of his incubation tank in uniform?" she asked, considering the way the tall boy stood surveilling the group, his back ramrod straight.

I laughed.

"I guess he's just trying to keep things together," I said.

"Soon as there's a break in the storm," she said, "I say we go for a long walk, find something cool, and burn it. Doesn't matter what it is, so long as it's flammable."

I smiled at her. She was reaching out, and I was grateful.

"Just my luck," she added, rolling her eyes. "We land on a new world—no parents, no security guards, no reeducation 'specialists' for thousands of miles—and there's nothing to incinerate but snow. I'd suggest we try setting Sevin on fire, but since he probably pees ice water, that won't work."

I laughed again, a real one this time.

"There you go," said Teada, encouragingly. "I knew there was a sense of humor in there. Pee jokes. Note to self."

"You're a very odd person," I said. "I like that."

"Oh right," she replied. "Like normal Sin-drones wander the streets at night by themselves."

"I guess not. But then I don't expect you think too much of normal."

"Till I came here, I pretty much loathed it," she said, a little ruefully. "Now, I confess I can see the appeal of a little normality, at least where toilets are concerned."

"You never spoke a truer word," said Trest, who was passing with a bag slung over his shoulder. "Brigadier General Sevin had me do some *investigations* re the plumbing. Don't ask me about it, because some things I will take to my grave, but I actually think I would rather freeze to death out there than reopen that waste storage tank."

"Well," I said, "we appreciate your sacrifice."

"You have no idea," said Trest with a shudder. "And I pray you never will. I figure we have another week before the tank needs to be drained again, or we find some other way of . . . But there I go again, crashing a conversation between pretty ladies with ruminations on sanitation systems. I'll leave you to it."

I grinned as he walked away.

"He's pretty cool," said Teada. "Wordy, but cool."

She said it as if she were agreeing with me, and I realized that I had thought almost the exact same thing only moments before. I gave her a quick look, and she flushed and looked away.

We said nothing about it, but we both recognized the way our minds had touched. The strangeness of that, the impossibility, was like hearing an alarm, shrill, insistent. Frightening.

CHAPTER

I T WAS A LONG DAY. THE STORM DIDN'T LET UP TILL LATE, so we were confined to the ship. Twice I got my comm pad out and fiddled with it, but it showed me nothing I didn't already know. There was nothing out there. No way of reaching back to Home. Hardly news, but it still bothered me.

"Sola," said Sevin. "I want to start cataloging everything we have in stores, beginning with our personal belongings. Can you go through your stuff first?"

He offered me his comm pad, which had been opened to a notepad app.

"Sure," I said. "Where are they?"

"Underdeck One," he said.

I hesitated, then tried to cover my unease with a question.

"Underdeck One?"

"The first level below this," he said. "Runs the whole length of the ship. The level below that is Underdeck Two, but it's not as large. Crew members call it 'the Well.'"

I nodded, but said nothing.

"What?" he asked, stooping to the lantern that sat by his feet. "It's just storage and engine access, vent and grav systems . . . There's nothing to be afraid of down there."

I bridled.

"I know that," I said, conscious that my face was getting hot. "I just . . . didn't know the layout. We haven't all spent half our lives on ships, you know."

And with that, I marched defiantly straight to the closest stairwell and descended the metal steps noisily, without looking back. I felt the eyes of others following me, felt—more specifically—a pulse of apprehension and relief that *they* weren't the ones going down into the underdeck. But I had, again, chosen the kind of defiance that permitted no second thoughts. Sevin called after me, but I ignored him and continued my pointed descent, my boots ringing on the stairs so that the lower I went, the more they echoed.

It was only when you came below that you realized the main decking had actually been designed with passengers in mind. Apart from the stasis pods and bathroom, there was room to move about: not much, perhaps, but the spatial layout was positively luxuriant compared with the underdeck. Down here, the passages were tight and flanked by towering steel cabinets and loaded racks. Though there were several points at which the walkways connected, their layout was irregular, dictated by the machinery of the ship's propulsion, life-support, and guidance systems, so that the whole felt like a labyrinthine tangle. One end of the maze split into two levels, though this was not, I thought, the Well that Sevin had referred to, which was accessed by a long central ladder that descended into the bowels of the ship.

And it was dark. A little light bled down through the stairwells from the upper deck, but once you turned a corner or two of the doglegged corridor, and long before you got near the Well, it was pitch black. I cursed myself for not bringing a light and realized that that was why Sevin had called after me. He had surely planned to give me the lantern.

I considered going back but rejected the idea, instead holding Sevin's comm pad up and using its meager, greenish glow to ease my way through the metal passageway. It gave me three or four feet of good visibility, a few more of shadowy impression, then nothing.

I moved slowly around counterintuitive corners that branched and doubled back around great incomprehensible pieces of machinery. I was quickly disoriented and unsure if I had already passed what I had come looking for. I paused for a moment, studying the racks and lockers, listening to the unnatural resonance of my feet, my breathing, in the confined space. Maybe if I focused on what I was doing, I would be less unnerved by the darkness and the strange noises that came out of it.

Being on the *Phetteron* was like being inside a living creature. After the crash, I had assumed that the creature was dead, but down here you couldn't be sure. The creaks and groans of sheet metal and overstretched cable sounded like the slumber of some great beast. It was probably just the extreme cold outside, or the tiny pressures and tensions created by my fellow passengers moving around above me, but at times I was sure the noises came from some other source, as if there were something moving about in the tight, dark hallways just out of sight.

There could be rats, I supposed. Ships of old were supposed to have rats, and I vaguely recalled that one of the last places domestic cats were kept was on vessels like this, to keep the vermin down. Then one day the people on Home couldn't remember the difference between cats and the rats they hunted anymore, and had found other ways of eradicating any nonhuman life onboard. So in my heart, I knew there were no cats aboard, no rats, though that didn't make me feel any better.

Focus, I reminded myself. *There's nothing there.*

I inched my way along the narrow walkway, scanning the storage bins and crudely labeled shelves with their restraining straps and plastic screens. I found the care packages thirty paces in. It was further than I had anticipated, and I reflexively checked the battery life on Sevin's comm pad. I didn't want to be stuck down here in the dark. There was a junction behind me, and, since it led into the center of the ship, I guessed that it wound its way eventually to the ladder down into the Well. I didn't like the idea of it at my back, the black heart of the *Phetteron* down deep in the ship's cold chest. As I opened the locker, my fingers fumbled with the catch.

I saw mine right away. It was a little less chic than most of the others, a little more battered from use. It was Sindrone gray, with fasteners of brushed nickel. I lifted it down carefully, setting the comm pad on the metal floor grille until I had my case open. I got to work itemizing the clothes: two pairs of trousers, four shirts, and six complete sets of underwear. I accounted for the minimal toiletries—soap, shampoo, personal hygiene kit, toothbrush and paste—but hesitated over the rest. There was an old map of Sindrone, decades out of date, and actually printed on folded paper. It had no practical value, but I liked studying it, imagining its ancient streets and buildings—the factories, offices, meeting halls, and cathedrals that had all been torn down over the years—as if I might be able to sneak out and walk them, discovering the city with my eyes, my nose, and the soles of my feet. It was doubly useless here, and revealing its existence would only embarrass me. I did not enter it into Sevin's log.

There wasn't much else. Memory chips and batteries for my comm pad. A folding multitool. A few candies in a bag, which I itemized, privately thinking that things would have to get very bad indeed for our fates to depend on half a dozen cream torps and a Chococone. Not much to show for the comforts of Home. Even without opening them, I could see how different everyone else's packages were. Muce's had plush ears sticking out of a side pouch. Carlann's was almost covered with decals celebrating music and flik stars. Most of their faces were familiar to me, but I didn't know their names. The one belonging to Herse was covered with pages from old books—actual paper books—yellowing and dense with cramped, small type. Yasmine's was small and elegant, a silvery backpack crammed, no doubt, with hairbrushes and makeup and glittery accessories . . .

You don't know that, I reminded myself.

True.

Dren's case was plastered with images from games: impressive aircraft and space ships shooting, racing, exploding. Sevin's was cadet issue, a sleek attaché case with brass fittings. Trest's featured an old-fashioned cartoon duck holding a fizzing bomb. Teada's was faux leather, charcoal gray trimmed with black, and marked with a red sticker that brayed "Caution: Danger of Fire!" Guessing she had put it there herself in mockery of her own antisocial habits, I grinned, though even this one drove home the fact that everyone's package said something about who they were.

Except mine. Mine was a blank, outside and in. The person who owns this, it said, exists. Probably. Nothing more.

There was the map, of course, but that was secret. And stupid.

I raised the light and scanned the stack, counting. Nine. I frowned and did it again. We were one short. I checked off the names on the list.

Bryce.

I frowned again and rechecked, but there was no mistake. Unless he had moved it, Bryce had no luggage.

Now it was true that the reeducation facility supplied basic necessities, including clothes and toiletries, but it was equally true that no one would willingly use something that might have been used by someone else. The idea of leaving home and packing *nothing* was more than bizarre. It was . . .

Something clanged in the passageway behind me.

I spun around, heart in my mouth, holding up the comm pad, but I could see nothing beyond the narrow walkway and the racks of spooled cable. I kept very still, listening. At first there was nothing to hear, but then, very faintly, there came the creak of the metal floor, only yards away, but round the corner and lost in darkness.

Just the further settling of the ship?

Or a footstep?

I remained motionless, unbreathing, feeling the cold of the vessel seep into my bones. And at last it came again, and this time I was sure. It was a footfall.

"Who's there?" I called.

My voice sounded panicky. Unsure of itself. I swallowed and tried again.

"I've got a wrench. If I have to come back there . . ."

I let the empty threat tail off. It echoed through the metal halls. The coils of cable had developed an eerie menace in the thin light, as if they might have heads, as if they might unwind themselves and come slithering towards me . . .

The corridors seemed to have grown tighter, squeezing the air out of the underdeck. I forced myself to take a ragged breath and felt my heart thudding in my chest. The comm pad light flickered in my unsteady hand.

The sound of the footstep came again, closer this time, followed by the soft squeal of something being dragged along the metal floor. I was almost overwhelmed by the urge to run, to pelt madly back the way I had come, along the doglegged corridor to the steps and up, out, in one breathless, panicky sprint . . .

I refused.

I didn't have a wrench, but I did have the utility tool. Fumblingly I opened it to the blade, held it out in front of me, and spread my feet for balance.

Two more footfalls, quicker this time, and something moved out from behind the corner. I realized too late that the comm pad was casting more light on me than it was on whoever, or whatever, had just appeared in front of me.

Who. Not what. There could be no what.

They were no more than ten yards away now. A second or two at a run. But I still couldn't see whoever was in the shadows watching me. Without thinking about it, I turned my head slightly and narrowed my eyes till they were almost closed, trying to sharpen my other senses. I heard nothing new, tasted only the metallic tang of the ship's innards, smelled only the trace of engine oil, felt only the cold . . . But then there was something else, a presence I could sense at the edge of my mind like a distant candle in a cave. I sharpened my focus, and it blossomed till I was sure I felt . . .

Fear.

Not mine. Someone else's.

And then a familiar voice.

"Sola? Is that you?"

I breathed out.

"Teada?" I answered.

She moved then, two halting steps that brought her into the light. She looked badly scared, her eyes wide, her face pale and uncertain. She studied me, as if not sure I was real, and then, finally, took the final, decisive steps that brought her close enough to touch. She exhaled, and her breath was rapid and heavy. She put her hands to her face as if to get a grip on her feelings. She was terrified.

"God," she muttered. "God. I thought you were . . ."

"What?" I asked.

Not what. *Who.*

"I don't know," she babbled. "My comm pad battery died. I've been wandering down here for . . . I don't know. Feels like hours."

"It's okay," I said, though I refrained from touching her. Old habits, they say, die hard. "Why didn't you say who you were when I called?"

"Your voice sounded so strange," she said. "Echoey. And I was . . . I don't know. Confused. Spooked."

"It's this place," I agreed, trying to sound consoling as my own panic faded. "You really had me going there."

"I guess so," she said, looking at the knife in my hand. Her eyes came up to mine, and something of the uncertainty was back.

"Just . . . a tool," I said. "Let's get out of here."

"Dren lent me his comm pad because mine was charging," Teada said as we moved down the hallway. "I bet he knew the battery was almost dead."

"What were you doing down here?"

"Just exploring," she said. "Forced myself to. Wanted to see what this 'roaming' was all about. Not my thing."

I smiled, but then caught something else from her, an embarrassment about what she had said that I didn't understand. She closed her mind off to me, but not before I had glimpsed—in the midst of her decision to go wandering the ship—my own face.

●

EVERYONE WENT TO BED EARLY, PARTLY OUT OF BOREDOM, partly because things were getting tense and fractious. Dren was giving everyone a smug, knowing look and kept expressing how people were feeling:

"Ooo, Muce doesn't like it when you point out how small she is."

"Herse, are you missing your mommy?"

"Check out Teada, wishing there was something she could set on fire."

In each case, the remarks came off as shrewd guesses, but each one stung, something Dren clearly relished.

"Give it a rest," I told him.

"Not missing *your* mommy, are you Sola?" he shot back, smirking. "Not at all. But I guess that's just a different kind of sad."

I got to my feet and closed angrily on him.

"Wanna hit me?" he said, delighted, slowly cocking his head onto his left shoulder and holding it there. "Wow, you really are the cavegirl, aren't you? Everyone else is dying to find a signal for their comm pads so they can message their parents, and you'd rather pick up a rock and smash my skull in."

"You're wrong, Dren," I said. "I suggest you shut your mouth."

"Or what?"

"Just shut up, Dren," said Sevin, stern. He was sitting against the wall by the window, his head tipped back. Dren grinned, conceding nothing, but fell silent, and eventually he climbed into his stasis pod and closed it.

I gave Sevin an appreciative nod, which he returned before shutting his eyes. The only other person still up was Herse. He was sitting with his knees up and a maroon sweater pulled over them, but his arms showed above it, spider-leg thin. For a moment, he didn't seem to realize I was there; his eyes were cast down on a sort of old-fashioned book or notepad, something you might write in by hand. As I remembered the printed pages pasted to his care package in the underdeck, he looked up, startled. He stuffed the book—or whatever it was—under the blanket, and gave me a guileless, sheepish look.

"You keep a journal?" I asked, trying not to sound like I thought it was weird.

He seemed to think about it.

"Not really," he said.

101

"But you write," I said. "With a pen and everything."

He looked away, and even in the low light I could see how his face burned. For a moment, he said nothing and avoided my eyes; then he turned suddenly and stared at me, his face set. He plucked the little book from under the blanket and flipped it towards me with something like defiance.

"Read it," he said. "I don't care."

He did, but he'd been caught out and was putting on a brave face. I shook my head, not looking to where the book had fallen on the deck between us.

"It's yours," I said. "Private, I'm guessing."

"Not much point trying to keep secrets here, is there?"

"What do you mean?"

He hesitated, then shrugged it off.

"It's poetry," he said. "You know what that is?"

I glanced at the book, its pages splayed open from the fall, and I could see the careful hand lettering. I'd never seen anything like it.

"I've heard of it," I said, "but no, not really."

"It's just . . ." He hesitated. "Words. Ideas and images. Feelings. Impressions, painted in words. I know it's old school and odd, but . . . Hell, we're all strange, right?"

I nodded and smiled.

"Like you for instance," he said.

I felt my body tense and waited in silence.

Herse looked at me, his brow furrowed with thought. He opened his mouth to speak but then thought better of it.

"What?" I asked.

He shook his head hurriedly, the color rising in his thin face.

"Nothing," he said, reaching for the little book and snatching it up as if I might make a sudden grab for it. He pocketed it hurriedly. "Going to bed."

I let him go, wondering what he had been about to say.

Back in my stasis pod, I thought about Dren. He had been wrong. I didn't want to kill him, or even hit him. Not really. But there was something about him that went beyond being a smartass or a bully, and I tried to remember if I had felt it from him when we first landed.

He seemed different now, colder, harder to read. And that look he had given me when he had taunted me for being primitive and violent—*cavegirl*—head cocked on one shoulder, eyes strangely vacant, reminded me unnervingly of the mysterious girl I had seen out in the snow the night before, that strange, sightless stare . . .

Coincidence, surely, but the idea raised the hair on the back of my neck.

Two hours later, everyone having turned in, the ship was in darkness. I slid open the cover of my pod and inhaled the cold, metallic air. The *Phetteron* was utterly silent, which was, in its own way, unnerving. On Home, it was never quiet. Not really. There was always the faint whine of electric lights, the low drone of air conditioning, the constant, almost inaudible hum of computer circuits. Here, there was nothing, as if the very air had died. And yet somehow, in spite of this curious sensory vacuum, there came the persistent sense that I was being watched.

I lay where I was, just breathing, thinking of nothing. I may have dropped off for a moment, but then I heard something. A whispered voice coming from the rear of the ship. There was the faintest glow coming from the same direction.

I strained to hear and caught a stifled sob.

"No," said the voice. A boy, I thought, though it was hard to tell.

If I sat up, I would probably see him. But would that be a kindness, catching someone in the depths of homesickness and anxiety—?

The thought had barely formed in my head when the voice came again, and I knew I had been wrong. This was not homesickness. It was terror. I could feel it now, my body taut and cold, pulse beginning to race.

"No!" it said again, more insistent this time. "Go away. You can't come in."

I lay perfectly still, gripped by the same terror I sensed from the boy.

Then I rolled, pushing myself onto my elbows and gazing into the darkness. Someone was sitting up in his pod, his back to me. Someone pale with short, fair hair.

Dren.

I say he was sitting up, but he was in fact cringing, his knees drawn up to his chest. His head was tilted up, and I followed what I took to be his gaze.

He was looking at the makeshift panel that we had lashed into place across the hole in the roof. The light from his stasis pod was soft and cast odd shadows in the dark, but it looked like the panel was shifting. Not the fluttering and guttering it did in the wind. This was different. It moved, straining against the ropes, then went still. Then it tugged violently several times as Dren clamped his hands over his ears.

I stared into the gloom, and my breath caught. Along the edge that was flapping, I was almost sure I could make out two sets of small, pale fingers gripping the edge of the panel from outside.

Someone was outside. On the roof. Someone or something, trying to work an opening under the panel.

For a moment I couldn't move. I was frozen with horror. I stared at those awful little hands, clawing to get in, the nails skittering like insects on the torn metal, and then I swallowed hard and took hold of myself. I got up and out of the pod before I could change my mind.

"Dren!" I called, mastering my fear as best I could. "Are you okay?"

He turned, aghast, and his eyes were wide and wet. He looked like someone I had never seen before. The easy smirk, the smug cockiness was gone, replaced by a fear so powerful it was shocking to look at.

It lasted only a second before evaporating, turning instantly to anger and resentment.

"Leave me alone!" he spat.

I was so taken aback I didn't know what to say, and in that stunned moment the flapping of the plastic panel ceased. I peered into the gloom but the hands—if they had ever been there—were gone.

I started to ask Dren what had happened, but he threw himself down into his stasis pod and closed the lid over him.

Eventually I did the same, but I lay there for a long time, listening for the sounds of movement on the roof, of thin, pale fingers scratching at steel, the impossible child trying to find a way in.

CHAPTER

T HE FOLLOWING MORNING, I SOUGHT DREN OUT,
catching him the moment he was away from the
others.

"You all right?" I asked.

He ignored me and went on flicking through images
on his comm pad.

"Dren?" I prompted.

"I'm fine," he said, not looking at me. "Leave me alone."

"Last night—" I began, but he cut me off, turning on
me with a baleful stare. There was none of the wounded
grief and fear I had seen in his face only a few hours before.
Only a defiant hostility.

"Look," I tried again. "If there is something alive on
this planet that didn't come here with us, you have a duty
to tell us what you know."

107

He cocked his head to one side and stared at me, saying nothing. It was the strangest look—like the girl's look—the eyes wide and hungry, the body very still. He licked his lips and gave me a fixed grin, mouth open, teeth bared, head still on one side.

It was unsettling enough that I snapped at him.

"And you can cut that out, too," I said.

"What?" he asked, still staring and grinning. There was something reptilian about his gaze.

"Whatever," I said, turning away so I wouldn't slap him. "But I'd suggest you keep that adolescent crap to yourself, or I'm going to get pissed off."

I said nothing to anybody about what I had seen—or imagined I had seen—and within an hour, as light filtered into the ship, I almost managed to convince myself that none of it had been real. There was already a dull anxiety on the *Phetteron*, and I didn't want to stoke it into real fear unless I had to. I considered telling Sevin or Bryce, but the former was ordering people about, and the latter was laughing quietly with Yasmine. Privately, even.

I ate half a protein bar, used the awful toilet, then busied myself getting supplies for our morning's reconnaissance, invigorated by the prospect of getting off the ship for a while. The storm had, apparently, blown itself out, and even Sevin couldn't come up with a reason why we shouldn't go. He was presiding over the stores and had completed the checklist of everything we had, noting it all down on his comm pad, which, in the absence of a signal, was now little more than a notebook. For all their fierce privacy, most of the others had given him permission to go through their belongings just so they wouldn't have to go down into the underdeck. I couldn't really blame them.

"How long will the food last?" I asked him.

"If we stick to one protein bar per day," he said, "a week."

I blew out my breath.

"Maybe while we're out, we'll find a food source," I said.

His brow clouded, and his lips got thin. He still wasn't happy about us leaving the ship.

"I can't imagine what," he said.

"That's sort of the point, isn't it?" I said. "We have no idea what's out there, and our supplies won't last us till rescue arrives."

He said nothing, but I felt his skepticism. Home was all we knew: the tech grid; our insulated, isolated rooms with our streaming classes and hangouts; the manufactured nutritional supplies delivered at the exact same time every day. We were completely unprepared for life out there. Besides, in the unlikely event that we found anything other than snow, ice, and rock, we had no way to know whether it was poisonous or not.

And in truth, even the thought of finding some naturally occurring food source was just bravado. None of us had ever eaten anything that wasn't synthesized in a lab and packaged by a vast corporation. To go back to eating plants or something would be like shedding a thousand years of evolution, regressing into animals in ways far worse than my clambering about the ship like some ancient monkey-hybrid. It would take extraordinary desperation to vanquish that kind of shame.

"Can we take one of those flashlights?" I asked, as if I knew what I was doing.

For a moment he stared me down, and I thought he was going to say no. But then he reached into the emergency crate and tossed one over, giving me a smile that did not reach his eyes.

"Thank you," I said.

He nodded.

"Better take this, too," he said, offering me a long-bladed knife in a sheath.

"What for?" I said.

"Like you said: we have no idea what's out there."

I scowled, but I took the knife, feeling its surprising weight before tucking it into my belt.

"I have that utility tool," I said. "In my care package."

"No you don't," he said. "I impounded that for use on board the *Phetteron*. I don't know what you'll find out there, but I doubt there will be screws and bolts."

I bit my lip, though I knew he was right.

"Right," he said. "No point in climbing out of the roof."

He walked the gangway towards the flight deck and stopped at the door through which we had boarded the ship. He pulled a lever, then began spinning a great metal wheel until the main hatch disengaged and the transport's door swung open. It was strange to see him straining to open the door, a task that tested muscle and sinew, instead of just watching it slide aside with a technological swish. It made me think of his body as a kind of engine, a machine of flesh and bone. Not just him either. All of us, including me. It was an unsettling idea.

"What?" he asked.

"Nothing. We should go," I said. "Listen," I added on sudden impulse, "last night, while I was trying to get to sleep . . ."

"What?"

"I don't know for sure, but I thought I heard something outside," I said, trying not to sound scared or sure. "Something on the roof. Like a person."

"Someone was out of their pod?" asked Sevin, irritated. "Who?"

"No," I said. "But I thought . . . It was like someone was trying to get in."

Sevin blinked, his face carefully blank, then frowned.

"You sure you weren't dreaming?" he asked.

"Pretty sure," I said. Sevin opened his mouth to say something; but then, aware of Trest watching from inside, he just shrugged and shook his head.

It wasn't just Trest. They were gathering behind us. Not only the recon party—all of them. I could feel their nervous apprehension as they peered out. The ship flooded with light and a rush of frosty air. I had put on two extra layers of clothes and my coat, but they were designed for air-conditioned hallways and transit tunnels. This was something entirely different, a biting cold. I reflected on the aptness of the phrase: a cold with teeth. We wouldn't be able to stay out in it for long.

I turned quickly back to Sevin and spoke in a low voice.

"What I was saying before," I said. "About last night? I wasn't the only one. Dren saw it, too."

Sevin stared at me, his face suddenly uneasy, then nodded to let me know he'd heard.

"Good luck," he said. "Be careful out there."

I descended the steps built into the lower hatch and onto the hard snow, scanning the ground for signs of those sharp blue ridges.

"Maybe this isn't such a good idea," said Bryce, cradling his splinted arm.

I shrugged.

"You don't have to come if you don't want," I said, trying to suggest that I didn't care either way.

I turned to look at him and saw Yasmine in the doorway. She was using one of the blankets as a kind of shawl and wearing sunglasses. Somehow she looked elegant and prepared.

Bryce saw her, too. He shook his head, standing a little straighter than he had been.

"No," he said. "It's fine. Might even be fun, right?"

I considered the frozen vista.

"Not quite so picturesque once you get out here, is it?" I said.

He looked confused.

"Picturesque?" he repeated.

"A bit cold for painting," I clarified. Practically the first thing he had told me about himself was his wish to paint—not on a comm pad but with an actual brush, like artists used to do. A private thing.

He winced as if stung, and color flushed his cheeks.

"I didn't mean I actually planned to . . ."

"Just keep your wits about you," I said, and began walking, head down out of the gale, eyes on the ground in front of me. I didn't know why I had so deliberately and spitefully snubbed him, but I was glad that he couldn't see my face as I marched away.

The last time I had set foot on the planet's surface, I had left only the shallowest of footprints because there was no more than a thin dusting of fresh snow on the ice. But yesterday's storm had deepened the snow considerably, leaving great drifts up against the *Phetteron* so that the ship looked like it had been there for decades or had grown out of the ground itself. It was, in its way, beautiful, but with my feet sinking to the ankle, sometimes to the calf, it was hard going. I tried to get a sense of direction based on the great blue mountains that sparkled ahead. We wouldn't go too far. This was just a look around to prove it could be done.

"We've got to get out of this wind," said Yasmine.

"Agreed," I said. My lips were dry, and though it wasn't much colder outside than on the *Phetteron*, the wind was savage, sometimes making it hard to breathe. So much for the storm having blown itself out. There was no snow falling, but the wind was—if anything—stiffer than it had been the day before.

I peered around. It was so bright, the harsh sun bouncing off the snow and ice, that I had to squint, shielding my eyes with my hands. "What about there?"

I pointed to where a shining blue ridge rose up like a great, slanting wall of glass.

"Should give us some cover," said Yasmine.

I gave her a nod. Yasmine and Bryce smiled at each other, and I felt his interest in her. It wasn't surprising. She was quite stunning. Still, it irritated me. He turned and gave me a look, part question, but also part defiance.

I stared at him and felt—as I had with Dren the day before—that he had sensed something about me. Something I wouldn't say. Perhaps I was not the only one whose hunches about other people's feelings were curiously heightened? I bristled at the thought. I didn't want anyone sensing anything about me that I wasn't prepared to put into words.

But then maybe I had imagined it. Perhaps I was letting the strangeness of our situation get to me. I needed to focus on staying alive till the rescuers arrived from Home, and getting paranoid about people—myself included—being able to sense thoughts wasn't going to help.

I trudged a little quicker through the snow, keen to put some distance between me and the other two, realizing with a jolt that this was the spot where I had seen the girl in the night. I didn't want to think about that, for several reasons, so I focused my mind on the aquamarine slash that sheared up through the snowfield ahead.

It was further than it looked. We walked for a solid half hour in the cutting wind before reaching the glass ridge, but we had been right. As soon as we got under its ice-blue shadow, the gale dropped to almost nothing. And not a moment too soon. I was beginning to lose feeling in my toes, and knew we were going to be out for a while longer yet.

Bryce and Yasmine were chatting about their favorite things to do in Sindrone: the best vapo joints, the best views of the glass server towers, the most fashionable hangouts for those rare times you just had to leave your house. Yasmine was doing most of the talking. Bryce was just agreeing, or asking noncommittal questions, and in my head I felt something at odds with his cheerful demeanor. He was worried, anxious that she might . . . what? Catch him out, somehow.

My eyes dropped to the ground ahead and tightened as I tried to focus my mind, but then I saw something that drove all other thoughts from my head. It was small and black and still, sitting impossibly on the snow.

A shoe.

It was tipped on its side, but had accumulated only the faintest dusting of snow, as if it had just been put there. It was small, a girl's. No heel to speak of. Soft, black syntholeather with a single strap and a high shine.

Lying there in the snow as if someone had stepped out of it at a party and . . .

And what?

I stared, then stooped. Bryce and Yasmine caught up to me. They were giggling at something.

"This yours?" I asked Yasmine.

Her brow furrowed.

"Right," she said. "Because I wear whatever shoes my mom wore when she was a teenager and then scatter them on foreign planets."

"Okay, Sola," said Bryce, grinning. "We'll keep up."

I gave him a quizzical look. He thought I'd put it there as a joke.

"I'm serious," I said. "I just found this. Here."

It was Bryce's turn to look befuddled.

"That's not possible," he said.

"Well, apparently it is," I said. "Because it's here."

He dropped into a squat and cautiously picked up the shoe in his good hand.

"It's dry," he said. "Looks new."

"To the fashion-challenged, perhaps," said Yasmine.

I shot her an irritated look.

"He means it's not been out here long," I said.

"Must have been sucked out of the ship as we came down," she said. "It probably belongs to someone on board."

I thought for a moment, then nodded. That must be it. I took it from Bryce and pushed it into my backpack, keeping my face out of the wind, trying not to think of the girl I had seen out there in the dark, watching, squatting on the roof of the ship, fingernails scrabbling to get in . . .

"What?" asked Bryce.

I shook the memory off.

"A little further?" I suggested, rising and eying a cluster of pillar-like rocks a few hundred yards away.

"Sure," said Yasmine.

116

We covered the distance at something close to a run, then slumped to the ground out of the wind. For a moment, we sat carefully against the strange aquamarine rock, motionless while we caught our breath for fear of discovering a razor-edged crease in the stone that would open us up. The edges were staggeringly sharp.

And they sang. As we moved along the canted wall, we came upon spaces between the outcrops where they had been carved by the wind into a series of irregular glass columns. As the wind blew through them, they produced a high clear tone, each one different, so that when the breeze shifted, the rocks seemed to play a faltering melody, harmonizing, rising, and falling with the breeze. There were no words in the notes, but they felt like voices, like the soft echoes of long-dead monks chanting through the halls and chapels of some ancient cathedral. Some of the pillars were no taller than me. Others were towering pinnacles like great icicles, glittering from turquoise to violet as they sang to us.

No one said anything, but we felt each other's unexpected bliss and smiled like little kids, happy without really knowing why. We were still relishing the moment when I saw movement off to my left.

An animal!

A real, wild animal. It was white. About the size of a large rabbit or hare, but with no visible ears and a slightly pointed face.

I put one finger on my lips, and used the other hand to point it out to the others.

It was perhaps fifty yards away. Yasmine beamed, and Bryce gasped. None of us had seen a wild animal before.

Not for real, I mean. I'd seen old fliks of animals, of course, and I'd seen recreations at the History Park in Sindrone, but that was about it. One time when I was roaming at night, I thought I saw something in one of the dumpsters—a trash bag moving, like there was something alive inside it—but I was too freaked out to look closely. For all intents and purposes, there were no animals on Home. Hadn't been for a century or more. Once we had eliminated the need for them in our own food supply, they were out evolved and out built. Although people fought to keep them around artificially for a while, everyone eventually lost interest. There were enough fliks of them that we could access at any time, so what did we need with the real, smelly, inconvenient things themselves? The people of Home were moving closer and closer to being minds, while animals were all instinct and body. They reminded us of what we'd rather forget about ourselves, so we stopped paying attention to them, and slowly, quietly, they went away.

I looked at the creature and acutely felt the blankness in its head, the tension of its muscles, its driving appetites, its instinct for survival. I was shocked to realize that such things were fast becoming my own concerns.

"It's so cute!" Yasmine said.

I gave her a look.

"Maybe so," I replied. "But that's hardly the point."

"What's the point?" she asked.

"I mean, we're not sightseeing or looking for things to . . ." I nearly said *paint*, and though I stopped myself in time, Bryce seemed to guess, his face hardening. "The point is that if there are animals here, that means there's food. Plants. Stuff we could eat or burn."

Yasmine looked unsure, embarrassed. We could tolerate walking around, but making fires, eating whatever we found growing? Even if we learned how to do so, the idea felt primeval, bestial.

"Okay," said Bryce. "But how do we know whether we can eat what Mr. Cute over there can eat?"

"We'll cross that bridge when we come to it," I said. "And don't call him that. We don't know what he eats yet, but we might be able to eat him."

Yasmine gagged.

"Meat?" she exclaimed, revolted.

"I was only joking," I said.

"Good," said Yasmine, shuddering. "We're not savages."

"Not yet," I said. "But I'm guessing the chances of finding a tree full of protein bars are slim."

The rabbit thing moved off through the blue pillars, oblivious.

"You don't really think you could eat that?" Yasmine asked me, appalled. "Skin it and everything? That's horrible."

"No," I admitted, "but if it's between that and starving, who knows?"

"You'd have to catch it first," Bryce observed. "You might have been a roamer back in Sindrone, but that hardly makes you a master hunter. You plan to shelve a few millennia of evolution in the next few days?"

I shrugged and smiled a little bleakly at how in sync our minds seemed to be.

"Might not be that hard," I said. "Might happen whether we want it to or not."

It wasn't a very encouraging thought, and the fact that it seemed absolutely right worried me. What if it took a month or more to be rescued? If we survived till then, how would we adjust to living here? What might we have to become just to get through these long white days and black nights?

I followed the creature around the ice-blue pillar. Close up, it looked more like an oversized vole than a rabbit. I studied the ground, looking for shoots and scattered seeds or nuts that the creature might be foraging for, but there was nothing. The wind sighed, and the pillars sang their eerie melody. The vole stopped, snuffling. At any moment, it might catch our scent and bolt.

I felt a prod in my ribs and turned to see Bryce pointing at the knife in my belt. I gave him a quizzical look, and he opened his hand. I drew the knife doubtfully and gave it to him, haft first. He took it in his good hand, hefting its weight, then gripped it by the blade and reached back to throw.

Yasmine grimaced and looked away as Bryce aimed at the white creature. I felt his focus and a hint of something else. Was he showing off? Something like that.

And then he flung it hard.

The knife sailed end over end, missing the vole-creature by several yards and clattering off one of the blue pillars so

A PLANET OF BLOOD AND ICE

that shards of rock scattered like needles. One slashed my cheek, and I slapped my hand to it.

The vole-thing loped off.

"Nice going," I said.

Bryce blushed.

"Thought it was worth a shot," he said.

"I guess you haven't devolved enough yet," said Yasmine, smirking.

"Give me time," said Bryce, stooping to pick up the fallen knife.

"No rush," said Yasmine. "Would hate for you to become some cave-dwelling thug with no conversation skills just as we were getting to know each other."

Cavegirl.

"Give me the knife," I said, irritated. "And let's discuss it before we start trying to impale the local fauna."

"You were the one who was talking about hunting for meat," he replied, defensive.

"I don't think bouncing knives off rocks ten feet from the target counts as hunting," I shot back. "All you did was spook it. Now we don't know what it might have been looking for . . ."

"It's there," said Yasmine, pointing through the blue pillars to a depression in the snow. "Look. Oh, it's gone."

"Yes," said Bryce, curious, "but gone where?"

The vole-thing had vanished.

"Probably has a burrow over there," I said, striding over, dabbing at the tiny wound on my cheek. I was cold and annoyed, wishing we were back at the ship.

It wasn't a burrow. It was a track that dropped steeply down into a ravine with the same blue, glassy walls, quite invisible except when you were right on top of it. It descended about thirty feet, then seemed to twist hard to the left.

"What do you think?" asked Bryce.

"Go down there?" said Yasmine. "No way."

"Worth a look," I said, pushing past them and heading down.

"We're not going to discuss it?" asked Bryce.

"You can discuss whether you're going to follow me," I said, not looking round. "But I'm going to see what's down here."

I kept going, feeling the rock wall cautiously with my right hand, eyes on the ground as the surface snow lessened, and I found I was walking on solid ice. At the bottom, the path turned, rounded an outcrop of glittering blue rock whose sides were fluted like curtains, and dropped another ten feet. The further I descended, the more the wind dropped—and with it the eerie singing of the stone—and the path now became a narrow passageway. The ice overhead had closed again so that the light became soft and tinted the same color as the rock. It felt strangely like being underwater.

I moved more cautiously, conscious of the others behind me, and it occurred to me that if there were creatures like the white vole, there might well be predators, too. I scanned the ice floor, but it was too hard for tracks. I slowed even more, but I kept moving. I didn't want Bryce and Yasmine to think I'd lost my nerve.

The path twisted around another sharp corner, sloping down even more steeply, and I used the wall to steady myself as I felt my boots slip. It was growing darker, but unless my eyes were playing tricks on me, a soft blue luminescence came from the rock itself, stronger than what little sunlight was fighting through the ice overhead. I felt a cold water drop land on the back of my neck and trickle under the collar of my jacket and realized that I could hear a steady plink in the passage ahead. It had narrowed to no more than three feet now, and the icy ceiling was starting to slope down. I had to stoop to round the next curve, conscious that the only light was now the strange glow of the rock wall.

I studied it, pressing my face to a smooth section of the chill, glassy stone and peering in. It struck me that the glow wasn't even or steady, but seemed to emanate from particular points under the surface, each one swelling, brightening for a few seconds, then fading again as another took its place. The color changed from deep indigo to a blue so pale that it was almost white, and then back again. The sparkling stone didn't just reflect the light. It produced it.

I wondered if it was just the rock down here or whether all of it—the columns, the veins beneath the ice, the very mountains themselves—did the same. That would explain the strange glow I had seen when I had gone out after the girl in the snow.

I was still considering this, secretly pleased by the idea, when I caught a shift in the quality of the air. I bent my head and pushed through the passage, which had narrowed sharply again like the neck of a bottle, and it was unmistakable. The air ahead was still, and—I was almost certain—fractionally warmer. And there was something else. I closed my eyes and inhaled cautiously, my body motionless.

"What's that?" asked Bryce behind me. He had smelled it, too.

"Shh," I said. "I'm trying to concentrate."

I felt his irritation flicker like the blossoming points of light in the rock, but I ignored it and sniffed again.

I was sure of it. The air was different. It didn't have the icy chill we had grown used to, and there was a faint but undeniable fragrance, sweet but not entirely pleasant. It was not as rank as the dumpsters of Sindrone, but touched with something like that. My pulse quickened. It might be the odor of death and decay, but it also smelled of life, albeit in some form I had never known on Home.

"Maybe we should go back," said Yasmine.

"No," I said. "I want to see."

And without waiting to see if they followed, I took three more steps and rounded a corner. The scent grew stronger as the passage opened into a miniature cave. The walls pulsed with slow, soft light, as if the place were alive. It was bare as the passage had been, but the ceiling dripped steadily, and a thin curtain of water slipped down part of the wall. It was unquestionably warmer here. My heart began to pound. Something was down here. Something remarkable. I could feel it.

The passage beyond the cave twisted and turned, the floor treacherously uneven and slick with water that, in places, had collected in puddles several inches deep. I tugged at the collar of my jacket. While I had been freezing only minutes before, I now felt clammy, and my shoulders started to sweat.

"What if something lives down here?" said Bryce. "It could be a den. Wolves or something. Bears."

Three or four hundred years ago, such creatures had roamed wild on Home, but they lived on now only in the holographic display parks, and even those digital zoos had been unfashionable and sparsely attended for at least a century.

"Bears?" said Yasmine. "Actual living bears? I thought nothing lived here."

"I thought that, too," I said, absently, not looking at her. "But we saw that vole thing. Rabbit. Whatever it was."

"Nothing lives on Valkrys," said Yasmine, more certainly this time. "I've seen the fliks. Everyone has."

"Yes," I said, uneasy, but not wanting to discuss the subject any further.

"You hear that?" said Bryce.

"It's just dripping water," I said.

"It's not," said Bryce. "There's something else."

He was right. I paused and caught it in between the steady plink of drops from the ceiling: a thin, piping pair of notes that could almost have been a call. I tried to home in on the sound, but I couldn't be sure. Maybe it was just water echoing oddly in the tunnel ahead. But maybe it was something different entirely, though I could not imagine what.

I reached another hard-angled bend on the passage and saw what looked like a doorway in the rock.

"Careful," I said, snatching my hand from the stone. "This is sharp."

That was an understatement. The rock jutted out from the right, narrowing to a knife-edge that ran floor to uneven ceiling. I flattened myself against the other side and eased around the corner, too busy avoiding the aquamarine glass inches from my face to notice what was ahead until I was completely clear of the lethal doorway. I felt it immediately: the openness, the warmth.

I stopped and spun around, gaping. I was on the edge of a precipice. The passage had opened up suddenly on the side of what looked like a great subterranean bowl. Laid out before me was a vast blue cavern roofed with ice and trailing what looked like vines, but were in all likelihood roots. It was as large as one of the ancient cathedrals of Home, like a vast piece of the sky captured and enclosed, radiant with light that filtered through the glassy ice above. Even from here, I could see at least three other access points where gaps in the ice-capped ravines formed slender passageways into the open center. Here and there the cavern was open to the sky through shafts that carved through the rock and ice, casting pale light in hard-edged shards like pieces of broken mirror. In places there were pools of clear water, and at their banks I saw leaves, green and lustrous. I stared, awestruck.

The air was warm and sweet. I heard the drip of water echoing through the cavern, and, as I gaped, a shock of orange flew across the expanse, piping shrilly: a bird.

"This can't be," said Yasmine.

"No," said Bryce.

They sounded awed, but also uneasy.

"And yet," I said, "here it is."

CHAPTER 12

W E MOVED CAREFULLY DOWN INTO THE BASIN, and it was like stepping into an entirely different world. The air warmed as we descended, and the light yellowed where the sun shone directly through the openings above. Some of the pools were clear, showing the bluish rock beneath, but others were dark and greenish, redolent with the smell of life and fringed with reeds. From time to time, the water stirred as things splashed briefly—frogs or fish, perhaps. Pale birds with orange napes fluttered and piped overhead, occasionally settling to tug at the vegetation or drink from the pools. Nearby was a cluster of slender trees with silvery bark, and Bryce picked up a long straight branch, testing it as a walking stick.

"Guys," said Yasmine. "Check this out."

128

She was standing close to one of the pools, where two oversized bushes were nestled. They were covered in large, waxy leaves and hung with globe-like fruit, amber colored.

"What do you think?" she asked.

We stared. No one had eaten fruit, real fresh fruit, on Home for decades or more. As the planet's population had grown, what agricultural land remained was turned over to factory production of various food substitutes. At the time—though it was hard to imagine now—some people had objected. But most people welcomed the move to cheap, prepackaged protein and nutrient supplements, and not only because they were so much easier to store and prepare than the meat and plant matter on which people had once lived. The culture had evolved. People who sought flavor and texture in food—the *experience* of eating—had become rare and embarrassing throwbacks who were too invested in their bodies, in sensation. The residents of Home took in fuel out of necessity, but the process of doing so hadn't been a source of pleasure for a century or more, and most people were glad to simplify the process still further. The notion of eating fresh fruit was about as strange and uncomfortable as that of eating meat, and the three of us eyed each other warily.

"I'm not saying we try it," Yasmine was quick to clarify.

"Could be poisonous," said Bryce, warily prodding the fruit with the end of his newfound cane.

They hesitated and looked at me.

I nodded my agreement, but the words came out anyway:

"Sevin said we only have protein bars for a week."

Another awkward pause.

"The birds are eating them," said Bryce, nodding to where one had alighted on the further bush and was pecking at the fruit.

"We're not birds," said Yasmine.

She almost shuddered, but I felt something under her revulsion, a curiosity she was ashamed of. I felt it too, and not only because the very thought of food had set my empty stomach rumbling.

I reached out and touched the fruit, cupping it in my right hand. It felt heavy and slightly warm, the skin silken. I squeezed gently and felt the flesh give a little. I gripped a little more firmly and gave the thing a twist. The stalk snapped and the fruit came free.

The others were watching me closely, eyes wide, lips slightly parted. Yasmine bit her lower lip, staring. I raised the fruit to my face and took a cautious sniff. It smelled sweet and fragrant, as I imagined flowers might. Though no one spoke, I could feel their secret thrill that I might taste it. I felt it, too. The embarrassment and wariness were still there, but they were fading beneath the desire to try it, which roared like blood in our ears, our lips, our throats.

I closed my eyes and bit.

The flesh burst in my mouth with a rush of juice so unexpected that I could barely keep it in. It was sweet and glorious, a complex rush of flavors unlike anything I had ever tasted. I bit again before I had even swallowed the first mouthful. Another bite, hungry, almost frenzied, and the juice ran down my chin.

Sweet. So very sweet, and soft beneath the skin, the liquid flowing over my tongue, flooding my mouth, so that there was nothing but the ecstasy of the flavor—the *sensation*—of the fruit . . .

I opened my eyes in time to see Bryce and Yasmine taking fruit of their own from the plant and diving in. In turn they closed their eyes, overcome by the rapture of the fruit, slicing with their teeth, cramming it into their faces as the juice ran through their fingers.

They laughed as they ate, and I joined them. It was joyous laughter, but also shocked at our own daring. It was the rapture of the illicit, and it was chased by shame, so that when we were finished, when we were sitting on the ground, full and spent, we avoided each other's eyes, even as we continued to giggle occasionally.

We washed our hands and faces in the clearest pool, awkward and silent again, shooting each other furtive, bashful glances but saying nothing. There was no need for talk. We all knew what we had felt.

Pleasure.

At sensation. At food that had grown naturally, untouched by scientist or nutrient corporation. We had delighted in that which grew wild, and that meant we were becoming wild, too.

"Should we . . . ?" Yasmine eyed the bush.

"What?" asked Bryce.

"I don't know," said Yasmine. "I just thought since we're going to run out of food on the ship, maybe we should—"

"Take some of the fruit back?" I concluded for her.

Yasmine looked hastily down till Bryce came to her rescue.

"Let's hold off for now," he said. "We could be rescued any day. No need to create more weirdness than we have. But I guess we should report back about this place."

"Why?" I said. "I mean, we don't know what we're looking at yet."

He and Yasmine looked at each other.

"I'm not saying we keep it secret," I said. "But we should at least take a look around first. Then we can tell the others exactly what we've found."

Bryce's doubtful look irritated me. Maybe it had been his use of the word "report," like we couldn't do anything without Sevin's permission first. And maybe it was because I knew in my heart that my penchant for secrecy was unhealthy. I pushed that idea away, annoyed by it.

"What's the big deal?" I exclaimed.

"We've been gone a while," said Yasmine. "They're probably wondering where we are."

"And when we get back," I said, "we can tell them."

There was an awkward pause, then Bryce shrugged.

"Maybe we should wait till we're sure it's not poisonous," he said. "Or at least till we know our bodies can handle it. I mean, we've never had real fruit before."

Yasmine and I nodded sagely, pretending this wasn't a dodge, that we weren't all ashamed to admit to the others what we had done and—paradoxically—that we wanted to keep the secret fruit to ourselves. In case we wanted more.

So we returned empty-handed, making the slow trek back through the icy passages to the world of glass and ice above. Bryce led the way, testing the snowy ground with his silvery wooden cane, partly using it to distribute his weight as he walked, but mostly because he just liked it. I hadn't ever held anything made of actual wood before, and I found my eyes straying to it, fascinated. It was a long walk, and snow had started to tumble from the sky in great swirling flurries, but we were silent as we hiked, remembering the taste of the fruit in our mouths and feeling the curious, silent tether that connected us, a bond that seemed to grow deeper with each step.

Looking across the white plain to where the skewed wreck of the *Phetteron* sat, its freezing, angular metal so different from the world we had just left, we stood for a long moment in the billowing snow, saying nothing, steeling ourselves for the return and what awaited us inside.

I had expected to be mobbed as we returned to the ship, everyone desperate to know what we had found. As it turned out, everyone ignored us. They were too busy fighting.

I T WAS CHAOS. THE *PHETTERON* WAS A RIOT OF SHOUT-
ing, everyone bunched together on the main deck,
Sevin trying to insist on some kind of order while
Dren and the thin boy, Herse, had each other by the
throat.

I stared in amazement as Trest joined Sevin in trying
to pull the two boys apart. Then I snatched Bryce's cane
and waded into the fray, yelling at them to pull themselves
together.

The cane was light and flexible. I hit Dren on the head,
not with all my strength, but hard enough that he shrunk
away, stunned. I was almost as shocked by what I had done,
but when Herse made to go after him, I pointed the end
squarely into his chest and pushed. He was all spidery limbs
and anger, but he backed off.

I could feel the rage coming off them like a terrible, burning heat. Their eyes went from me to each other and back, and then Sevin stepped between them, speaking in a commanding tone that shut everyone up.

"What the hell is going on?" he demanded. Maybe it was his authoritative manner or the still fairly crisp uniform with its brass pips at the collar, but he seemed older than the others, like a parent blundering into kids' squabble. I reminded myself that these kids were big and strong enough to do each other real damage, or to turn on him if the uniform failed to work its magic.

Dren glowered and smirked but said nothing. Herse spoke up.

"He's been reading Carlann's journal," he said. "She asked me to talk to him."

"I didn't read her stupid journal," said Dren. "Or Herse's idiot *poems*."

He tossed that last word spitefully, and several people gave Herse curious and baffled looks.

"You're a liar," said Herse, straining to get away from Trest, who had his arms around him.

"Who you calling a liar?" Dren shot back, wriggling to get past Sevin.

I brandished the cane at him, and he shrank back, knowing I would use it.

"That's enough!" roared Sevin. His voice echoed through the *Phetteron*, and everyone fell silent. "Sit down, both of you," he added, angry at the disorder, at the flouting of his authority. "Carlann," he said, nodding at the girl in the choker whose head I had stitched. "What made you think Dren had been reading your journal?"

The girl flushed and looked down.

"See?" said Dren, still defiant. "She doesn't have anything on me."

"Carlann?" Sevin prompted. She still said nothing.

"Did you see him with it?" I asked. Sevin shot me a look but didn't try to stop me.

Carlann shook her head.

"You thought your journal had been moved or something?" I asked.

"Don't put words in her mouth," snapped Sevin.

I opened my mouth to protest, but Carlann shook her head again.

"It was nothing like that," she whispered.

"So why did you think he had been reading it?" asked Sevin, his irritation showing through.

"Because he said . . ." Carlann looked up, her face hot, eyes shining. She glared at Dren but couldn't finish the sentence.

"What did he say?" I pressed, as gently as I could.

"Things he could've only known if he'd looked at it," Carlann finished weakly. "He knew things. Private things."

"Like what?" asked Sevin.

But Carlann shook her head and would say no more. I looked at Dren. Though his head was down, he managed to meet my gaze.

He knew things. Private things.

I was alarmed, but not surprised, when Dren shot me a furtive smirk. I saw it in his face. He hadn't been reading Carlann's journal. He just knew what was in her head, some of it at least, and the others had sensed as much. It was no wonder they were scared and angry. Dren hadn't just violated their privacy; he had altered their sense of the universe.

I made an effort to close my mind. Dren was the last person I wanted peering into my thoughts.

Sevin inhaled.

"Okay," he said, finally. "Everyone listen very carefully. I don't know how long we're going to be here. It won't be easy, cooped up like this, and sometimes we'll get on each other's nerves. But there's no room in here for fighting, you hear me?" He paused, scanning their faces. Some of them nodded. Others, including Herse, looked down, chastened. Dren just stared at Sevin, an insolent half-smile curling his lip. "Our survival," Sevin continued, "depends on us working together as a group. Turn on each other, and we're dead. You hear what I'm saying?"

The earnest certainty of his tone, along with his hard, level stare, was compelling. Eventually even Dren looked away. The group murmured its assent. "All right," Sevin concluded. "Find something useful to do, or go somewhere quiet to get your heads together for a moment. Get in your pods if you want. Council meeting in ten minutes. Sola, you and the others will report back then, yeah?"

I nodded, immediately anxious about what I was going to say and what I wasn't. Dren looked at me, his head cocked slightly as his knowing smile returned. I stared him down, but he made me uneasy. I turned hurriedly away. As I did so, I saw Bryce and Yasmine talking urgently together, standing so close they were almost touching. Feeling my gaze, they both looked swiftly up with the same sheepish smile. Guilty, but of what I wasn't sure.

●

THE COUNCIL MEETING WAS A SUBDUED AFFAIR. HERSE AND Carlann never looked up from the metal decking, while Dren's eyes constantly wandered around the circle of faces, considering each, thoughtful and amused, before moving on. At one point his gaze settled on Bryce, and something passed between them. Bryce was—I felt sure—ignoring him deliberately, something Dren seemed to find bleakly funny.

I did most of the talking. I told them about the cavern, how far it was, how we had gotten there, and what it was like. It was warmer there, I said, at least partially sheltered, and full of growing, living things. I did not mention the fruit I could still taste in my mouth. I avoided Bryce and Yasmine's eyes, feeling transparent, but everyone was too elated at the prospect of spending time off the ship to question what they were hearing.

"You think we could make a camp there?" asked Sevin.

I frowned.

"There are passages and caves, but the main cavern is wide open," I said. "There'd be no privacy, and I'm not sure

A PLANET OF BLOOD AND ICE

what we'd sleep on, but I think it would be a good place to spend some of the daylight hours."

"Any sign of anything that might be edible?" asked Teada.

Yasmine looked down quickly—too quickly, I thought—but no one seemed to notice.

"We didn't spend enough time there to know for sure," I answered, meeting Teada's eyes deliberately. "We could go back tomorrow, though."

"We could all go," suggested Trest. "Much as I love spending every second inches from nine other people in a little metal tube, it might be nice to see the sky and, you know, anything else at all."

"Someone needs to stay on the *Phetteron* at all times," said Sevin. "In case a ship from Home tries to contact us or a rescue party lands."

"Aye aye, Brigadier General," said Trest.

"I've told you not to call me that," said Sevin.

"Wing Commander then," said Trest, deadpan. "Field Marshal."

Teada smirked. She wasn't the only one. Sevin, knowing there was no point arguing, threw up his hands and said, "Hilarious. But my objection stands. We can't risk missing any response to our beacon. Someone has to stay on board."

It was a sobering thought and it rather took the air out of the group's excitement. Trest shrugged, conceding the point, and fiddled with his ear chain. I was almost glad of it, because it meant I didn't have to face quite so many enthusiastic questions. When it was all over, I busied myself with going through the contents of a storage locker that hadn't been catalogued. There was nothing of obvious value, but I sat there anyway, doggedly turning things over in my hands—bits of machinery, circuit boards, fragments of Home that now seemed to belong to a different universe entirely—while my mind strayed back to the fruit, the gush of juice in my mouth, the sweet, tender flesh between my teeth.

I didn't really understand my own shame. On Home, I would have. If I'd heard of people eating something growing on a bush, I would have been baffled and appalled, but now I struggled to recall the logic behind such revulsion, even as I still felt its stigma. Were such feelings like the machine parts in my hands, remnants of a civilization that no longer had any meaning for us? And if so, what were we becoming? I thought of the meds we had all taken every night before bed. We had done so without knowing what they did. But now that we didn't have them, I supposed we would all change in some small way, on some deep molecular level, though I could not say exactly how. Maybe it had already started.

I sensed Dren's eyes boring into me and turned to find that knowing smile playing unsettlingly round his lips. I shrugged them off, and then remembered.

"One last thing," I said aloud to the group, fumbling in my backpack. I pulled out the little black shoe and held it up. "Whose is this?"

Blank faces. Shrugs.

Muce peered at it, but it was too big to be hers, and she eventually shook her head. Teada pulled a disdainful face: not her style.

"Must belong to someone," I said, scanning the faces.

"Where did you find it?" Sevin asked.

I hesitated.

"On the deck back there," I lied, nodding vaguely toward the back of the ship. I felt Bryce and Yasmine looking at me. And Dren.

"Must have belonged to someone from a previous journey," said Sevin, giving the shoe a cursory look. "They never clean these things out properly between trips."

That must be it, I thought. A previous journey. Some passenger left a shoe in a crevice between the lockers. After the roof tore free during the crash landing, the shoe was sucked out and falls on the planet surface.

Makes sense.

So why, I wondered, was I trying to remember if the spectral girl I had seen out there in the night, the one who scrabbled to get in through the hatch in the roof, had been barefoot?

●

THAT NIGHT, AFTER FIDDLING POINTLESSLY WITH MY COMM pad, I lay in my stasis pod thinking of the fruit and listening to the muted whistle of the wind. The snow had grown steadily heavier over the course of the evening, and the *Phetteron* was now at least as cold as it had been when we first landed. I wondered how the plants that grew in the cavern survived. The roof was, after all, open to the sky, even though the great bowl in the rock seemed to protect it from the elements. Perhaps it had once been closed? That would explain why everyone on Home treated Valkrys as entirely barren and lifeless. I had a hunch that the cavern wasn't an isolated instance, that there were pockets of life all over the planet, even if Valkrys's frozen crust and asteroid cloud suggested the opposite. It was hard to believe that Home's understanding of the place had been so wrong. Though I had been called a rebel, the thought still came as a surprise. Everything I had ever known or experienced had been filtered according to what the government deemed appropriate, and I had simply accepted it.

Home looks after its own. No contrary position is viable.

But maybe Trest was right. Maybe we had been misled. Or maybe we just hadn't asked enough questions. Life on Home was so easy. It had never occurred to us to probe beneath the surface. We talked about the government as if we knew what that meant, but there were no elections, no great debates. Hadn't been for decades. And so long as our beds were comfortable, our nutrition prompt, and our entertainment satisfying, we hadn't cared to ask why.

The thought kept me awake for a while—so when the space above the transparent cover of my pod glowed suddenly amber, I saw it immediately. I had seen this before.

The light shifted as if moving around the silent hold, brightening and dimming before finally vanishing completely.

I hit the cover release button and peered out into the dark and frigid belly of the ship. There was no sign of the light, and I slid soundlessly out. I glanced at the tiny image of the angel, asking for her protection, then paced barefoot along the gangway, feeling the penetrating cold of the metal stinging the soles of my feet through my socks. I slowly paced straight to the back of the ship, where the plastic cover shifted in the breeze, but it looked quite secure and there was no sign of the light. The other pods, too, were still and dark as graves. I was the only person stirring.

The thought pleased me.

All unease and fear melted away, and I felt the familiar rush of being out and alone at night: unseen, unheard, queen of a nocturnal world no one else knew, like the angel soaring above the town. I turned and walked slowly back along the gangway, but as I got closer to the viewer, my composure melted away. I felt cold and full of dread. I knew what I would see when I looked out. She was there again. The impossible child. I knew it.

I inched closer but stopped at a familiar sound. I listened, trying to decide what it was.

The clunk of the main cabin latch.

Without thinking, without even deciding to do it, I dropped to my knees and flattened myself against one of the main braces to which the gangway was attached. It was rough and cold to the touch and not quite wide enough to conceal me completely if anyone came looking closely.

I peered round it as the door to the flight deck cracked open with a dull *thunk* and the scrape of its slightly buckled doors being forced apart. Someone came out, their body momentarily silhouetted against the gray expanse of the forward viewers. Someone tall. Almost certainly a boy, which was a kind of relief. At least it wasn't that girl in the old-fashioned dress.

I kept very still and watched, but the figure carried no light, and when the doors closed behind him again, the hold was plunged into darkness. I waited, trying to home in on the sound of his feet, the soft hiss of a stasis pod opening, but I couldn't be sure which one it was.

When I was satisfied that he—whoever he was—had gone, I inched my way back to the window and looked out, though I knew that there would be nothing now. I felt it in my own ease. The fear had gone. There was no one out there.

I returned to the pods, feeling for the raised numbers that marked each one till I found mine. I wondered why anyone would be in the main cabin at night. The controls were dead. There was nothing there you couldn't access in some other part of the ship, except the comm system, and we all knew that there was no signal with which to reach anyone. So why would anyone creep in there at night?

For the same reason I was walking around the *Phetteron* by myself? Could it be that simple, that there was there another roamer on board chafing against the claustrophobia of the stasis pod? Maybe. I couldn't think of any other reason, but I decided to check the cabin as soon as it was light enough to see what someone had found so fascinating.

Before I climbed into my pod, I pressed my face to the freezing porthole and gazed out into the night.

Nothing, I thought, vaguely relieved until I reminded myself that whatever I had seen out there may already have found a way onto the ship.

CHAPTER

I WAITED TILL FIRST LIGHT TO EXPLORE THE FLIGHT DECK, but by then everyone was already up and discussing the cavern, so I stayed where I was. Sevin asked if I would lead the group, and I agreed, torn between the desire to have some time on the *Phetteron* by myself and wanting to get back to the cavern and all it contained. Everyone wanted to come along, and when Sevin asked Bryce and Yasmine to stay behind and watch the ship, they couldn't think of a reason why not, though their faces fell.

The prospect of leaving them alone together bothered me, too, for reasons I didn't want to consider too closely.

"See you later," I said to Bryce.

"Yes. Happy hunting or whatever . . ." he said.

He was smiling, trying to be jovial, but I could sense his awareness of Yasmine moving around near her stasis pod. He was being friendly to me, but he was also waiting for me to leave.

Snow was falling gently as we headed out. So much had accumulated overnight that the *Phetteron* was furred with white, losing its hard edges and becoming something new and strange, like a creature emerging from a chrysalis. Sevin watched the sky cautiously and said that we would have to abandon the trip if it got much worse, but he was clearly as curious as the others to see what we had found.

Our footprints from the previous day were utterly buried, and it took me a moment to find the blue ridge and figure out which direction to go. I was, naturally, the leader, the others trailing out behind me in a straggling line. The mood started out buoyant, gossipy and excited, but within minutes Carlann had started to complain about the cold and how long we had been walking.

"You sure it's wise letting them all come along?" I asked Sevin.

He turned to consider the group trudging and wading through the snow, some laughing, some, like Carlann, already miserable and whining. He frowned.

"Probably not," he admitted. "I couldn't think of a reason why they shouldn't come, and you said we had to make decisions collectively. How much further is it?"

"I'm not sure. Half an hour? More? We're moving slower than last time, and the snow makes the landscape look quite different. It may take a few minutes to find our way in. We're making for that outcrop there."

"Okay," said Sevin. "Have a word with Carlann, will you? She trusts you."

I nodded and dropped back to where the stragglers brought up the rear. As I did so, Dren gave me a look.

"Think the intrepid adventurer can shut her moaning up? Getting on my nerves."

I ignored him, but as I labored past, I felt something hard and bright coming off him, almost like sound. It was intense and confused, a wave of anger and cruel joy touched with something still more unsettling: appetite. Not for food. For other things I couldn't see clearly and didn't want to understand. Dren was hungry. He wanted things, and his desire jutted out like spikes of electricity. It was frightening.

I picked up my pace, avoiding his eyes, and reached the back of the line where Carlann was sobbing quietly and Herse was trying to comfort her. Carlann was bundled up in a gray overcoat with a hood, the most weather-appropriate thing I'd seen anyone wearing. Herse was in the same maroon sweater he had worn yesterday, supplemented with a blanket wrapped hopefully round his shoulders. He looked frozen.

"Hey," I said.

"I want to go Home," said Carlann between gasps. Her face was tear-streaked and miserable.

"We will," I said. "But first we're going to check out this awesome place—"

"Not to the stupid ship," Carlann snapped. "I hate the ship."

"We all do," I agreed, trying not to think of the underdeck. She ignored me.

"I want to go *Home*," she said. "To get off this awful planet and go Home."

"Oh," I said. "Yes. We all want that."

"I want to get away from you all," Carlann spat. "I don't want people touching me. You people. Weird people. Looking at me. I want to get back on the grid. Go back to my own room, my own things. I want to see my family."

Herse gave me a significant look.

"You'll see them soon enough," he said. "And in the meantime, you're making new friends."

"Delinquents," she snapped back. "Deviants. People who walk around outside and write poems."

Herse winced as if stung, but then nodded and forced a smile.

"That's right," he said. "You ought to fit right in. Why did they send you here?"

"No reason," said Carlann. "It was a mistake. I'm not like you."

"Okay," said Herse, as if he believed her. "That sucks. Well, we'll get you home soon, and you can yell at your parents for not packing you warmer clothes."

She scowled at him, but he grinned back. Grudgingly, she nodded.

"It's freezing here," she said. "All the time."

"Not where we're going," I said. "The cave is warm. There's water and plants and bushes with—"

I stopped myself, and they both looked at me.

"With what?" asked Herse.

"Beautiful leaves and flowers," I said.

Herse looked skeptical, but Carlann nodded again and said, "That sounds nice."

"It is," I said.

"I can't wait to see it," said Herse, mainly for Carlann's benefit, and this time she managed a real smile.

"Why don't you see if you can catch up with the others," I suggested.

She considered the idea for a moment, then nodded and broke into a stumbling trot so that I was alone with Herse at the back.

"Good of you to look out for her," I said.

"That's what we have to do, right?"

"Right," I said.

There was a pause.

"Last night," he said, as if he had been saving the words up, waiting for the right moment, "when I showed you the poetry book."

"What about it?"

"When everyone had already turned in and we were sitting on the main deck . . ."

"I remember," I said, pressing.

"I had the weirdest sensation," he said. He looked directly ahead as he walked, avoiding my eyes. "I felt . . . No, I knew—I don't know how or why—that you were thinking about an angel. Not a real one. More like a picture."

I stopped him with one hand and turned him to face me, though he kept his eyes down.

"Why would you think that?" I demanded.

"I don't know," he faltered. "It just came to me . . ."

"I wasn't," I said.

"I just thought—"

"Why would I be thinking about an angel?"

"I don't know," Herse replied, shaking his head in embarrassment. "I guess you wouldn't."

"That's right," I said. "I wouldn't."

It wasn't exactly a lie. I hadn't been thinking of the angel. Not at the moment he was talking about. Earlier, I had, but I held onto the idea that he was wrong. It made the half-truth easier.

"There's a picture of an angel on my stasis pod," I said, more reasonably. "You probably saw that, associated it with me, and—"

"Right," said Herse, glad of something that made sense, eager to end the conversation. "That must be it."

"The picture was there when I got on board," I said. "I didn't put it there."

It was a stupid and unnecessary lie, and I saw in the flicker of his eyes that he recognized it as such. I looked down and blew the air from my lungs so that fog blossomed around my head.

"That's not true," I said, eyes still on the snowy ground. "I did put it there. I was thinking about it. I don't know why I lied."

He nodded, and when I managed to look into his face, I saw that he was smiling sadly with something like sympathy.

"I wrote you a poem," he said suddenly. "I don't mean anything . . . you know . . ." He pulled a face and shook his head hurriedly.

Nothing romantic, he meant.

"It was the idea of the angel," he said, struggling to clarify what he already regretted mentioning. "It's not very good or anything. Dumb, really. But maybe I'll show it to you when we get back. If you like, I mean," he added with a deliberate shrug.

"I'd like that," I said, because it was what he wanted me to say.

He nodded, then changed the subject.

"I'm sick of being on the ship," he said, his voice suddenly taut with frustration.

"Me too," I said, glad of his response and the compassion it implied.

"It's not just the . . ." he fought for the words, "whatever this is." He pressed two fingers hard against the center of his forehead on "this" and I knew what he meant. "It's all of it. None of it makes any sense. What are we doing out here? No one is asking that, not out loud anyway. We talk about rations and toilet rosters and how we're going to survive—and that's good and important—but no one's asking how the hell we finished up here. We're on Valkrys! The nav system malfunctioned and sent us to Valkrys? How is that possible?"

"I really don't know," I said. "And maybe once we're settled, we can try to answer that question without going nuts. But for now . . ."

"I know," he said. "We figure out how to get from one day to the next. We stick together."

"Right," I said. There was a pause. "Yesterday," I added, "what you did, confronting Dren. It was a nice thing to do."

"Stupid," he answered.

"That too," I agreed, "but nice. Standing up for Carlann, I mean."

"She's had a rough trip," he said.

"We all have."

"Yeah," he agreed. "But she's the only one who's had her head stitched and her secrets read."

"Dren," I said.

"Dren," he echoed, the word leaden in his mouth. "There's something about that guy. I mean, I know we're all supposed to be deviants of one kind or another, and I know our crimes are supposed to be real serious and all, but let's be honest while we can. We're petty criminals at worst. Most of us are Section 4F violators: Breakers of Home Decorum. I'm not even sure what *decorum* is, but I know that what we do doesn't get other people hurt. Or killed."

"You think Dren is different?"

"He *feels* different," said Herse. "I know that sounds nuts, but yeah. And I'm not the only one. Bryce knows something."

"Bryce?"

"I saw them when we boarded back on Home," said Herse. "They recognized each other. Bryce was not pleased to see him, I can tell you that."

"Are you sure? Bryce?"

"Pretty sure," said Herse.

He would have said more, but we had suddenly caught up with the others. The line had stopped. I stood as tall as I could to get a better look. At the head of the irregular column, Sevin was kneeling on the snowy ground.

My first thought was that he'd inadvertently cut himself on one of those glassy ridges, but when I fought my way to the front I found that he was unharmed.

"What is it?" I asked.

He looked up, and even in the pale reflected light from the snow, his face was ashen. Saying nothing, he jabbed a gloved finger at the ground.

It was a great print, almost a foot across and pressed deep into the snow. It was made up of a single large depression roughly the shape of a rounded, inverted Y, with four smaller marks above it, each one circular but scored at the top by a spike a couple of inches long.

I stared.

"What is it?" I said.

"A paw print," said Sevin.

"Of an animal?" I said, astonishment making me stupid. "What kind?"

"How should I know?" he snapped back.

The others were pushing to get a look now, but they were hushed.

"Bear?" said Trest, quietly.

"Wolf?" wondered Teada.

"Cat," said Muce. It wasn't a question. Everyone looked at her.

"How do you know?" asked Sevin.

"About a hundred and fifty years ago," Muce said, "back when people still kept pets, some ancestor of mine had a cat. When it died, he had a cast made of its paw print. I found it in a drawer when I was little and asked if I could keep it. It was way smaller than that, like this," she said, making an O with her tiny finger and thumb, "but otherwise it was just the same."

A cat.

Though this would be—what? Twelve feet long? More? Like the tigers that historians say once lived on parts of Home, only bigger. I felt a chill deeper than the wind. Sevin looked at me.

"You saw nothing like this when you came out here?" he said in a low voice.

I shook my head.

"And the snow is new, so the print is fresh," he mused, trying to figure out what direction the beast might have gone. "I think we should go back."

"I agree," I said.

The word "cat" was being muttered around the group. Sevin stood up and raised his hands to get their attention.

"The snow is getting harder," he shouted over the wind, "and I don't want us to be out any longer than necessary, so we're going to turn back. We'll try again another day."

I had expected disappointment, a collective groan, perhaps a few protests, but that wasn't what we got. They exchanged anxious looks and then started to move back the way we had come, but in a ragged and uneven scatter. I felt their panic.

Sevin should have mentioned the paw print. Should have said the word they were already whispering: cat. His dodging it just confirmed their fear. If Sevin wasn't going to be honest about why we couldn't go on, things must be really bad . . .

In seconds, the sense of order and calm had collapsed. Some were walking briskly, others straggling, some running outright. And that wasn't the only source of the mounting confusion. The snow had indeed picked up, and the swirling flakes lowered visibility to no more than a few yards. Sound was muffled, too. In seconds the group which had been a single, unified huddle was divided and confused. There was a cry as someone—Teada, judging by her pale-green jacket—fell face forward in the snow. I made to help her, but she was up and scrambling, her eyes wild. Others were already out of sight, fear trailing in their wake like smoke.

I saw Sevin, running and yelling for order, and then Herse and Carlann blundering after him.

And then I saw something else.

It came out of nowhere. A white shape appearing amongst us out of the storm. It was pale and huge, with canine teeth like long, curved knives that grew down over its lower jaw. It leapt, slashed once with one impossibly powerful foreleg, and pounced.

Herse's blanket fluttered to the ground and lay there. The great white cat ignored it, lowered its jaws to the nape of the boy's neck, and bit once.

I stood, unable to move, staring in horror. One of Herse's hands reached up into the air, fingers splayed as if looking to grab a lifeline that would snatch him away. Then the hand spasmed and fell to the ground, quite still.

I felt his mind go dark, and knew, with a sudden, agonized certainty which took my breath away, as if it had been driven from my body by the frigid wind.

He was dead.

Carlann began to scream, turning and running away from the creature and right at me. Her infectious panic stirred me into motion. I grabbed her hand as she passed, and we fled away from the monstrous cat, away from the others, away from the *Phetteron*.

We ran and ran, blind with tears and terror, lost and speechless. We didn't know where we were or where we were going, but we knew we had to keep moving. So we pounded on, stumbling drunkenly through the snow, dragging each other forward, screaming inside.

CHAPTER

I HAD LIKED HERSE. I HADN'T KNOWN HIM. NOT REALLY. But I had liked him, and the idea that he had been protecting Carlann when he was killed was doubly cruel.

Killed.

There was no doubt he was dead. Carlann kept asking if there was a chance he was still alive, but there wasn't and she knew it. When she inquired a third time, I snapped and told her not to ask again.

We had run without stopping till we could barely stand up and collapsed under the blue shadow of a rock outcrop. It was still snowing hard, so I had no idea where we were or if the beast had followed us. I was guessing it hadn't, but that might have just been wishful thinking.

There was no sign of the others. Whatever would happen next, we were on our own.

Carlann continued to sob, and I sat with my arm around her. My own tears were dry, grief drowned out—at least for now—by practical concerns. Even if the cat was long gone, I doubted we could find our way back to the *Phetteron* in the storm. My sense of direction was badly skewed by the panic of our retreat, and in my heart I suspected we could end up wandering aimlessly for hours. What might stumble upon us in the meantime, God alone knew.

We sat in silence, breathing, sucking in the cold air as our bodies recovered from the harrowing sprint and the shock of Herse's death. We each had half a protein bar and ate quietly, trying to replenish some of the energy we had burned off, though neither of us had any appetite. We drank from our water bottles, too, remembering only after we had emptied them that we should fill them with snow.

"Which way is it?" asked Carlann, peering around the blue rock cautiously.

"The ship?" I said. "Back over there, I think. But I don't know if we should go that way."

Carlann shuddered and said nothing.

"Maybe we should make for the cavern," I said, thinking aloud.

"Why?"

"It's sheltered. There's water."

She sensed something in my hesitation and looked at me.

"And?" she asked.

I looked away and swallowed.

"And there's food," I said.

"What?" she gasped.

"Fruit," I answered, avoiding her eyes. "There are bushes with fruit. I tried it," I said, deliberately keeping Bryce and Yasmine out of it, "and it seems safe."

"You ate some? Right off the bush?"

She was aghast, horrified.

"Yes," I said, finding a little defiance. "The protein bars won't last forever. And if we can't get back to the ship—"

"I'm not eating fruit of a bush," said Carlann. "It's disgusting. It's animal."

"It might keep us alive," I shot back.

"What's the point if we sacrifice all we hold dear in the process?" she said primly, echoing the old Home slogan about deviance being unattractive.

"Fine," I snapped. "Don't eat the fruit. How much of your protein bar did you save?"

Her eyes got big, like she was a little girl.

"None," she said.

"You ate the whole thing?" I asked, astonished.

"I was hungry."

I put my face in my hands.

"I'm sorry," she said, like I was her mother or her teacher. The girl was no more than a year younger than me.

I sighed and snatched the protein bar from my pocket. I had only taken one bite. I broke what was left in half and gave her one of the pieces.

"Don't eat it now," I said. "We could be out here for a while."

She took it meekly, without protest, and muttered a "thank you" as she put it away.

I stood up, brushing the snowflakes from my nose and hair and rubbing warmth into my cheeks.

"We can't stay here," I said. "It's too exposed, and when the sun goes down it's going to get dangerously cold."

"Do you have a positioning unit?" asked Carlann.

"No," I said.

"That's too bad."

"Not really. They work from satellites. We're on Valkrys, remember? Not a lot of nav sats in orbit."

"Right," said Carlann, chastened. "Sorry."

"It's okay," I said, trying to sound conciliatory. "I just need to figure out which way to go."

The truth was that I already knew which way to go, at least in the short term, but that meant going back to where Herse had been killed. I just didn't think I could do that, even though the thing that had killed him might be miles away by now.

Unless it had settled there to eat.

I pushed the image away. Perhaps we could circle round to the *Phetteron* by a different route?

That sounded good, but if my sense of the ship's location was wrong . . . we could wander for days, or however long it took to freeze to death. But I couldn't see a better option, especially since I now knew that the cavern wasn't safe either. If we could get in, so could the sabertoothed cat. This assumed, of course, that the *Phetteron* was safe, that the great beast—or other things just as lethal—couldn't find a way in, or wouldn't try, and that might not be true. Either way, it was difficult to see the ship as a haven, all that cold metal and the darkness in its belly . . .

Still, no point thinking about that.

"Okay," I said. "Ready to go?"

"You know where we're going?" asked Carlann in her little-girl voice. It was clear that she wouldn't offer any suggestions. She had relinquished all decision-making to me, whether I wanted it or not.

"I think so," I said, "and I'm not going to get any better ideas sitting around here, so let's go."

"What if you're wrong?"

I gritted my teeth, then rounded the edge of the rocky shelter and faced down the storm.

"Let's hope I'm not," I said.

●

BUT I WAS. WE WALKED FOR AN HOUR AND FOUND NEITHER the cavern nor the *Phetteron*, and though the snow eventually stopped enough for us to see in all directions, we caught no sign of the others. The sun was still high but past its zenith, and we were now on the clock.

I responded by walking faster so that Carlann began to trail a few paces behind, even though I knew that I might be taking us still further off course. The snowfield was featureless except for occasional slopes swelling like dunes and clusters of blue spines rearing up from below the surface like teeth. After another ten minutes, I got the nagging impression that some of those clusters looked all too familiar, and if it wasn't for the absence of tracks, I'd swear I'd been there before.

The mountains looked the same as before, but they were so far away that distance was impossible to judge accurately. We could have walked right past the *Phetteron* in the storm, straying further and further afield the longer we walked.

Carlann had grown sulky, her tears for Herse tainted with something like spite which was directed primarily at me. She scowled when I told her to catch up, and muttered to herself darkly as she trudged along. I could feel her resentment, her self-pity. How I could sense those things I did not know, and was too weary to consider.

My heart was beating faster, partly due to the exertion, partly from a swelling sense of alarm. Perhaps the ship would be over the next rise, I told myself. And, when I got there and found the same empty white space rolling out in front of me, the next. Maybe if we could find some high ground, now that the snow had stopped, we'd be able to see further.

I scanned and saw where a great pinnacle of the blue stone stabbed up over to our right.

"I'm going up that," I said. "You might want to wait at the bottom."

Carlann's surly stare melted into fear and despair.

"You're–you're leaving me?" she stammered.

"Just so I can get a view from the top," I said. "I'll only be a few minutes, but the rock will be sharp and hard to climb. It's very easy to cut yourself badly. Just wait for me out of the wind. Get your breath back."

"What if something comes?"

"Nothing is going to come. Look," I said, surveying the snowfield. "You can see for miles now. Nothing is going to creep up on us."

"It crept up on Herse."

"It was snowing then, and we walked right into it," I said. "Five minutes, okay? I'll come right back."

She pouted.

"I wish Herse was here," she said.

"Five minutes," I said, walking away.

She trailed disconsolately after me, and I had to stifle a wave of irritation. I reminded myself that she had been through a lot, which is what Herse would have said if he had still been alive to say it.

She watched me climb apprehensively, not, I felt—perhaps unfairly—fearing for my safety so much as fearing for what would befall her if something happened to me. I stopped looking down and made the ascent carefully, using my hands and knees as well as my feet, moving slowly, judging the sharpness of each ledge, and sticking where possible to those portions of the rock face that had a heavy accumulation of snow.

Five minutes had been overly optimistic. It took me nearly ten to reach the top alone, but the view was worth it. I could see triple what had been visible from the plain, and I revolved slowly, studying the ground in every direction.

I saw it right away.

Over to the right, at the end of long, ragged scar in the ice field, was the half-buried wreckage of the ship. It looked odd from this angle, unfamiliar, and not at all where I had expected it to be. It was perhaps a half-mile across open country, and had it not been for a couple of low, undulating drifts, I would have been able to see it from the bottom.

I waved and shouted to Carlann, laughing with relief, forgetting my irritation with her. We would be home within the hour.

Well, not *Home*, of course. But safe, and that would do for now.

"You saw it?" said Carlann, joyful and a little desperate, when I reached the bottom. "You really saw it?"

"I really saw it," I said, striding through the snow. "We'll be there in no time."

I could feel the tension in my thighs and calves from all the hiking. I knew they would ache and stiffen up later, but for now I was elated. The awful day would end better.

Carlann walked beside me now, and as we came to the second rise she even pushed a little ahead. I watched her as she crested the drift and felt something of my former anxiety returning, but then she was jumping and pointing and clapping her hands with delight. She could see the ship.

She ran now, seeming to forget I was even present. I felt the strangeness of being alone out there in the snow and jogged after her as best as I could. The snow had hardened here, and the going was faster. I was driven by relief that, for the moment, staved off the inevitable exhaustion and the other kinds of pain that would come back when I had time to think. I ran, laughing under my breath, and it took a moment for me to realize that Carlann had stopped only yards from the ship.

She was standing with her back to me, gazing fixedly up at the transport. My approach, my questions did nothing to break her fascination, and in spite of my good humor I felt a prickle of annoyance.

"What?" I said, as I drew up next to her. "What are you looking at?"

She said nothing, but pointed a wavering hand at the barely legible lettering beneath the side viewers.

It read "*Hynderon.*"

Not *Phetteron*.

It was a different ship.

CHAPTER **16**

I T WAS AN OLDER VESSEL THAN THE *PHETTERON*, ITS SHAPE cruder, more angular, and its faded paint and rust-pitted exterior suggested it had been there some time. Years, probably. But there was no doubt that it had originated on Home, which was unsettling in lots of ways.

The *Hynderon* had accumulated a good deal of snow and ice, but its touchdown looked to have been comparatively smooth, and there was no sign of the kind of damage visited on the *Phetteron*. From where I stood, I could see no hull breach, no shredding of the engine nacelles such as we had suffered.

So how to get in?

Snow and ice had built up around the main hatch, and I could walk up without the need of stairs or a ladder. I kicked at the accumulated icicles that hung from the doorframe, then pulled the knife from my waistband and set to chipping at the frozen seal. If the door was locked from the inside, none of this would make a difference, but it was just possible that the only thing keeping it closed was the ice.

I worked till sweat rolled down my face while Carlann watched, saying nothing, doing less. At last I stood up, my back aching, and reached for the latch handle. I took hold and pulled it down, hard. I heard something inside disengage, but the door did not move. I tried again, cursing under my breath, then went back to working at the door seams with my knife. Carlann was crying again.

I pulled at the door with all my strength, and something at the top gave way so that it popped an inch or so out of the frame, though the bottom remained stuck fast.

"What's that?" said Carlann. She was gazing back the way we had come. "Was that there before?"

I stared out into the dunes and ridges, blinking the sweat out of my eyes. There was a low, white mound that might have been the still, crouching cat.

"Did you see it move?" I asked.

She shook her head, eyes wide.

"Watch it," I said.

Back to my hands and knees. Back to the knife. Then up again and pulling as Carlann breathed my name and pointed to where the white mound seemed to have shifted ominously.

This time the ice gave way entirely, and the door fell open as far as the accumulated snow would let it. I pulled the flashlight from my backpack and leaned inside, shining the beam around and dragging the door shut behind us. Carlann took up position by the window and stared out at the hazy shape.

I wasn't sure what I had expected. Carnage, perhaps. Bodies. But there was none of that. What I got instead was a powerful memory of boarding the *Phetteron* for the start of our flight. This was a different ship, even more basic and utilitarian, but its familial link to the *Phetteron* was clear. For a moment I was right back there, hunting abashed for my stasis pod, the transit agent poking me and repeating regulations over and over as if I were too stupid to have grasped them the first time. Sound echoed in the same way around its bleak metal deck. But unlike the *Phetteron* now, there were no holes through which the whistling wind could enter.

I climbed in. It was too much to hope that the electricity worked, but I pulled the auxiliary power switch anyway, and gaped as the emergency lights eased on.

"Oh my God," I muttered aloud.

"What?" asked Carlann from behind me.

"The ship," I said, amazed. "It looks pretty much intact."

"You mean we could fly it out?"

Her question thrilled me. But despite the hope the unexpected ship represented, we needed to keep our heads clear.

"Let's not get ahead of ourselves," I said, though I could feel her anticipation building like an engine accelerating.

I gazed around the deck. It was all weirdly familiar but slightly off, as if reflected in a distorting mirror. Hold.

Stasis pods. Stowage lockers. Staircase down to the under-deck and engine room. All recognizable and roughly where they were on the *Phetteron*, but from a slightly different era, and all furred with frost and dripping icicles.

As if to make the point, there was no ident reader on the flight deck doors, just a keypad. Even if there was power running to the circuit, that was going to prove a huge stumbling block. The doors were molded in two parts, solid enough to provide an airlock should the cabin be manned, and unless they had been left unlocked, it would take the code or a blow torch to get through them.

I tried them to be sure, brushing away the ice crystals that had formed on the metal, but the handle did not move one iota.

So much for flying back to Home.

And if we could get through, the controls would be protected by similar codes. It was too much to hope that Sevin's cadet status would give us access to a machine that had probably not been flown since he was born.

I moved into the passenger quarters, feeling the cold of the ship. Turning on the emergency lights had also started a fan somewhere in the bowels of the vessel, and it creaked and squealed as it turned. The air that moved through the hold was as frigid as that outside. It took a moment to see why. A series of vents in the roof had been left in the open position.

Why would anyone do that? And, more to the point, where was whoever had done it?

I stooped to the nearest stasis pod, wiping the frost from the glass—and recoiled in horror.

"What?" asked Carlann, who lingered timidly just inside the doorway. "What is it?"

It was possible that she had sensed my feelings as well as seeing my physical reaction.

There was someone in the pod. A boy, about my age. His face was pale, the lips blue, his eyes frozen and staring. He was dead.

I placed my hands over my mouth and blew till I could feel my fingers warm slightly. Then, deliberately not giving myself time to think about it, I moved down the central aisle, wiping the glass on each stasis pod, looking in, and moving on.

As on the *Phetteron*, there were ten pods. Nine of them were occupied. They were all kids like us. All dead.

I sat on a luggage rack at the rear of the ship and looked at the floor, quite still, saying nothing, ignoring Carlann's babbling inquiries and pleas for consolation. I just sat there. Any hope I had felt moments before was gone, replaced by the sheer weight of death around me.

Kids.

I don't know how long I sat there. Five minutes? Ten? Maybe more. I didn't wonder who they were or whom they had left behind. Nor did I speculate on the petty crimes that had brought them here, though I was sure in my gut that they had been deviants like us who had been bound for reeducation and never arrived. I didn't know where that conviction came from, but it burned in my mind like frozen metal. I was also sure that before I left this place, I would have to open one of those stasis pods. The idea of what I might find haunted me, like a monster in a dream whose presence you could feel but not quite see.

But it didn't make sense.

The ship might not be airworthy now, but it seemed to have landed without suffering the trauma the *Phetteron* had. So what had killed everyone on board? Some sort of toxic leak, perhaps. Had the stasis pods failed or locked so the kids couldn't get out? But then the pods would have shown signs of violence, surely. They weren't so sturdy that someone whose life was in jeopardy wouldn't be able to kick their way out.

Reluctantly I returned to the first pod and, ignoring Carlann's sobs as she begged me not to, flicked the cover release. It came free immediately—the boy inside certainly would have been able to escape if he had been alive. So either he had remained unconscious the whole time, or someone had put him back into the pod after death.

I didn't like that idea, but it settled in my stomach like a stone.

I avoided looking at his face. His clothes were old-fashioned, and the comm pad in his jacket pocket was like the one I had had when I was five, gray and just a little clunky. It took all my strength to turn him over. He was quite rigid, which somehow helped me swallow back the nightmare of what I was doing. The corpse didn't move like a person. More like a statue or mannequin like they made in the old days to sell clothes. Even his hair was frozen and broke when I tried to move it.

"Sorry," I said.

It was a stupid thing to say, and almost brought the sadness and horror screaming out, but I pushed my feelings back and studied the back of his head.

I knew it would be there, the tattooed triangle.

Once I had seen it, I put him back, laboring to get him into position so that I could close the lid without breaking one of his fingers.

"How did they die?" asked Carlann, still keeping her distance.

"I don't know how all of them died," I said, my voice blank and flat.

"That one then," she said, slightly petulant.

Her phrasing—like the boy was just a thing, not what had once been a person—annoyed me, but I shrugged the feeling off and considered what I had seen.

There had been no marks of starvation on the body. He looked like he had been quite healthy. There were no lacerations from the teeth or claws of a great cat like the one that had taken Herse. There was just a single hole in his chest, small at the front, slightly larger at the back. There wasn't a drop of blood in the stasis pod, which meant he had died outside of it.

"Sola?" Carlann said, as if I had drifted off. "How did he die?"

I stood up and considered the boy's frozen face in the window of the pod cover before turning and answering her.

"He was shot."

CHAPTER

I SCOURED THE SHIP FOR ANYTHING WE MIGHT USE—
extra blankets, lamps, food—but there was surprisingly
little to be found. Either they had built a camp somewhere else or they had been even less prepared for survival
on the planet than we had been, and died shortly after
arriving. It was possible that they hadn't been killed here
at all, that they had died and *then* were loaded into the
transport, but there was no blood, no sign of a struggle.

The boy wasn't the only one who had been shot. I saw
three other bodies with the same holes, two more with
head wounds that might have been caused by rocks, and
three with gashes that might have been done by claws, but
looked more like knife wounds. I couldn't be sure, but an
awful possibility lodged in my gut like a blade.

They had done this to each other.

The thought made my heart thump and my skin crawl, my brain imagining their last, horror-stricken moments and projecting them onto the underside of my eyelids.

I said no more about it to Carlann and, to force my mind into the present, started examining the ship. I made only one useful discovery. As on the *Phetteron*, the ship had a computer station in the hold. It didn't give access to all the ship's systems, but through it I could access the nav log.

The story it told was eerily familiar. The *Hynderon* had left Home twelve years ago bound, according to its initial trajectory, for Jerem and—I was guessing—the reeducation facility there. But not long after breaking Home's atmosphere, the ship's course had altered. There was no sign of an incident that had disrupted the vessel's functions, no catastrophic collision, no unscheduled rendezvous in which the ship's heading had been accidentally reset. The ship just changed course and made for Valkrys, where it braved the asteroid field and landed. The comm system broadcast an SOS for several weeks before the ship powered down, though whether that was some automatic protocol or was done by someone on board, I had no way of knowing.

What I did know was that the nav sensor screen showed incoming signals as well as outgoing ones. Now that it had been reactivated, it was picking up a periodic blip: not from off-world, but from a broadcast being made close to our current location.

The *Phetteron*.

It had to be. Sevin had set the ship to send out an emergency pulse in the hope that a rescue vessel would detect us.

So the good news was that if I was reading the frozen gray monitor screen correctly, the *Phetteron* was only two miles to our north. We would have to be alert for predators, and we couldn't keep the signal with us. We'd just have to use the information from the nav screen to give us to get our bearings and then hope we could keep true to course till we reached our ship.

Carlann had, predictably, mixed feelings about the news: delight that our separation from the group was nearly over, dread and boredom and irritation that we'd have to walk two miles to reach them. She didn't say it with her lips, but she blamed me for taking her so far from the rest, and I didn't bother to argue. And besides, how was I supposed to protest a feeling she hadn't actually put into words

So after carefully scrutinizing the landscape for any sign of the great cat, we closed the *Hynderon*'s door, leaving the ship largely as we had found it, and set off walking. I had plotted a path to exactly where I thought the nav system was pointing us, picking a violet spot on a distant mountain as the point to make for. With luck we'd run into the *Phetteron* long before we reached it.

I told Carlann that stealth was our best safety and that talking might alert hunting animals to our presence. That kept her quiet, though I still felt the ebb and flow of her fear, hope, and irritation as we trekked in silence. She neither said nor did anything that suggested she was aware of what was going on in my head, but she had the little tattooed triangle as well as I did, which meant we had been marked as similar a long time ago. Maybe the mark was somehow related to our impulse to bend rules and social codes, but I was beginning to think it meant something more. What the bond between us was, I wasn't yet prepared to say.

To avoid thinking about the *Hynderon*, I filled my head with songs from Home and hummed under my breath till I sensed that even that was annoying Carlann. I grinned bleakly to myself, adjusted the collar of my jacket against the bitter wind, and kept humming.

We saw the *Phetteron* after about forty minutes, lying off to the left and no more than a couple hundred yards out of our way. Carlann gave no sign that she was impressed or grateful, but I enjoyed a sense of achievement despite all that had gone wrong that day. I savored the moment, because for all the relief of finding our way back to the ship, I was apprehensive. I thought of the bodies on the *Hynderon*. How long had they lasted after they had touched down? What had happened that had led to them to be stored away in their stasis pods forever? And the unavoidable question: Were we already inching along the same path?

•

BRYCE CAME RUSHING OVER AS SOON AS I OPENED THE door, his face suffused with relief and concern. Sevin just stood up and looked at me from across the hold, nodding slightly when I caught his eye. It was enough.

Bryce asked if we were okay and said how worried they had all been, and I told him we were fine and fought back the impulse to collapse in his arms, weeping. If we'd had to, I would have walked through the snow for hours, but now that we were here and safe, the exhaustion and grief was suddenly unbearable. The ship was awash in sadness and despair, and our return only reset the balance a fraction. Trest got up and came towards me, but hesitated when he saw how close I was standing to Bryce. Yasmine was watching, too, smiling with relief. If there were other feelings there, feelings connected to the way Bryce had drawn me into his chest with his good arm, I could not sense them.

And for a moment, I didn't care.

I took a long shuddering breath, taking in the scent of him, the warmth of his body—and then heard Carlann say, in a voice meant to carry, "We found another ship, didn't we Sola?"

She said it, I was sure, to get attention, and it worked.

Everyone stopped speaking, and those who had been sitting leapt to their feet. As they thronged about her, I felt her pleasure.

"Is this true?" Sevin demanded. His face was carefully neutral, but I sensed his excitement.

"Yes," I said. "Two miles to the south. It's an old ship. Been there years."

"From Home?" asked Muce.

"Where else would it be from?" drawled Dren.

"Yes," I said to Muce, smiling. "From Home."

She grinned, glad to see me, and I felt a curious urge to hug her.

"Could you get in?" asked Sevin, again careful.

"Yes," I said. "The flight deck door was code-locked, but the external hatch wasn't."

"There are dead people inside," said Carlann.

The others looked at her.

"Full of kids like us," she said. "All dead in their pods."

A tense silence descended on the group.

"But we might be able to fly the ship," Carlann concluded. I scowled at her and sighed, but when all those eyes turned on me for confirmation, I said, "Well, I'm not so sure about that. As I said, the flight deck is sealed. But the ship seems largely undamaged, and its backup systems are certainly functional."

A wave of excitement bubbled through the ship. I met Sevin's eyes and shrugged, waiting for the others to connect the two pieces of information Carlann had laid out like mines. It was Trest who made the link, his face clouded.

"So if the ship is intact," he said, "why are the people on board dead?"

"We don't know yet," I said quickly, shooting Carlann a warning glance.

There was a momentary silence, then Dren said, "Sure you do."

Several of the others gave him baffled looks, but I stared at him, feeling my face flushing.

"No," I said, "I don't."

"You know what killed one of them," he said, his face tightening with concentration.

Unbidden, the image of the dead boy rose in my mind, the tiny, bloodless hole in his chest . . .

I closed my eyes and shook my head violently, trying to shut Dren out, but when I looked at him again, he was smirking knowingly.

The others were watching us, curious and wary, but then Teada asked when we were going to back to the other ship, and their attention wandered. Dren held my eyes for a moment, then winked, and I turned away. As the others buzzed over the discovery of the *Hynderon*, I found a quiet corner at the rear of the hull and sat there in the shadows, head in my hands, saying nothing. I had no idea what time it was, how close we were till nightfall, but I suddenly wanted nothing more than to crawl into my stasis pod and go to sleep under the abstract gaze of the angel in the picture.

"I'm sorry about Herse."

I sat up and opened my eyes. It was Yasmine.

"It must have been terrible for you," she said.

I couldn't think of anything to say that would begin to express what it had been like. In the end, I just shook my head sadly and said, "I didn't know him well. But he seemed nice."

Yasmine nodded thoughtfully.

"We're going to have a memorial service," she said. "We were just waiting for you and Carlann to get back."

I sighed again. I was physically and emotionally drained. I didn't feel like sharing my feelings with the others.

"Okay," I said. "When?"

"In about an hour, Sevin says."

"Okay," I said again. "Wake me, will you?"

As I made for my pod, she drifted over to Bryce. I thought about what Herse had said about Bryce knowing Dren, how he had recognized him when they were boarding the ship back on Home and wasn't pleased to see him. If it was true, they had both hidden the connection and were continuing to do so. That was worrying, and for a moment—one I instantly regretted—I hoped Herse had been wrong.

●

THE SERVICE, SUCH AS IT WAS, WAS JUST ABOUT BEARABLE. Teada produced a candle and lit it as we sat in a circle. Sevin, predictably, presided, but he did it well, talking about how Herse had been a strong young man, quick to stand up for others, and that we would not forget him. He made his death sound like a sacrifice, as if Herse had confronted the cat to protect the rest of us. Maybe that was true—I hadn't really seen. And it seemed like a good way to remember him, one that gave his life and death a sense of purpose, so I nodded with something like satisfaction. I didn't cry, and when Sevin invited the rest of us to contribute our thoughts, I didn't say anything. Trest said Herse had shared a tube of fizz jellies with him right after the crash, before we knew what was going on.

"The good kind, too," he said. "Not the little silver ones that taste like toenails. That was cool of him. Telling, you know? So . . . thanks, man."

He nodded at the guttering candle flame as if the spirit of the dead boy lived inside it.

Carlann talked about his kindness toward her, her voice cracking. Yasmine threw a long, elegant arm around her shoulders, her silver hair spilling over the shorter girl as she sobbed.

"I'll miss you," Carlann said. "I know you saved my life, but I would rather you were still here."

I watched her as the circle leaned in to comfort her and felt the warmth of her satisfaction at being the center of attention. She wore their sympathy like the choker at her throat, a frail and tragic princess. I scowled and turned away, only to find Dren looking at me. His eyes flicked towards Carlann, and he pulled a dubious face like he understood. The color rose in my cheeks, and I hurried away from the circle, feeling disloyal and transparent, just like when I had lied to Herse about the angel.

When no one was looking, I opened Herse's stasis pod and located the slim little book he had offered me not so very long ago. I took it to my own pod and climbed in, muttering an apology and taking a deep breath before opening the book to the last page. A handful of lines had been penned in careful, even script:

I dreamed of an angel,
Her wings like driven snow,
Though warm and soft as down
When she folds them round us
To keep out the bitter wind,

But also swift and keen as the air
On which she rides,
Gathering us to her,
Lifting us up
Till we rise like flame
Into the still night,
Hot and bright and pure
Because she is holding us.
And we burn with her light
So that even before the dawn
We can almost see ourselves.

I read the poem slowly, turning each phrase over in my mind until I got to the end, then I read it again and again till I could almost hear the words in Herse's voice. Long after I shut the light off, they resonated in my head like the chiming, distant bells of a forgotten cathedral.

●

MAYBE THE NAP I HAD TAKEN EARLIER HAD DONE ME MORE good than I realized, but I slept for only an hour or so before waking and finding my old restlessness was back. Some of that impulse, I admit, came from the fear of waking up in the night to find the strange, pale girl looking in at me.

But when I opened the stasis pod to the cold night air, I found that I wasn't alone. Sevin's light was on, and when I climbed out, he opened his own—as if waiting for just such an eventuality.

"Can't sleep," I said.

"Let's sit in the flight deck," he said, sitting up. "That way we don't have to worry about disturbing the others."

Or being overheard. He was thinking it, too. I was sure of it.

He closed the heavy doors behind us, and I nodded at the keypad that locked it.

"Think you could do that on the *Hynderon*?" I asked.

He shook his head.

"If it's as old as you say, no way."

"So we won't be flying back to Home anytime soon," I said, settling into the copilot's chair.

"Hard to believe it really is airworthy," said Sevin, "but if it is, there may be other ways to get in, even if takes weeks. When you activated the radar that led you back here, did you see anything else on the long-range scanner?"

He asked casually, like he was just curious, but I felt an anxiety beneath the question. He had wanted to ask me this since I first came back.

"No," I said. "I didn't think to switch the scanner frequency. Why?"

"No reason," he said. Lied. He caught my look. "I'm getting worried that there's no rescue coming," he conceded. "Happy? I'm anxious. Scared. I thought that by now . . ."

He inhaled. Exhaled long and slow.

"People think I'm in charge," he said. "The others. Not you. So I try to look like I know what I'm doing, partly because I think I can help us survive, and partly because they need someone to tell them it will be okay. I can't let them know that now I'm not so sure. I don't know. Seems we should have heard something by now."

There was still something he wasn't saying, something he was struggling to muffle in his mind so I wouldn't see it, but some of what he was saying was true, too. He paused, and I sensed him preparing to ask something important. It was a curious sensation, feeling his mood as if it were something I could reach out and touch. It reminded me of how he had felt when Carlann had announced that we had found the ship. He had been excited. Not surprised, I thought—though maybe that was in there, too—but whatever it was, his response had been quite unlike everyone else's. They had been excited because the new ship spelled the possibility of escape, of rescue. Sevin's exhilaration had been purer, a genuine thrill, though what motivated it was lost to me.

"You said there were bodies," he said.

"Yes."

"You saw them?"

"I only looked closely at one," I said. "A boy. But yes, I saw the others."

"How many were there?"

"Nine," I said. "There was one empty pod."

"Nine," he repeated. "Are you sure?"

"Positive," I said. "Why?"

He shook his head.

"Nothing," he said, though I could feel the effort it took to keep other more powerful emotions out of his face and mind. I caught the whiff of them all the same, echoes of feelings he was working to keep in check: confusion, excitement, even fear.

"What do you know that you aren't telling us?" I asked.

"I don't know what you mean," he said.

"You're lying," I answered. It wasn't an accusation, just a statement of fact. "I can sense it, and you know that, too. That's why you keep trying to lock your mind down, to put it in a safe so that nothing leaks out where I might see it. I assume you can do the same to me."

He hesitated.

"Read your thoughts, you mean?" he said. "Yes. Some. Maybe not as well as you can. Or Dren."

"Dren's scary," I said. "He's too good at it, and I don't trust him with anything he might learn."

"Have the others realized what's happened to them since we left Home?" asked Sevin. "That their abilities have sharpened?"

I shrugged.

"I sensed that Bryce and Yasmine were aware of it when—" I caught myself imagining the taste of the fruit in my mouth and tried to block the memory from my mind. "When we were out at the cavern."

"Those two seem to be getting very cozy," said Sevin.

I bristled at his manner, and at the idea that he was probably right, but I said nothing. His eyes betrayed no awareness of what had gone through my mind.

Odd.

I thought of the girl I had seen out there in the dark, allowing the strangeness of the memory to work on my imagination till the hairs on the back of my arms prickled. I closed my eyes and gave myself up to the moment, allowing myself for the first time to linger on the uncanny and unnerving image that had haunted me since I first saw it.

When I opened my eyes, Sevin was fiddling with the controls in front of him. Unless he was an extraordinary actor, he was completely unaware of me.

Very odd.

He bent forward to study the details of the nav screen, and I reached over and grabbed the back of his head with one hand. He squirmed, but I gripped harder and said, "Hold still. You have something in your hair."

I fumbled, parting the black, short tufts, moving them.

When I stopped, he gave me a quizzical look.

"Just a bit of lint," I said. "Gone now."

He did not have the tattoo. Everyone else on board had it, I was sure. So did everyone on board the *Hynderon*. But Sevin did not.

I watched him, and he seemed cautious, guarded.

"What do you think it means, this other ship landing almost in the same place as us twelve years earlier?" I asked.

He shook his head and looked away.

"Probably nothing," he said. "A coincidence."

I stared at him in amazement, feeling again the effort to keep his feelings hidden. He was lying, recklessly so.

A coincidence?

Two ships from the same fleet landing on the same dead planet halfway across the solar system? It was absurd. He couldn't possibly believe that. He was still avoiding my eyes, staring off into the darkness through the front viewers.

I decided to let it slide till I had real ideas.

"How are the supplies?" I asked.

He puffed up his cheek and blew the air out.

"Getting low," he said. "We need to start eating less."

"That's not going to be a popular decision."

"It's too bad there were no more supplies on the *Hynderon*. We need to find a food source, but that doesn't seem real likely. That cavern you found," he said. "You think there might be anything edible in there?"

I shrugged, trying not to break eye contact and failing.

"We didn't have time to really look around," I said.

"Maybe we should go back," he said.

All that I was not saying—the guilt of keeping the fruit secret and the shame of having reveled in eating it (*cave-girl!*)—weighed on my chest. I opted to change the subject.

"Is this your sanctuary?" I asked him, gesturing at the flight deck. "Your bolthole."

He seemed poised to deny it, but nodded.

"I come here from time to time," he said. "Just to sit and be by myself. Amazing how crowded ten people can make a ship."

"Last night?" I prompted. "You came in here then?"

"Might have," he said, prevaricating. "Yes, I think so. Why?"

"Did you see anything odd?"

"Odd?"

"Strange," I said. "Out of place."

"On the ship?"

"Outside."

His face creased into lines of bafflement. Then it cleared, and he shook his head.

"Should I have?" he asked.

My turn to frown.

"Not sure," I said. "If you ever do, tell me."

He considered me.

"You're an odd one, Sola," he said.

"Odder than the others?"

"Definitely."

"Can't all be cadets," I said.

"Careful," he said, grinning. "That ejector seat still works, you know."

I got up.

"Going to try sleeping again," I said on my way out.

He turned as if about to say something, and I felt a surge of confusion and hesitation, unusual for him.

"What?" I asked.

He shook his head, and now I sensed only frustration and disappointment.

"Nothing," he said. "See you tomorrow."

●

Outside the flight deck doors, I paused to gaze out through the side viewer, but there was nothing to see in the night except the darkness and the bluish gray of the snowfield. That should have made me feel better, but it didn't. I scanned the silent stasis pods, alert for the telltale golden glow that had so bothered me on the first night, but all was still. I groped my way back to my pod feeling ill at ease, my mind tumbling with questions. Tomorrow we would return to the *Hynderon*. That seemed unavoidable. I didn't want to go, but I knew I had to. There were things to learn there that I had missed but that mattered to us. Things, I suspected, that Sevin already knew.

I was about to get into my pod when I noticed a curious, repeating pattern on the metal of the gangway. I stooped to get a better look, and my breath caught. Up and down the main walkway, unmistakable even in the soft glow of my stasis pod, were a set of prints made by small, bare feet.

I WAS UP LATE THE NEXT DAY, AND THAT MEANT THAT I was at the back of the line for the bathroom. While we had been out yesterday, Bryce and Yasmine had collected snow in a bucket to replenish the water tank, but it hadn't all melted, and everyone was complaining that the stream from the tap was thin and ice cold. The bathroom smelled, too: a sour, unpleasant aroma that was not confined to the cramped metal room, but contaminated the entire deck. My family's apartment in Sindrone had three separate bathrooms, one for each of us. The idea of sharing a toilet was repellent, even when it didn't stink.

I watched Bryce moving around the hold, going through his bag of belongings and pulling out a clean tee shirt. He slipped out of the one he was wearing with difficulty, dragging it over his broken arm with a look of frustration and discomfort. For a moment he stood there, shirtless and pale, and I thought how strange it was that he could do something in front of people that would have mortified him less than a week ago. But getting the new shirt on was even harder than taking the old one off, and I couldn't help feeling for him as he wrestled with it.

I took a step out of the line to go and help him, but Yasmine just appeared beside him, grinning and taking his shirt. I stopped quickly and half turned so it wouldn't look like I had been heading over, but I couldn't not watch the way she threaded his arms through the holes, how she pulled the fabric down over his shoulders, his chest, smoothing it before taking her hands away, and the look on their faces as their eyes met.

"You going in there?"

I turned. It was Trest.

"What?" I said, regrouping.

"The bathroom," he said, smiling. "Morning sanitary procedures and all that. Sorry to ask. It's just that you seemed to be in line, but now I'm not so sure. Never been great at reading girls. Women. People of the opposite . . . So, yea or nay on the bathroom?"

"Yea," I said, smiling back at him. He had seen me watching Bryce but hadn't said anything, and for that I was grateful.

"Fair enough," he said. "Enjoy. I mean, not enjoy. Good luck or—something. I'll stop talking now."

"I know what you mean," I said.

"Thanks. Words, huh? Easier to use over a comm link."

"I guess so," I said.

"Put me in virtual chat mode, and I'm totally cool for hours," said Trest. "But actual people standing next to me, looking at me? Different ballgame entirely."

"I thought you had adjusted better than most," I said, honestly.

He made a theatrical gesture that was almost a bow. *It's an act*, said the gesture. *I'm faking it.*

"But if we're here much longer, I guess everyone will see right through that, too," he said, ruefully. "You know how we evolved as a culture, leaving behind all that body stuff that the primitives used to care so much about? You ever wonder what we put in its place? I do. I mean, are we smarter now or something? I don't feel like I know anything. Especially here, when what little I do know doesn't add up to anything useful."

He shook his head, and I realized he was being more serious than usual.

"I know what you mean," I agreed. "Take away our comm pads, and we seem pretty useless."

He looked at me thoughtfully, and his hand went to the chain around his ear, as it often did when he was distracted or uneasy. Then he lowered his voice.

"You ever think it's odd, our being here? Considering that other ship, I mean."

"Not sure I follow," I said, caution tautening around my thoughts.

"I mean, a ship from Home goes off course by accident and crashes here," he said, his eyes flashing around as if making sure we weren't overheard. "I can just about buy that, though it's not easy, considering the guidance systems on these ships. But let's say it was just a mistake—and still no one comes looking? Either they can't track a lost ship to Valkrys or they don't bother to come and recover the bodies?

"And let's say we can accept all of this, that the weird interference from the asteroids or all this blue rock or something makes it impossible to find the crashed ship. That's all perfectly reasonable. But then a decade or so goes by, and it happens again? In the same spot? No. That's beyond coincidence. It's borderline impossible. I know I'm hardly the brains of the outfit—as Field Marshal Sevin would be quick to point out—but it seems obvious to me that this all stinks worse than the toilet. So what I want to know is, why is no one else asking the question?"

I just looked at him, sensing his thoughts, and was as sure as I could be that he had no other agenda. He was hiding nothing. He just wanted reassurance that he wasn't alone in his questions.

"Maybe they aren't ready to face that possibility," I said.

He nodded.

"Are you?"

"I'm not sure," I said, "but I guess I have to be." I eyed the bathroom door. Suddenly I wanted to be alone. "Going in now," I said.

"Understood," he replied, managing a tight smile. "But let's talk about this soon, yeah?"

"Yeah," I said. I watched him go, then stepped into the bathroom.

The smell drove out any thought about what he had just said. They weren't kidding about the water either. It was freezing. I wondered if we would be better on the *Hynderon*, where there was more power and functional systems, but I remembered the bodies in the stasis pods. I couldn't imagine sleeping in those even if we could manage the ghastly business of lifting the corpses out.

Back on deck, I replaced my meager toiletries in my pod and turned at a familiar voice.

"You have any candy?" asked Muce. "I'm really hungry."

She looked so small and lost. I smiled as kindly as I could, reminding myself that it must be especially hard on someone as young as her to be stuck out here without her family.

"I'm afraid not," I said. "I don't think anyone has anything like that left. We collected it all, remember?"

"That girl did," said Muce. "She offered me some, but I didn't like it."

"Which girl?" I asked, glancing around the bustling hold.

Muce just shrugged, eyes downcast.

"Muce?" I prompted.

She raised her head, but her eyes didn't meet mine.

"Something wrong?" I asked.

Muce shook her head, then said, "Just hungry. I'll ask Sevin."

And she walked away. Her lie was obvious. So was her fear.

I went after her.

"Muce," I said, turning her around and dropping to a squat so that our faces were level. "Did you see someone else on board? Someone who didn't embark with the rest of us on Home? A girl?"

I could feel her shutting her mind down. It was like standing outside an apartment building and watching the lights go off. She shook her head again, short, staccato movements, emphatic and rushed.

"I saw someone," I said, taking a chance. "A girl in a dress like they used to wear on Home years ago."

"You did?" asked Muce. Her eyes widened, and a few of the lights in the building of her mind came back on.

"Yes," I said. "Out there."

I nodded to the side viewer.

"Is that where you saw her?" I pressed.

She shook her head again, though it was different this time. More lights came on.

"Down in the underdeck," she said.

"*On the ship?*" I exclaimed.

Muce looked around to be sure no one had overheard, then nodded.

"I was exploring," she said. "I woke up really early. Before it was light. And there was nothing to do. And I was bored. And—I went downstairs. I'm sorry. I know we are supposed to stay on the main deck—"

"It's fine," I said, conscious that my pulse had started to race. "What did you see?"

"The girl with no name," said Muce.

"You mean you didn't know her name, or she wouldn't tell you?"

"She had a name once," said Muce, "But she forgot it."

She said it with certainty, and the hair on my neck stood on end.

"What did she look like?" I asked.

Muce frowned.

"Ordinary and weird and the same time," she said. "Like this."

She tipped her head onto one side and opened her mouth. It was chillingly familiar.

"Was she wearing shoes?" I asked.

Muce thought for a moment, then shook her head.

"Barefoot, even though it was cold. And when she talked, it was like the words just appeared in my head."

I felt icy, as if snow water were running down my back.

"What did she say?"

"She had candy. Said I could have some. That she could get more."

"And?"

"I didn't take it."

"Why not?"

Muce scowled, upset by the memory but unable to express it. She shrugged a little too large, and her eyes welled.

"I don't know," she said, the effort of speaking making the tears brim and course down her cheeks. "I just didn't like it."

"It's okay," I said, putting my arms around her and drawing her into my chest. "It's fine. But let me know if you see her again, yeah?"

Muce nodded into my shoulder, but said nothing.

"Everything okay?"

It was Sevin.

"Fine," I said, standing up. "A little homesick is all."

Sevin gave Muce a sympathetic look. I hadn't bothered to hide my lie, and I could feel Muce's unease and confusion, but Sevin couldn't. I was sure of it.

He turned to me, all business.

"Think you can lead a group of us to the other ship?" he asked. "I hate to make you go out there again . . ."

"It's fine," I said. "Yes. Who is coming?"

"I thought maybe Trest and Dren. Teada?"

"You're picking them?"

"As opposed to?"

"Asking who wants to come and thinking it through as a group," I said.

He pursed his lips and took a breath.

"Why do you have to make everything difficult?" he snapped.

"Not trying to make everything difficult, Sevin," I said, reasonably. "Just reminding you that you aren't actually in charge."

"You want to give the orders?"

"What orders?" I shot back. "There are no orders. This is not a military maneuver. We're not cadets. Call the council you invented, and let's talk, as a group, together."

He took another deep breath and unconsciously smoothed the front of his uniform jacket.

"Fine," he said, contemptuously. "We'll talk."

As he stalked away, I marveled at the extent of his anger and how pointedly it was directed at me. Then I made my way to the back of the ship and inspected the panel fastened across the hole in the roof. The ropes that held it in place were different.

"Who has been messing with these ties?" I asked Dren, who was sitting close by.

"The panel came loose while you were gone," he said, his face neutral. "We had to start over. I guess Muce isn't as good with knots as she thinks."

I stared at him, but as I probed, reaching for his mind with mine, he tipped his head onto one shoulder and gave me an odd, empty stare.

I took a step backwards. Only then did his usual self-satisfied smile slink back into position. He drew part of a protein bar from his pocket and raised it halfway to his mouth.

"Sevin's put us on half-rations," he said. "Guess we'd better get rescued soon, huh? I'd suggest you share with Bryce, but I think he's giving his to Yasmine."

He considered the protein bar as if he had never seen one before.

"How do you know Bryce?" I asked.

Dren's face clouded.

"Same as I know you," he said.

"You're lying."

"Yeah?" he said, then took a bite of the protein bar. It was a curious motion, quick and savage, and I glimpsed something strange and ravenous inside him.

I saw his lips, the dark hollow of his mouth, the edge of his teeth, and then, unbidden, unwanted, came the taste of juice in my mouth, the fruit bursting as I chewed . . .

Dren looked up quickly, his eyes fixed and hard on mine.

"You know where there's food!" he exclaimed.

I muttered that I didn't know what he was talking about, my face hot, my eyes flashing around for an escape. Bryce was staring at me from across the hold. He looked anxious. Had he heard?

"Fruit!" said Dren, his tone both accusatory and triumphant, deliberately loud. "You found fruit, and you ate it!"

There were other eyes on me now. All around the ship, the sounds of activity were slowly stilling. I turned and caught Teada's gaze. It was questioning. Hurt. My guilt burned in my skin, glowing like a beacon. Denial would only make it worse. I hung my head.

"Sola?" said Trest. "He's got it wrong, yeah? Because if you'd found food, you would have shared it with the rest of us, wouldn't you? I mean, why wouldn't you? Right?"

It wasn't supposed to be damning. He wanted me to explain that there had been a misunderstanding, that Dren didn't know what he was talking about, but I couldn't.

There was total silence for a moment. Then, as I stood there with my head down, humiliated and ashamed, a voice spoke up.

"We found it in the cavern."

Bryce. I couldn't look at him, not yet, but I almost cried out with gratitude. Not that his confession helped the situation.

"You did what?"

That was Sevin. He was staring at us with astonishment and fury.

"You found fruit in the cavern, you ate it, and you kept it secret?"

He sounded incredulous as well as angry, and when he looked at me I felt something else burning at the heart of his indignation: disappointment. Betrayal. Knowing he was right, I lowered my eyes again.

"We were embarrassed," I admitted in a small voice.

"We felt . . . uncivilized."

That was Yasmine. She had taken Bryce's hand. I was standing on the other side of the ship and felt lost and alone, cut off from them by a great abyss.

"I see," said Sevin, though it was the kind of "I see" that the corrections officer says after you explain why you were out after curfew. The sort of "I see" he says before pronouncing sentence.

"I suppose I should have expected this kind of behavior from people who . . ." his voice tailed off, but he continued to stare us down.

"Is there more?"

It was Trest who asked.

"More fruit, I mean. I can't say I'm too keen on the idea personally," he went on with a nervous smile, "but if it's between eating the stuff we find on plants or starving to death . . ."

He shrugged. Carlann gaped as if he had just admitted to some unspeakable crime, as if she had never seen his true self before. But Teada gave him an appraising look and nodded slowly.

"Well?" snapped Sevin. "Is there more?"

"Yes," I said, straightening up for the first time since the ordeal had begun. "We only had one each. There's a lot more, and I'll bet we could find more bushes in other caverns." I hesitated and said something they wouldn't believe but that I knew in my heart was true. "We would have told you before we ran out of food. We wouldn't have kept it secret. We figured you'd just see it when we took you to the cave. But then we never got there and . . . I don't know. But we would have told you."

Carlann gave me a look of pure contempt, despite the fact that she apparently considered the idea of eating the fruit disgusting, but some of the chill fury in the room had thawed a little.

"Okay," said Sevin. "Okay. I'll lead a team to the *Hynderon*. Carlann, you're with me. Trest, and anyone else who thinks they could help hack the controls for the flight deck doors, likewise. You three," he said, nodding to Bryce, Yasmine, and me, "will return to the cavern and bring back whatever you can carry that we might be able to eat."

"It's not safe out there—" Yasmine began.

"No," said Sevin, with finality. "It's not. So don't take longer than you have to."

A PLANET OF BLOOD AND ICE

He turned away, and as if he had broken a spell, the group immediately began to disperse, muttering. Only Dren lingered to give me his considering smirk before wandering off to his storage locker.

My outrage was muffled by a lingering sense of shame, and I took a step toward Sevin, intending to offer him a private apology. He turned when he saw me coming, and I was shocked to see him smiling mirthlessly, though he quickly wiped his face blank. Moments before he had been outraged and anxious, but now I sensed something like relief. Whatever the problem had been, our confrontation had somehow solved it. His anger at our secrecy had been real, but somehow I felt sure that we had also played right into his hands.

"Er, guys," called Trest from the rear of the ship. He looked abashed. "I really hate to say it, but I think the toilet is backed up. It's kind of . . . full."

●

SEVIN AND TREST HAD GATHERED TOOLS FROM THE MAINtenance locker below decks and were trying to get access to the toilet's waste tank, which, they said, would have to be drained. This announcement caused a kind of horrified stillness onboard as the sheer stinking awfulness of our situation was once more made apparent. People nodded silently when Sevin announced the repair plan, and then looked away, pretending it wasn't happening.

While Bryce, Yasmine, and I got together our things in preparation for braving the hike to the cavern, I pondered what had so pleased Sevin. There was only one possibility: He was glad that I wasn't going back to the *Hynderon* with him. Our revelations about the fruit had given him the excuse he had been hoping for, and now he would explore the other ship without me standing over him.

Why? What did he think I might see? What secrets did he plan to act on while we were harvesting in the cavern?

I brooded unproductively on these questions as we walked back toward the singing pillars by the entrance to the cavern. I had taken Bryce's cane and, with Muce's slightly grudging assistance, had lashed the knife to one end, fashioning a crude spear in case we ran into the creature that had taken Herse. I doubted it would make much difference, but I had to feel like I'd done something to protect us.

Poor Herse. There had been no new snow, so the place where he had been attacked was all too clear, the ice splashed with russet and crimson. There wasn't much, but we had been alert for it. My pity was touched with anger and sadness. We would never be able to take his body back to his family when the rescue ship arrived. It seemed particularly unfair. For all its beauty, Valkrys really was the cruel, inhuman planet we had been taught about on Home, and I had been stupid to think otherwise, even for a moment.

"You think we should explore the cavern more?" asked Bryce. "We didn't see much of it last time."

I shook my head.

"Let's just get what we came for and go," I said.

We did not speak again for fifteen minutes, by which time we had found the winding blue passage that led us down into the great basin in the rock. We had seen no sign of any living thing.

The descent was as treacherous as it had been the last time, wet and icy at the same time, the rock rippling with lethal blue ridges. Even so, I felt my heart leap the moment we spotted the bushes with their glorious swollen fruit, and I forced myself to take it slow.

Bryce was still cradling his arm, and Yasmine was sticking close to him, but I could feel their excitement building, too.

"There," she said, pointing to the bush still heavy with globular fruit.

My hunger became savage, selfish. A part of me wanted to just stay here and eat till I was stuffed, ignoring Bryce, ignoring Sevin's pompous orders, just to sit in the relative warmth of the cavern and feed myself the succulent flesh of the plant till I was sick. I didn't, of course, but it took more effort than I would have expected not to.

In fact I ate nothing, deliberately not even smelling the fruit as I picked one after another and stowed them in my backpack. Bryce and Yasmine did the same, working in silence till both bushes were bare. Our bags were bulging. We couldn't have carried any more if there had been any.

"I've never walked so much in my life," said Bryce. "My legs are killing me."

"What's over there?" asked Yasmine.

She was gazing off beyond one of the longer pools, where a bird was flitting across the surface, to where the cavern seemed to almost close.

"Probably just another passage or alcove," said Bryce.

I found myself leaning forward to get a better look but couldn't make out anything.

"It looks sort of regular, you know?" said Yasmine thoughtfully. "Like a doorway."

"The rock is crystalline," said Bryce. "A lot of the formations are straight, angular."

"Yeah," she agreed. "Still."

I took another look and could see what she meant.

"Might not be a bad idea to see if there are more bushes," I admitted. "What we have here will only feed us—all of us, I mean—for a couple of days. Might be good to see if there's more close by."

Bryce frowned doubtfully.

"What happened to 'get what we can and get out'?" he asked.

"We're here," I said. "The worst part of the journey is between the cavern and the ship. If we're planning to come back, I'd like to know for sure it's worth the trip."

He looked ready to argue, but he saw—or sensed—Yasmine's anticipation and capitulated with a shrug.

"You're the one with the spear," he said.

I led the way. On the other side of the pool—which was almost big enough to be a lake—was another bush, but it was small and boasted only a few small fruit.

"Leave those," Yasmine said. "Best let them grow."

I felt the sweat running down my back and unfastened my jacket. The difference in climate down here was amazing. The sky, where it was visible was blue and clear, sending shafts of golden light down into the cave, about which flowers grew and insects buzzed. There had to be more food down here somewhere.

But as we walked, I found my attention was occupied by the strange, hard-edged entrance that Yasmine had indicated. It looked like a gateway. At first I resisted the term, but the closer we got, the more apt it seemed.

Nonsense, of course. The opening must have been an accident of wind and the splitting of rock as it froze and thawed over the centuries. But, then again, it had enough symmetry and grace that it was hard not to imagine some guiding hand at work in its construction. Two tall posts rose up from the surrounding wall of blue, flickering rock, and the space between them was crowned with a distinct arch. The nearer we came, the more perfect it seemed: evenly balanced as if carefully, elegantly carved. It stood perhaps twenty feet high, and its surface was slick, perfect. Elsewhere, these glassy surfaces had always been marred by spines, ridges, and drape-like ripples in the rock. Here there were none, so that the wall on either side of the great arch looked as if it had been polished smooth. It glittered in the fractured sunlight, and I felt a new eagerness in Bryce and Yasmine, this time touched with apprehension.

What had we found?

There was only one way to find out. We did not discuss it. We simply stepped through the arch and came to a faltering halt.

"This isn't possible," Bryce whispered, staring about him as if gripped by a sudden madness.

"It looks like . . ." said Yasmine, but she couldn't say it.

"It looks like a city," I said.

CHAPTER

T O BE ACCURATE, IT LOOKED LIKE IT HAD ONCE BEEN
a city. The arch led us through a kind of gatehouse,
a portal in the rock that made up the perimeter
wall, and then the ground fell away before us, forming a
long, straight road. On each side of the road rose tall, regular structures of the glossy blue stone. Most were roofless,
their tops jagged and uneven, and some were little more
than fragments and rubble, but there was no question that
they had been built by people long ago. Some were so well
preserved that it was impossible to determine whether they
were ancient ruins or the wreckage of some recent disaster.

The great ice cavern lowered as the buildings receded so
that a few hundred yards away the tops of the empty buildings brushed up against the frozen crust of the planet's surface. It was impossible to guess how extensive the town—if

that indeed was what it had been—truly was. How much more was buried beneath the snow and ice, we could not say.

In places the remains of towers rose up, some open, some with ornate spires, one capped by a cracked globe that reached into the frozen canopy and was half buried in a massive drift. One imposing structure was especially impressive, and though the tops of its walls and parts of the roof were fractured and uneven, it was still monumental, tall and stately like those ancient cathedrals that had so occupied my thoughts. Perhaps that was what it had once been; perhaps its translucent stone had once bathed a prayerful congregation in soft, blue light. At its foot was what seemed to be the auditorium of a great theater. Blue stone benches were arranged in horseshoe-shaped rows, rising with the natural slope of the ground. Directly ahead was a broad walkway flanked by the remains of stately buildings with large windows and decorated trim. One had apertures flanked by columns and friezes carved with geometrical patterns. There was a central square with pale stone terraces, through which ran a long open channel of water—with hard, sheer sides like a canal—spanned by elegant bridges with slow, graceful curves. The river eventually extended into a great sideways slant of snow and ice where the planet's frozen surface had engulfed everything that had been built here.

Because none of this was natural. It had been built by the people who had lived here. Whatever Valkrys was now, it had once been home to an industrious and sophisticated people. They were gone now, and the city they had built was uncannily silent, but the town they had left behind echoed with their genius, their artistry.

I stared, realizing with a start that I sensed nothing from Bryce and Yasmine. It was as if our minds had been momentarily wiped clean by the staggering discovery, and—perhaps for the first time since crash-landing on this rock, I was alone in my head. I felt awe, certainly, and surprise at the beauty of the place. But there was more to it than that. The city—the fact of it—revealed that all I had been taught about Valkrys was wrong. With that revelation, the universe—my universe—had shifted. It was unavoidable evidence that I had been given bad information, had been fed it by my teachers and by the technology I had always trusted implicitly and completely. Trest had been right. What we thought we knew, what we were so sure of that we never questioned it for a second, had proved unreliable.

We had been lied to. All our lives.

Bryce and Yasmine felt it, too. I didn't sense it from them because since we had entered the city I had felt nothing from them, but I saw it in their faces, their mute awe, their troubled eyes. The cosmos and our place in it had just been kicked unexpectedly out of kilter, changing everything.

We wandered through the ruined city in silence. Even Bryce and Yasmine drifted apart, as if each of us had to process the enormity of the place and what it meant, alone. Their minds continued to be closed to me, and the more I moved around, the more I became convinced of something that was really no more than a guess the walls of the buildings were like screens, though how the rock itself could shut out the others' thoughts, I had no idea.

I found a great chamber that was half flooded with clear water. Steps descended into the pool, and around it were cubicles and cubbyholes, as well as larger chambers with domed roofs and vents in the walls and floors. I remembered history fliks about how people had once bathed together for sport and recreation, and wondered if this was such a place. In another area I came across what seemed to have been a formal garden, its earth charred and marked with the blackened stumps of long-dead trees, the whole crisscrossed by stone paths with benches and ornamental follies. I looked up, trying to decide if the city had once been open to the sky or if it had always been covered by the great frozen roof of the cave, but I couldn't be sure. Maybe the entire area had sunk into the earth in some massive seismic event.

It was a place of mystery. There were structures whose function I could not guess: waist-high counters with well-like holes in them, mosaic floors depicting fanciful beasts, alcoves carved into undulating shells. I found stone pinnacles that appeared merely decorative but may also have served a purpose I could not imagine.

I approached one palatial structure—its walls marked with little ice-blue turrets—and saw a circular platform surrounded by columns, some fractured and fallen but others still standing and bearing a circular frieze on elaborately carved capitals. It felt like a temple, a place of worship, and

I would have been respectfully quiet if one thing hadn't stopped my feet, my heart, my very breath.

Motionless, I stared in stunned disbelief.

In the center of the circular platform stood a great three-sided column that towered above, and at its feet, some ten yards away and just large enough to stand on, was a round platform. Inlaid into the blue stone was a red triangle.

It was exactly the same as the one tattooed on the back of my head.

●

FOR A LONG MOMENT I JUST LOOKED AT IT, THEN I BROKE the silence, calling to the others. Somewhere a startled bird trilled. Then Bryce answered. Then Yasmine. They found their way to me and stared at the triangle in the stone for a long minute, speechless. Yasmine's right hand strayed to the back of her head, and she glanced, bewildered, at Bryce. She had it, too. He had checked her, found it, told her.

None of those things surprised me, but to come across the mark here, of all places . . .

"A coincidence?" said Bryce. "A triangle is a pretty common symbol."

"A red triangle?" said Yasmine. "In a city where every-thing is blue, we find a perfectly carved *red* triangle that matches the ones tattooed on our heads?"

Bryce said nothing.

"Is it just me," I asked, glancing around the structure, "or does this look like a temple or a church?"

Yasmine gazed up through the columns.

"A cathedral," she said. "Yes."

"And that has what to do with us?" asked Bryce.

"I really couldn't say," I said. "But it feels . . . I don't know. Relevant."

"It *feels* relevant?" Bryce echoed. "What does that even mean?"

"I don't know," I admitted. "It's like we've been here before. Long ago. Like I almost remember it."

"Or it remembers us," said Yasmine.

I looked at her, beautiful under the strange colonnade, the great triangle at her feet. I nodded vaguely, till I saw the way Bryce was frowning.

"Sounds a bit mystical to me," he said. "We should be getting back."

"There's another one here," said Yasmine.

I looked to where she was pointing, another ten yards or so to the left: another circular platform a couple of feet across, marked with a red triangle. I imagined looking down from above—the watchful angel again—and saw the way the chamber arranged itself around the massive triangular column in the center. I pointed to the right.

"Bryce," I said. "Check over there."

I heard him grunt in mild surprise.

"There's another," he said.

Of course there was. Three platforms, each the vertex of a triangle etched into the base of the temple—or whatever it was—and in the center a triangular pillar . . .

"Step onto it," I said, absently. "Yasmine, too."

"What?" asked Bryce. "Why?"

"Just . . ." I couldn't explain the hunch. "Just do it."

He did, frowning, and Yasmine did too, stepping onto her triangle like a wandering statue returning to its base. I did the same.

It happened as soon as I stood up, a shrill but not unpleasant whistling in my ears, like the song of the wind-blown stone columns in the snow, and then I felt the sudden, strange awareness of Bryce and Yasmine as if we were huddled together sharing a single thought.

No, not a thought. A memory.

Because in that second, I saw the cathedral as it had once been: not fractured and lifeless, but whole and thronging with energy. Above us, the ceiling rose in great vaulted arches of cobalt-blue crystal, and the sun shafted down as if through deep, clear water. The place felt glorious, holy.

And then the great column descended, sliding down into the floor until—with a distinct, mechanical thunk—its top was flush with the ground and we were back in the ancient ruin and ourselves again.

Bryce gasped curses and questions as Yasmine stared happily around her, enraptured. I said nothing, waiting for my breathing and heart rate to return to normal.

Apart from the central column that had lowered into the earth, there was no sign that anything else had occurred, and when we stepped off and back on our little triangle-marked platforms, nothing further happened. Once the strangeness of the event had passed, Bryce suggested that it had probably just been weight activated, that stepping on the stones had triggered some purposeless forgotten mechanism.

I wasn't so sure. Thought I could not guess what the machine—if it was a machine—had done or why, it felt curiously like it had been waiting for us, our tattoos, our deviance . . .

I didn't say so, though I caught the look in Yasmine's eyes and wondered if she felt it too. Bryce seemed reluctant to talk about it, so we let it alone. Clutching our heavy bags of fruit we left the city the way we had come and crossed the cavern floor without speaking. We would keep no secrets this time. We had to tell the others, even if we didn't know what we had found.

We passed the stripped bushes and began the slow, difficult climb up to the twisting tunnel that would lead us to the planet's surface. As we walked, I found myself rehearsing how we would present the news to Sevin and the rest.

A lost civilization beneath the icy surface of Valkrys.

It was staggering, and as we climbed back through the frozen cavern and away from the city, I began once more to sense Bryce and Yasmine at my back, their awe, excitement, and confusion blending with mine so that it was hard to tell which was which. I focused on the frost-split rocks in front of me, avoiding the glassy ridges of razor-edged stone, feeling my heart labor as we left the warm, fragrant air below and trudged up towards the snowbound surface. Halfway up the treacherous path that wound its way out of the great basin, I paused to look back at the others and, a long way past them, at the tiny, almost invisible gateway that had so altered my sense of everything.

Yasmine sensed my thought and smiled up at me. As she did so, she took an awkward step and slipped. Her ankle twisted as she tried to regain her balance. Her foot came down on ice, and then she was falling.

She slipped sideways off the icy path and along the blue ridge beside it. She screamed as she careened down, forty, fifty yards or more, and I was horrified to see a fine spray of blood shoot up in her wake.

No.

I felt paralyzed, frozen, the present racing away from me along with Yasmine's careening body. It had happened so fast. I reached out for her, but she was just gone . . .

Bryce cried out, and that woke me, if only partially. Now I moved without thinking, running down the path as quickly as I dared. The perilous ledge in places was almost a chute, the ice wet and slippery underfoot. I could see exactly where she had slipped, every detail registering with impossible clarity as I blundered after her.

After the dreadful speed of her descent, Yasmine now rested quite still against a rock at the bottom, unmoving. A long, ugly stripe of crimson pointed right to where she lay, tracing exactly which way she had fallen. It grew unnervingly thicker, more vibrant closer to her body.

Bryce, ungainly with his strapped arm, was even slower than me, so I reached her first. There was blood all the way down. At one particularly cruel ridge of blue, a knife edge slashing diagonally across the angle of her descent, the red droplets became heavy, and at the bottom, the rock and ice were streaming red.

She had come down on her back. Her shades were gone, and her eyes were wide with shock and pain.

"It hurts," she gasped, tears streaming down her cheeks.

I dropped into a crouch beside her.

"It's going to be okay," I said, keeping my eyes on her face, not on the spreading crimson pool beneath her.

I didn't want to look.

"We'll need to roll you over," I said.

Yasmine said nothing. She was starting to sweat, beads of it breaking out on her forehead and running with her tears. Bryce shuffled into position.

"On three," I said, bracing myself.

I counted, and we flipped her over as gently as we could. She cried out as she moved, a thin wail of agony and despair. I gritted my teeth and looked.

Her stylish jacket was cut to ribbons and soaked in blood. Only the collar was still intact. I unbound the knife from my makeshift spear and used it to slit the collar rather than trying to get her arms out of the sleeves. I peeled apart her ravaged shirt and the sheer camisole she was wearing underneath.

I heard Bryce's intake of breath.

Her shoulders were undamaged, pale and perfect, and most of her left side looked fine, apart from a few minor cuts. But just to the right of her spine, a long, clean-edged wound opened from below her shoulder blade down to the small of her back, as if someone had taken a scalpel, pushed it deep into her flesh, and then drawn it up in a long, savage sweep. It was bleeding heavily.

I had no idea what to do.

There was too much blood to see how deep the gash went or what kind of damage had been done inside, but it was also clear that if we didn't staunch the flow, she would die. Quickly.

"Did you bring that sewing kit?" Bryce managed.

I shook my head. "Go back for it," I said.

"Me?" he sputtered. "What are you going to do?"

I tore my eyes from the wound and looked at him. He was scared.

"I'll stay with her," I said. "I'll try to stop the bleeding."

He nodded, his face pale, and I think he was relieved that someone was taking control of the situation, even if he didn't really believe I knew what I was doing.

"Don't go, Bryce," said Yasmine. "Don't leave me."

"I won't be long," said Bryce. "Sola will stay with you."

"Yes?" said Yasmine, twisting her head so she could see me. "You'll stay?"

"Of course," I said. Then, to Bryce, "Be quick."

He left without a word, but his ascent was painfully slow. I used my hands to squeeze the slit up Yasmine's back closed as best I could, but the wound was too long. Too deep. It took an age for the sound of Bryce's footsteps and labored breathing to fade to nothing.

I said nothing. The silence was terrible, but I did not know how to break it. At last, she spoke.

"He's nice," said Yasmine in a slow, dreamy voice that frightened me. "Bryce. Bryce is nice." She giggled at the rhyme, but the movement pained her, and she stopped, wincing. "You're nice, too. But you're scared," she added, thoughtfully. "I can tell. Why can I tell? Since we woke up on the ship, I can feel things. Other people's minds. I thought I was imagining it, but I'm sure I'm not. It's not all the time. Not clearly. But sometimes I get a feeling, like it's my thought, but it's not. It's someone else. I just feel it in my head. Anger. Sadness. Excitement. Why can I feel it?"

"I don't know," I said, glad of something to talk about that wasn't the cruel slit up her back. "I feel it, too. I think the others do as well, but I'm not sure."

"So you can tell I'm afraid."

"I don't need any special gift to guess that," I said, smiling. My hands were slick with blood. Again. I tried to stretch the skin back into place, but it wasn't working. As soon as I let go of one spot to close it somewhere else, the wound reopened. It was still bleeding heavily. I tried not to think about her chances in case she sensed my thoughts.

"So, a roamer, huh?" Yasmine whispered, clearly trying to take her mind off her pain. Her breathing was labored, as if it hurt to inhale.

"Yep," I said, casual as I could. "I do love a little stroll. Always fun. As you can tell."

She laughed at that, tiny ripples of mirth shaking her shoulders till the pain forced her to stop.

"That's not the only irony," she murmured. "Guess what I was going to reeducation for?"

"Shoot," I said, managing a grin, as if this were chat room gossip between girlfriends.

"I cut myself," she said, with another tiny tremor of mirth, bleaker this time. "Not usually up my back, but still."

"That's funny," I said, not laughing or feeling anywhere close to doing so. "Why do you do it?" I asked, not because I wanted to know so much as to take her mind off her injuries.

She sighed.

"Why does anybody do anything?" she said.

I wanted to press her further, but knew that I shouldn't. The self-deprecating irony still showed in her eyes, but the touch of sadness beneath the pain reminded me of how little I knew her. She was the beautiful girl and nothing much more—not to me and, I suspect, not to anyone else either. I admitted to myself that what she had meant to me, her worth, was mostly about how that face of hers, that silvery hair, and how that lithe, slender body affected Bryce. Without really meaning to, I reached for her cheek and touched it softly.

It was a curious thing. You would think that getting flashes of insight into other people's minds would make you feel closer to them, but my experience on Valkrys had been the opposite. Everyone was so complex and full of contradictions that the more I glimpsed, the less I felt I knew.

"Hold still," I said.

I tried to pull the skin together at a point midway up her spine where the bleeding was worst, but it didn't make any difference. Another inch to the left, and the cut would have exposed bone. It was amazing she was still conscious.

Then I had an idea. A terrible, necessary idea.

I took my hands from her back and untied the laces of my boots. My fingers fumbled as I tried to work fast, and each second it took me to get the laces out, Yasmine seemed to lose more blood than she could spare. Next I drew the knife and tested its tip against my palm. Not as sharp as I would have liked, but it would have to do. I had, after all, done something similar only a few days before.

"Don't move," I said. "This is going to hurt."

It was no different from what I had done to Carlann's scalp with the needle and thread, I told myself. Just bigger. I worked quickly, methodically, placing the knifepoint just to the side of the gash. Pushing the tip quickly through the skin, then taking it out and repeating the action on the other side of the wound. Threading the shoelace through the ragged holes and tying it off, then moving down a couple of inches and doing it all again.

At first Yasmine cried out with each puncture, but her responses diminished as I worked, so that after a few minutes she barely even winced as the knife went in. Whether that was her getting used to the pain or losing sensation, I didn't know, but my sense of her agony was fading, which, I was sure, was not good. I looked at what I had done.

If any major veins or arteries had been severed, nothing would save her. Even if they hadn't been, mine was butcher's work, not surgery. I could only hope it would slow the blood flow and maybe buy her an hour or more . . .

By the time I was done, I was sweating and Yasmine had grown chill and silent. I covered her with the blanket she had been wearing as a shawl and tried to keep her conscious with casual talk. I didn't know how easily she could sense my thoughts, but I hoped that conversation would keep the desperate nature of her condition out of my head. I used her shredded shirt to mop up the blood and put pressure on the seams of my savage joinery, but it looked even worse now than before I had "stitched" her up, like some nightmare corset made of flesh. It was too horrible to look at.

Bryce seemed to have been gone hours. She took that moment to speak, faintly, dreamily.

"Bryce likes you, too," she said. "He's confused."

I nodded, smiling a tight, sad smile.

"I think he likes you more," I said.

For a long moment, she said nothing. I thought she was asleep, then she murmured, "I'm sorry, Sola."

I wasn't sure whether she was talking about Bryce or her fall. It didn't matter either way.

"Don't be," I said. "It's just, you know . . . life."

She said no more.

I checked the back of Yasmine's head for other injuries I might have missed, and as I pushed at her beautiful hair, clearing the scalp, I saw what I knew I would.

A triangle. Tattooed in red ink. Blurred and faded, but unmistakable on the back of her head. The same triangle that adorned the temple of an ancient civilization on an alien world, a world where I had arrived by mistake long after their city had crumbled to shards of ice-blue rock . . .

I looked up, and my heart jumped with a terror that wiped all thought of the tattoo from my mind.

Standing only twenty yards from me, utterly silent and pale as snow, was a great cat.

CHAPTER  20

I T LOOKED LIKE THE SAME BEAST THAT KILLED HERSE, though I had then seen little more than a blurry shadow leaping out of the blizzard. This was quite still, its yellow eyes locked on me. It was huge, with teeth that curved outside its lips like swords. It had been stalking towards us across the cavern floor, but now that we were aware of it, it had become impossibly still, a statue gazing fixedly and unblinkingly at us.

Yasmine began to whimper, but her tears were spent, and she could only grimace in fear and misery.

I rose unsteadily, holding out the knife in front of me like a talisman. The creature seemed to consider for a moment, then took a step closer, its muscles rippling beneath its fur like waves. I shouted, a wordless cry of defiance coupled with a flourish of the knife.

It was an empty gesture. The sabertooth was immensely powerful. I would have known that even if I hadn't witnessed how easily it had dispatched Herse. If it attacked, I couldn't possibly fight it off.

The beast seemed to know as much, and it took another step towards us. It was close enough to spring now and seemed to gather itself, its great haunches tightening and flexing as it gauged its moment.

And then there was another cry, this time from up the cliff path. Bryce, Sevin, and someone else, someone small, roared at the sabertooth as they made their clumsy, skittering way down.

The creature's yellow eyes flicked to them, then back to me, as if calculating the odds, and then there was a colossal bang, a sharp, flat sound that reverberated around the chamber. The cat winced, shrinking for a moment, then turned and bounded away, noiseless as falling snow.

I watched it go, then turned to where Bryce and Sevin were picking their way down the cliff path. The third person was Muce. The source of the bang was visible in Sevin's right hand.

"You have a gun?" I sputtered, as soon as he was in earshot.

"Fortunately for you, yes," he returned, his face hard.

"Where did you get it?" I pressed.

"From the emergency stores."

"There was a gun in the emergency stores?" I repeated in disbelief.

"Yes," he said, staring me down, daring me to contradict him.

"Why didn't you say so?"

"Let me see her injuries."

Still scowling, I squatted beside Yasmine and gingerly lifted the blanket. Sevin's brash confidence left him instantly, but he turned his shock into an attack.

"I knew this was a bad idea," he said. "What the hell did you do to her?"

"I was trying to stop the bleeding," I began, but abandoned the protest. He didn't just mean my attempt at surgery, and I was too weary to argue.

"It wasn't her fault," said Bryce. "How is she?"

I shook my head but said nothing. He stooped to her.

"Hey Yasmine," he said. "You still with us?"

She smiled faintly.

"Just," she mouthed, so softly I barely caught it.

"Muce," I said, turning away. It was painful to look at Yasmine, pale and blood-streaked, scarred by my awful sutures. "You have that sewing kit?"

Muce looked at my work.

"I'll do it," she said.

"Good," I said, not bothering to conceal my relief. "And when you've sewn her up properly, we need to get those shoelaces out. She'll get infected. You have alcohol?"

Bryce held up a plastic bottle and a cotton swab.

"Clean the wounds as best you can," I said. "Yasmine, honey? I'm sorry, but this is going to sting."

"Okay," said Yasmine, dreamily, still smiling.

I didn't like it.

"We need to get her back to the ship," said Sevin, watching Muce work. The girl had a steady hand and a level of composure I wouldn't have believed possible.

"No way," I said, taking a couple of pointed steps away and leading us out of earshot of the others. "Moving her will just reopen the wound."

"She can't stay down here."

"Why not?"

"Apart from the tiger or whatever that sabertoothed monster was, you mean?" Sevin spat back.

"We'll just have to keep watch on her," I said, not liking the idea.

"Overnight?" Sevin returned, aghast.

"Probably a couple of nights, minimum," I said. "There's no need to stay in the ship. It's not as cold down here. There's water. Food."

He gave me a look at that, and I nodded at the over-flowing bags of fruit.

"You're not serious," said Sevin. "The ship is our base. It's where our supplies are, our stasis pods, and it's what any recovery team from Home will be looking for. And it's a lot less likely that that giant cat will come hunting inside a steel ship."

"We don't all need to be there," I said, half-conceding his point. "It's cramped, and it's getting uncomfortable and tense."

"Tense?" he said, giving me a thoughtful look.

"Just . . . you know. People in close quarters. They're getting on each other's nerves."

He gave me another look, doubtful, probing, and I glanced away. He let it go.

"There's no toilet down here. No shower," he said.

"We can designate a sanitary area," I answered. "Dig a latrine. Somehow. Can't be much worse than the toilet on the *Phetteron*." Sevin pulled a sour face. I took a breath. "Look. I know it's not ideal, but if we try to carry Yasmine back to the ship now, she'll bleed to death."

"She might do that anyway," Sevin replied.

"You think I don't know that? You think I don't feel responsible? I led her down here. I know that. Now I'm going to do what I can to make her safe, and that means staying with her down here till her wounds have healed some."

"And this has nothing to do with you not wanting to spend another night on the ship?" he asked.

I stared at him, but kept my face blank.

"What do you mean?" I asked.

"No one wants to go into the underdeck. Some of the kids have been saying . . ." he began, then thought better of it. "Nothing. Forget it."

I waited, but he said no more. As he turned to rejoin the others, I stopped him with a touch to his arm that made him flinch.

"There's something else," I said.

He waited, expectantly, and I pointed across the great cavern.

"Over there is a gateway," I said.

His forehead creased, but he said nothing.

"A gateway," I continued, "that leads to the ruins of an ancient city."

I waited, watching him blink, feeling his mind race. He was caught off guard, alarmed even, but then something else registered: doubt.

"A city," he said, his voice carefully neutral. "Are you sure?"

"No contrary position is viable," I said dryly, eyes and mind burning into his.

He gazed at me, and I sensed he felt suddenly lost, like a boat on a wild sea tossed by monstrous waves, poised to sink without trace at any moment. He stilled the feeling with an effort that smacked more of desperation than certainty.

"That's ridiculous," he said. "No one has ever lived on Valkrys. You must be mistaken."

And without waiting for me to react, he turned and walked back to Yasmine, Bryce, and Muce, saying, "We're going to need to make a fire."

●

THERE WAS NOTHING I COULD DO FOR YASMINE THAT THE others couldn't do as well or better, so when Sevin said they would need more supplies from the ship if she was to stay in the cavern overnight, I volunteered. Sevin gave me a curt nod and did not argue the point. Bryce looked up from where he was lying beside Yasmine, and in his eyes was a kind of apology I pretended not to understand.

It wasn't his fault.

I had fastened the knife to the cane again and carried it beside me, point upwards. Sevin had a gun, so I wasn't concerned about leaving the others unprotected. I asked him about it again before I left, but he stuck to his story about finding it in the emergency stores.

"Why didn't you say you had it?" I asked once more.

"Didn't know who I could trust," he said, as if it didn't much matter.

"Would there have been a gun on the *Hynderon*, too?"

"Older ship," he said. "Who knows what standard procedures were twelve years ago. But I wouldn't be surprised if there was. Why?"

"Might be worth trying to find it," I said.

I didn't mention the bullet hole in the boy I had seen in the stasis pod. Sevin probably already knew about that.

So I walked, lugging two bags of fruit, climbing my slow, cautious way out of the basin and through the winding passageway to the surface, watching and listening for the cat that might be stalking me.

I liked to work my body a little, but Bryce was right: I'd never walked so much in my life since landing on Valkrys, and I could feel it in my calves and thighs. It wasn't a bad feeling, exactly, though it could be quite painful. It felt like a part of myself was waking up after years of slumber. My sore muscles kept my mind off all the terrible things that had happened, and there was value in that.

Herse was already dead. Yasmine . . . I just didn't know. My guess was that if we could keep her alive and uninfected for a couple of days, she might recover, but what did I know? What, for that matter, did any of us know? About anything?

All our lives we had been taught not to know things—which was the way of the ancient world—but to be able to find them. That was what the tech grid gave us: infinite knowledge at our fingertips so that we didn't need to keep any of it in our heads. Trest had once said that we had evolved away from bodies without really putting anything in their place, so we didn't actually know anything useful anymore. If he had seen what I had down there, he'd be even more sure. In the old days, people had spent their lives mastering a single subject. Now we mastered navigating the strands of the tech grid so that we could find our way to whatever we needed or wanted from any subject imaginable.

But what if the grid—as Trest had implied—was wrong? What if its data was flawed or compromised? Other kinds of information were long gone, consigned to the trash heap of irrelevance by progress. No one had ever lived on Valkrys. Sevin had said so, said it with the same certainty I would have before seeing those towers and temples. He was wrong. The tech grid was wrong. And if it was wrong about Valkrys, what else was it wrong about? Did I have to roam the universe, testing everything I had ever read with the senses of my own body to be sure?

I thought of the angel in the picture, caring, gliding overhead, and again felt the need for someone like that looking out for me. That thought transformed almost immediately into a burning desire to be the angel herself, my great feathered wings unfurling at my back as I left the world and its problems behind; beneath me, a great, soaring ecstasy in the chill, empty air, no thoughts but mine in my head, and those only of the uncaring joy of flight . . .

I thought as I walked, occasionally breaking into a stumbling trot through the snow, keen to get out of the open, whatever might be waiting for me on the ship.

As a result, I made good time getting back to the *Phetteron*, but though it was only midafternoon, the ship was quiet, subdued. The smell wasn't as bad as it had been. Evidently they had made some headway on the toilet tank, though I preferred not to think about that, and when I saw Trest obsessively washing his hands, I just nodded. For once, he didn't seem keen to chat.

Along with several of the others, Teada had already retired to the solitude of her stasis pod and closed the inner blinds, so I had to knock on the cover to get her attention.

She lowered the screen and gave me a quizzical, irritated look before opening the cover itself.

"What?" she said.

"Yasmine is hurt," I said. "She's going to have to stay overnight in the cavern."

Teada sat up, rubbing her eyes.

"That's terrible," she said. "What do you need?"

"You," I said. "They're going to need a fire, but I doubt they'd know how to make one even if they had a lighter."

"So you thought you'd consult the resident pyromaniac?" she said, very slightly put out. "Yeah, okay. Let me get my stuff."

"You brought a lighter on a trip to the reeducation facility where you were being punished for lighting fires?" I asked, amused and impressed.

"You ever sat through those lectures?" Teada replied, rolling her eyes. "Two of those, three tops, and I knew I'd have to burn something."

I grinned, and she matched it, abashed.

"I'm going to the storage locker below deck," I said.

"What?" she gasped, her eyes flicking toward the staircase. "Why?"

"Have to get some protein bars and another couple of blankets," I said, matter-of-factly.

"You want me to come with you?"

God, yes!

I hesitated, feeling her dread.

"No," I said, with all the casualness I could manage. "I'll be fine. Loads of battery in my flashlight, see?" I snapped it on and dazzled her till she winced away, smiling. "I'll be back in a few minutes. In the meantime," I said, producing one of the pieces of fruit, "eat this. Don't pull a face. Just try it."

"I don't think I could—"

"No one is looking. Take it into your stasis pod and pull the blind down if you like. Trust me."

She took it reluctantly, as if it might explode. Leaving her, I moved quickly along the gantry and down the rattling stairs into the belly of the ship, as if nothing could be easier or more natural.

It was an act.

I hated the underdeck with the kind of unreasoning loathing that could only come from fear. At the foot of the steps, I paused, directed the flashlight, and took my first step into the cramped passages that snaked around the ship's mechanical innards. In flight, I guessed this place was humming with the drone of the engines, the clank and groan of gears, the creak and whine of torque on its moving parts. Now it felt dead. It was utterly silent, except when something echoed down from above. And that was okay. So long as there were no sounds from this level or—worse—from below, the place they called the Well, I'd be fine.

It smelled different down here. It reminded me of what the ship had first felt like before we landed and contaminated the ship's aroma of machine oil and bare metal with our inadequately cleansed bodies. But there was nothing comforting in that thought. The underdeck felt like the *Hynderon*: an abandoned vessel, lifeless and left to slowly fall apart. A place of death and darkness.

I inched my way around corner after corner, counting off the bays and racks, feeling my pulse increase as a cold sweat broke out on my face and arms. It was amazing how far you could walk down here given the size of the ship, as if the thing had been designed to provide the most inefficient route no matter where you were trying to go. Or, worse, like the ship had folded itself into knots just to keep you here, creating blind alleys and false turns so that you might never find your way out of the maze.

I swallowed, took a deep, deliberate breath. I kept my eyes on the flashlight beam, edging forward till I found what I was looking for.

It was a metal locker as tall as I was, its door dented and edged with rust.

A minute, maybe less, I thought, *then I can leave.*

I wrenched the door open, listening to the silence, trying not to think of the darkness just outside the reach of my flashlight. Inside were a stack of folded thermal blankets, smooth to the touch; a spool of strong nylon cord; and three sealed packs of protein bars, six in each. I took the cord and the blankets quickly, and one of the food packs, considering with a start just how little there was left, and closed the locker door.

Behind the door, hidden from view till I snapped it shut, was the girl.

CHAPTER

SHE WAS WEARING A THIN WHITE DRESS THAT HUNG shapelessly about her, but which I knew would billow around her knees in a breeze. Her skin was pale and bluish with cold. Once, I suspected, she had worn flat black shoes of shiny syntholeather, but now she was barefoot. Her fingernails were ragged, I assumed from scrabbling at the plastic panel on the *Phetteron*'s roof, but there was no sign of blood. Blond hair hung lank around a face that was unnervingly blank, and her head was cocked onto her left shoulder in a way that—given her stillness—made her look like a doll or a puppet. But it was her eyes that revealed her truly unearthly quality more than anything else. They glowed with an eerie amber light.

As I stared, horror-stricken, her mouth opened.

She did not speak, and her lips did not move, but words appeared in my head as if she were whispering into my ear.

You want candy?

I took a step back. She did not move, nor did the expression on her uncanny, lifeless face alter. Instead the words came again, not from the slack, frozen mouth, but in my mind.

You want candy?

I shook my head, but when I tried to speak, I found that my mouth was dry. The words would not come out, and the hair on the back of my neck and arms was standing on end. The passageway seemed impossibly empty and silent, and I longed for someone—Teada, even Dren—to come blundering down the stairs from the passenger hold . . .

What do you want? said the voice. It was soft, sibilant, fading in and out so that the volume peaked in the middle of the sentence.

"Nothing," I managed to say, the flashlight fixed on her, if unsteadily. "Who are you?"

You want to live, said the voice.

Yes, I thought. *More than anything else. Just let me live.*

But that awful stare, the empty mouth, filled me with dread.

"I asked you who you are," I said. My hands had begun to tremble slightly, but I balled my fists and squeezed till the nails bit into my palms.

I can help you live.

"I can do that by myself," I said, fear making me bluster.

Almost out of food, said the voice as the girl tipped her head onto the other shoulder, mouth still open, golden eyes still fixed and staring. *Friends dead or dying. Great beasts on the hunt. Your companions lying to you. You won't survive without my help.*

I took another step back. It wasn't just the words that were in my head. She was, too. She could sense my fears, my anxieties. Even so, I couldn't stop myself from asking, "And how could you help with that?"

A kind of coexistence that replaces most of your physical needs, said the voice. *A sharing.*

"Sharing?"

Your body.

The words lingered in the silence. Then I took another step away.

"No," I said.

It will be better, said the voice.

"No," I said again.

If you refuse, you will not survive.

Despite my dread of the girl, the remark kindled a little fire in my heart.

"I can look after myself," I said. "I can survive the cold, the hunger, the danger."

The voice fell silent. The girl's head rocked slowly back to the other shoulder, and the mouth closed, but otherwise she did not move at all. Behind her, I noticed, were wet footprints on the metal floor. She stood there for a long moment, and then as the mouth opened again, the words appeared in my head, slow and sure and cold.

You cannot survive . . . us.

And then I ran.

●

WE SEARCHED THE SHIP AS SOON AS I HAD ROUSED THE others, but there were too many passages, too many alcoves. Somehow, she had either hid away again or slipped by us, and in truth we were all too keen to stop looking and get out of the underdeck for good. Dren was openly scornful of the whole thing.

"You imagined it," he said, as we regrouped on the main deck. "Or made it up to get attention. You think we're babies? Trying to scare us with your ghost stories. It's insulting."

"I didn't say it was a ghost," I shot back. "Ghosts don't leave footprints. She was real."

"The ship's not that big, Sola," Dren remarked. "If she's real, where is she?"

He enjoyed making me look stupid, but there was something else that he was hiding.

"Maybe we should take another look," suggested Trest. He didn't want to. No one wanted to go back down there. He was just being supportive.

I shook my head.

"We looked everywhere," I said.

"Not in the Well," said Trest.

That was true. The Well was the third level where the engine room and antigrav unit were. I had gotten close to it, felt its total darkness like a pit, but the prospect of climbing down the ladder had been too much for me, for all of us.

I shook my head wearily, not even bothering to reason my way out of it. I didn't want to go down there.

"Maybe she came up and got out," I said, rubbing my temples.

"She couldn't have," said Trest. "The passages were too narrow, and there were too many of us. She would have had to get past one of us."

"I guess," I said, noncommittal.

"Meaning what?" Dren demanded.

"Nothing," I said.

"No," said Trest. "You do mean something. You think one of us was helping this girl, whoever she is?"

He sounded shocked.

"No," I said, trying to shut down the *yes* that was ringing in my mind. Trest gave me a long look and frowned. "You said she would have had to get past one of us to get up here, and I agreed. That's all."

"I don't know, Sola," he said. "I thought we were all on the same side, but lately . . ."

"What?" I said, giving him a hard stare.

"Maybe you are more like Sevin than you realize," he said, "which, I'm guessing, will please him."

I felt my anger flare, but I was also confused by the tail end of his remark. He seemed to have sensed as much.

"Does it seem odd to you," he said, coming in close and lowering his voice, "that a cadet would be sent to Jerem for reeducation with a bunch of random deviants like us? I do. I think that if I were a cadet and violated some law, it would be dealt with—as they say—*in house*. But maybe you and Field Marshal Sevin are so much on the same page now that you never thought to wonder about that?"

My confusion deepened. And I saw the passion beneath the words, the hurt. His face—usually so mild, so self-deprecating—was flushed with frustration.

"Trest," I began, apologetic but unsure of what to say.

"It's fine," he said, shaking his head so that the chain around his ear swung. "I'm sorry. I shouldn't have said that. It just gets a little old, you know? Being the funny one, the goof, the one no one takes seriously. But yeah, it's fine. I'll leave you to it."

I stood there, flustered into useless, clueless silence. As Trest walked away, I felt Dren's pleasure without having to look at him.

•

"You ready?" I asked Teada. Since the fruitless search of the ship, she had been withdrawn and wary of me.

"Am I staying in this cavern, too, or am I coming back?"

Her reference to "this cavern" reminded me that she, like many of the others, hadn't seen it yet.

"I don't know," I said. "But I think you might like it there better than here."

She glanced around. Dren was playing on his comm pad, ignoring the warning to conserve energy. Carlann was sulking in a corner while Trest tried to engage her in conversation. He avoided my eyes.

"Maybe," said Teada.

She shot me a look from under her dark fringe.

"Thanks for the fruit," she said. "It was . . . nice."

She looked away, embarrassed, and I laughed at the inadequacy of the remark.

"Think you can carry those?" I asked her, indicating a pair of metal bars that had been used to stop anything spilling from the stowage bin. "They're just slotted in place."

"I think so," she said, taking one end and wrenching them free. They were about seven feet long, sturdy, but made of some light alloy.

"Maybe use them as tent poles or something," I said.

She considered them, then gave me a shrewd look.

"You really think there was another girl on the ship?" she asked. Either she wanted to believe in me, or she just wanted assurance that there had been no such girl.

"Yes," I said. "And if you don't mind taking a detour, I think I can prove it."

●

IT WAS RISKY RETURNING TO THE *HYNDERON*, EVEN THOUGH I was sure we had more than enough light to reach the cavern before nightfall. Teada was skeptical, but she was not cowed by Sevin's brand of cadet discipline. In another place, I think we might have been kindred spirits, though perhaps that went for several of those misfits and deviants who had boarded the *Phetteron*. It wasn't an entirely comforting thought.

In the end, I appealed to her sense of fun and adventure as much as to logic.

"Roam with me," I said, and her eyes had finally lit up.

So we made the long hike to where the other ship sat in the snowdrifts, constantly scanning the open ground for predators, though we saw nothing. Teada carried the two metal poles over her shoulder, pleased to be doing something useful.

The *Hynderon* was as I had left it, except that Sevin and the others had emptied its stowage bins, including the emergency locker. There was no gun there, and while I tried not to worry, the absence of the weapon bothered me. I forced myself to examine the stasis pods again, paying particular attention to the only empty one. The decking beside it was smudged. A footprint? Perhaps.

While I searched, Teada accessed the ship's computer from the workstation beside the still-locked flight deck and pulled up the passenger manifest.

"I'll tell you now what you'll find," I said, deliberately keeping my distance so she knew I wasn't looking over her shoulder. "There will be an entry for each body we have here and one more who should be in Pod Nine: a girl, pale and blond. About sixteen, medium height. Strange eyes, though maybe they didn't use to be."

Teada tapped at the keyboard, then blew out her breath noisily.

"Yes?" I asked.

"Yes," she said. "How do I know you didn't look through this when you came here the first time?"

"I guess you don't," I said. "But why would I lie about it? Anyway, you'd know if I were lying, wouldn't you?"

As I said it, I dropped the mental guard I had gotten used to keeping around my thoughts. Teada gasped. Her face flushed, and she looked down, embarrassed by the intimacy of what I had done.

"See?" I said, raising the barrier again.

"Why can we do that?" she asked.

"I don't know," I said. "I think we always could, but that it's gotten stronger since we left Home. Maybe it's being around other people like ourselves. Maybe it's because we're not on our meds anymore. I don't know. But we can, and that means you know I'm telling the truth." I paused, thinking it through. "Twelve years ago a ship left Home for the reeducation facility on Jerem. It never arrived. Instead it came here, along with ten kids all marked with the same tattoo, which—I think—means that they were like us: able to sense people's thoughts, if only a little.

"They came here," I went on, "and they died. Killed each other, I think. All but one. A girl who survived somehow, and waited for more than a decade till another ship arrived."

"What does she want?" asked Teada.

"I have no idea," I answered, "and I'm not convinced it's really her. Not anymore."

•

BEFORE WE LEFT, I PULLED UP THE NAV LOG ONE MORE time and switched to the scanner I had used to locate the *Phetteron*. It was still there, a little blip that indicated the emergency beacon we had launched. I reset the scanner to its maximum range, but there was nothing. I brought it down a little bit, so that it would pick up anything in the 25,000-mile range, but the signal immediately began to break up. The asteroid field, no doubt. I watched as something twinkled, then vanished. It came again, faint and inconsistent, then disappeared. It was probably just solar radiation bouncing off one of the metallic rocks orbiting the planet. I fiddled with the controls but could get no stronger lock, and nothing at all from any of the other range settings.

•

I WAS WARY OF MAKING THE TRIP FROM THE *HYNDERON* TO the cavern because I'd never done it before, but there was no snow falling, and visibility seemed to go for miles where the ground was high. I spotted the turret of blue rock from which I had first seen the second ship, and used that to steer us back to where Herse died. Then we veered south, scanning the area for the singing columns.

"Is that it?" asked Teada.

She was pointing to the left of where I had been look-ing, to where a snow bank arched its back like some prime-val serpent, then dove into a flinty cave mouth, the stone grayer than the blue we had become accustomed to.

"No," I said, thoughtfully. "But the cavern has more than one entrance point. Maybe this is one of them."

I hesitated. The last thing I wanted was to lead us down some blind alley—or worse—but I was far from sure how to find the passageway we had used before, and knew only too well the perils of wandering out in these frozen wastes.

"I'm not sure," I admitted.

Teada's face tightened with concentration.

"Let's take a look," she said. "We can always come back out."

I nodded my agreement, and she grinned unexpectedly.

"What?" I asked.

"You like having someone to share the decision-making with," she said, matter-of-factly. "I'm surprised. Pleased, but surprised. You seemed so . . . I don't know. Aloof. Independent. It's reassuring to know you aren't always sure of what to do. Weird, huh?"

"That that's comforting, or that you can sense how I feel?"

"Both, I guess. I'm assuming you can see into my head, too?"

"'See' isn't quite the word," I said, "but yes."

"And?" said Teada. Her smile this time was shy, almost bashful, which surprised me. She had seemed at least as tough and aloof to me as I had to her. It was an invitation, of sorts, so I stopped walking and came close to her. She didn't flinch, but closed her eyes, still smiling softly. Her embarrassed patience was lit from within by something like anticipation, as if I were going to kiss her. I put one hand to the side of her head to focus my mind.

For a moment, it was like those fliks you see of looking through a heat-sensing camera, the landscape is all blue and the people are yellow and orange and red around their core: a flare of emotion that registered like color. The images reduced and stabilized, though I could not tell which of us was bringing them under control. I felt the backdrop of her anxiety, but it was dominated by the exhilaration of letting me into her mind, and then I saw a sweeping collage of impressions, as if she were offering up a slideshow of her life.

I felt her isolation, a sense of abandonment that reached deep into her past, long before she came to Valkrys. I had no idea if it was true or not, but she felt unloved, rejected, even within her family. She thought herself dull and unintelligent, with no gifts or skills. Things she had once cared about—music, perhaps some kind of visual art—had been dropped with a sense of failure: she had not abandoned them; they had abandoned her. Till all that was left was fire, the joy of starting it—no, of setting it loose, watching it grow, a force that consumed and terrified but that she controlled. Most of the time.

I felt the thrill of it and gasped.

Teada opened her eyes and took a step back. She was sweating. We both were, as if the fire in her mind—our minds—had been real. Our eyes met, and she smiled again, that same shy, uneasy smile, and I was reminded of eating the fruit with Bryce and Yasmine, the way the moment had been chased by embarrassment at the joy of the thing, intimate and illicit as it had been. I wanted to say something, but after so close a connection, words seemed clumsy, rough tools that would surely shatter whatever had just formed between us.

I smiled deliberately, waiting till my heart rate and breathing had slowed a fraction before inclining my head toward the cave.

We moved toward it in silence. I forced myself to focus on simply putting one foot in front of the other, on watching for the sharp blue ridges that would slit me open as they had Yasmine, on scanning for signs of life that might spell other kinds of danger.

The gray rock was indeed different. It was less translucent, more like slabs than crystals, though its rough surface still sparkled in places. As soon as we stepped into the cave mouth, the light halved, and though the tunnel was broad enough for us to walk side by side, it got steadily darker as we pressed on. I paused to get the flashlight from my backpack. For a moment, I had the irrational fear that I would find the doll-like girl from the *Hynderon* standing silently beside me, her head cocked, her mouth open, but when I turned the light on, we were quite alone. I wondered where in the cavern—if indeed the passage led there—it would come out. We would need to find Yasmine as quickly as possible or this would all be a waste of time.

Maybe it already was. Her wounds had been terrible. I didn't know how long she could be expected to survive without proper medical attention. For a moment, I allowed myself to think that she was already dead, and immediately my mind slid to Bryce, mourning her but maybe taking comfort from me, seeing me as if for the first time . . .

It was an appalling and disloyal thought, and I banished it with a shake of my head and a grunt of disgust, but it was too late.

"Bryce?" said Teada out of the gloom. "You're in love with Bryce?"

For a moment, I could think of nothing to say.

I shook my head, but realizing that she probably couldn't see my face clearly, said. "No. I barely know him."

"But you like him," she said, and her voice had a knowing bitterness to it. "You're attracted to him."

"Doesn't make any difference, does it?" I said, angry at her response, that she had stumbled onto my stupid, childish crush, that I wasn't alone in my own head. "He's with Yasmine. End of story."

"Right," said Teada, and her mind was closed to me now, locked up and bolted. "End of story."

I walked faster, recklessly so, given the fact that I didn't know the passage at all. The blood was ringing in my cheeks, my ears, and for the first time since this had all begun, I felt truly angry at the injustice of it all. I heard Teada struggling to keep up, the metal poles clanking against each other and ringing on the stone, and I was glad that she was winded, as if the petty display of my own fitness would somehow teach her a lesson. But I knew in my heart that it wasn't her I was mad at. In fact I felt a kind of pity for her, as well as real affection, and that made the sense—however irrational it was—that I had failed her all the more bitter.

If I hadn't been so consumed with these feelings, so blinded by them, I would have smelled the cat sooner.

CHAPTER

THE PASSAGE STRAIGHTENED AND DROPPED. FIFTY yards ahead I could see the bluish light of the cavern quite clearly, and could even guess where it opened up in the great basin. But between us and that exit, so tantalizingly close, was a chamber that opened to the left of the path. The floor was strewn with hides of pale, matted fur and gnawed bones, and the place was rank with the stench of blood and offal and urine. I thrust a splay-fingered hand back at Teada to halt her, reaching for her mind, commanding her to stop and be silent.

I don't know whether she felt it or just reacted to my movement, but she went still and did not ask why I had frozen in place. As our footsteps stopped, I heard it: the low, growling breath of a large animal.

Awake or asleep?

I had no idea, and wasn't sure it much mattered. Such creatures would have preternaturally heightened senses, surely? If we tried to pass the mouth of its lair, it would awaken and kill us.

We had to go back.

I felt Teada's despair as her mind registered my certainty, but she did not object.

I turned the flashlight back the way we had come, and with agonizingly slow steps, we inched our way back up the tunnel. I was screaming inside with fury. Now we would be too late, Yasmine would be dead, and—somehow—it would be my fault. Teada moved impossibly slowly, cradling the metal poles carefully so that they made no sound against the rock, and while I understood why, I felt like telling her to just leave them. They weren't important. I don't really know why I didn't, except that she had decided they mattered, that she was helping.

We crawled out into the open air, still not speaking, and found that it had begun to snow again.

"Got to find those columns before the storm gets bad," I said. The presence of the sabertooth and the brutal reality of our situation had made all our other feelings irrelevant. Teada just nodded, businesslike, and asked what the columns looked like. I told her as we walked, my mind on nothing but finding the passage as quickly as possible. This had already taken much longer than I had anticipated, and now that we were outside again, it was clear that the diminishing light wasn't just because of the storm. We were getting dangerously close to sundown.

So we walked, as we always seemed to be doing on Valkrys, jackets fastened tight against the mounting wind. but even as I cursed it under my breath, it saved our lives.

"Listen," said Teada. "What is that? Music?"

"It's the columns!" I exclaimed, homing in on the sound and pivoting to face it. "Come on."

We ran then, and there they were, the jagged blue spines like the pipes of some ancient organ growing out of the rock, whistling in shifting harmony.

"This is it," I said. "The way down. Just watch your footing. It's slippery."

It was, but it was also familiar. Using the flashlight, I picked out our best route, and within minutes we were emerging into the great cavernous basin. Teada gaped and stared, relaxing so that I could feel her relief and pleasure at what she was seeing. Down where Sevin and the others were, I saw a soft glow: a lamp.

"Nearly there," I said.

We were at almost the exact point where Yasmine had fallen, when Teada lost her footing.

She slipped toward me, moving fast. I felt her alarm before I realized what was happening and dropped to my knees, arms spread to catch her. She hit me hard in the chest with her knee, but I didn't go down with her, and she was able to claw herself stationary.

"Thanks," she managed, as we lay there, as close as we had been when I had looked into her mind. "And sorry," she added. "About before. I didn't mean to . . . I wasn't assuming—"

"It's fine," I said. "I should have said something. It's this place. Wandering into each other's thoughts, it's not natural. Not for us, anyway. Not yet."

"Not yet?" she asked.

I just shrugged and said, "Come on. The others will be waiting."

I tried to hide how much I hoped that was true, that they would all still be there, alive, that I would have nothing else on my conscience.

●

IF I WAS EXPECTING A NOSTALGIC REUNION, SEVIN SMASHED that the moment he saw us.

"Where the hell have you been?" he demanded. "You've been gone hours."

"Nice to see you, too," I said. "How's Yasmine?"

"About the same," said Bryce, looking up at me and smiling sadly.

"I have food and blankets," I said. "And these."

I indicated the metal rods Teada was carrying.

"I thought we could fashion a stretcher with the blankets and this cord."

"We can't carry her up to the ship," said Sevin. "It's too steep. If we slipped—"

"I didn't mean to the *Phetteron*," I said. "We should take her over there. To the city."

That silenced them. Sevin gazed in the direction I was looking.

255

"Why there?" he asked.

"There are buildings," I said. "Some of them virtually intact, protected from the elements and predators, easier to keep warm. I see you've made no progress on building a fire."

Sevin looked away, stung by his own inadequacy, but Bryce spoke up.

"Yes," he said. "We should take her to the city." He gave us a look that said that that he was speaking for Yasmine. Sevin did not object. "Let's get to work on that stretcher."

Yasmine was barely conscious, but she smiled at Bryce and squeezed his hand.

"We're taking you somewhere safe," he said.

"That's nice," she whispered. "Hi Sola."

"Hi Yasmine," I said, shielding my thoughts as best I could. She looked pale and exhausted. The blood that had dried around her wounds was black. Teada shuddered, but it looked better than before, thanks to Muce's perfect, miniscule stitching. My ragged shoelaces lay neatly coiled beside her, and the only evidence of my battlefield surgery was the pattern of ragged holes that I had made with my knife.

"The bleeding has stopped," said Muce. "I couldn't have done it if you hadn't closed her up like you did."

I put my hand on the back of her head and drew her into a grateful hug.

"That tiger-thing came down again," said Sevin. "Watched us for maybe twenty minutes then went away again, but I wouldn't be surprised if it came back. I don't think the pistol will stop it."

"Another good reason to move," I said, gazing across the cavern to a dark opening that, I felt sure, led to the cat's den.

It took ten minutes to rig the stretcher and almost as long to get Yasmine onto it. We lay her face down, one of the clean blankets arranged on top of her. Her hair trailed over the side of the stretcher like a waterfall, but she was too weary to gather it back together.

Darkness was falling in the cavern now, and I offered to lead the way while Sevin brought up the rear, pistol in hand. I reached into my backpack for the flashlight Sevin had given me back at the *Phetteron*, and as I fumbled around, my blind fingers strayed upon something unexpected. It felt like a rectangle of folded paper, but when I drew it out and shone the flashlight on it, I found that it was an envelope of the kind people used to send letters a hundred years or more ago. I stared at it. On the front was a single word, not laser typed but written by hand in a cramped and unpracticed script.

Sola.

Who would write to me in such a strange and archaic fashion?

I turned it over, found the sealed edge, and slid an unsteady finger under it. I found the same spindly writing inside, on a single sheet of yellowing paper. Something portentous was looming, like the great cat coming ghost-like out of the cavern shadows. I turned it over and found the last line. My breath caught. It read, "Your misguided but ever-loving mother."

She must have slipped it into my backpack moments before I boarded the ship. I fumbled with the paper, over-whelmed by a nervous apprehension that made my hands unsteady as I turned it over and read from the beginning.

Dear Sola,

Forgive this strange letter, as I will ask you to forgive so many things. For some time now, I have been looking at my life: its few achievements and its single great failure. Cancer will do that to you. I have realized that it is time to face up to what I have kept hidden for most of my life. It is too late for me, but not — I think — for you.

These last few months it has been my belief, my conviction, that you feel you have failed your father and me, that you have let us down. I want you to know that this is not the case. It is us — and more particularly me — who have failed you.

I should have known this would happen. You see, my dear Sola, you and I are far more alike than you could possibly know. I realized this long ago, even before you first started getting into trouble, but I did not know how to respond. I asked the wrong people — which is to say I asked the officially right people — and they gave me bad advice. Not merely inaccurate advice, well meaning but incorrect. They gave me willfully misleading advice, designed to protect not me and certainly not you, but to protect themselves. I will act on such advice no longer. I will believe that contrary positions are, in fact, viable.

When you return, we will talk, you and I, as a mother and her daughter should talk. There is much I have to tell you. Even things — or at least one thing — to show you that will, I hope, demonstrate the connection between us, a connection that goes far beyond the parent-child bond as Home understands it. I hope, I pray, it will lead to a new understanding between us and to other good things, including, though I do not deserve it, your forgiveness.

Sincerely,
Your misguided but ever-loving mother

I reread the letter three times, eyes blurred and hands trembling. I did not know what it meant or what I'd learn if we ever saw each other again, but my eyes returned over and over to that unevenly scrawled signature. "Your misguided but ever-loving mother." The paper was blotched in swollen, uneven circles, and in places the ink had run a little. Tear drops.

Ever-loving mother.

She had never said such a thing before. Not so far as I could remember. I never really thought about it because expressions of affection—public or private—were rare on Home, the kind of outmoded behavior we had come to find embarrassing and a little distasteful, though all of a sudden I couldn't imagine why. I read it again, blinking back the tears in my own eyes, and in my mind my mother's face was now that of the angel in the picture, distant but thoughtful, smiling faintly as she watched over me. The shock of realizing that this was what I wanted—every day for years now—made it hard to breathe. I wanted my mother. I sat down and stared at the ground, slipping the letter into my breast pocket, close to my heart.

Contrary positions are, in fact, viable.

It was like she was throwing out everything I had been taught, everything she had been taught, but then, sitting in this impossible place, I was ready for that. The great blue structures around me were themselves a contrary position. They proved that everything I had learned about the universe on Home was wrong.

I looked around, trying to focus on what we had planned to do, and found Sevin watching me. He looked wary, thoughtful. I felt sure he had seen me reading the letter, and I gave him a steady look till he turned away, his face still clouded with thoughts I couldn't grasp. For a moment I watched him, but my mind kept straying back to phrases from the letter.

You and I are far more alike than you could possibly know.

There is much I have to tell you. Even things—or at least one thing—to show you . . .

What things? And now, stuck here on this barren and abandoned world, would I ever find out?

●

THERE WAS NO SIGN OF THE SABERTOOTH, AND THE CHAT-ter of birds had dropped to nothing. I led the way, lost in my own thoughts. Bryce and Teada were at my back, carrying Yasmine, while Muce trailed behind them. Sevin brought up the rear, eyes flashing around for signs of danger. We picked our way around the reedy margins of the pools until we reached the great blue gateway. Sevin passed the beam of his flashlight over it, saying nothing but studying it with mute astonishment. Whatever else he knew, the city was—I felt sure—completely unexpected, and it unsettled him as much as it had me.

He marveled at the road and the elegant buildings that reared up on either side, completely deferring com-mand as I chose the sturdiest, most intact ruins in the shadow of what I already thought of as the cathedral and led the way inside. There was a vast circular hall inside the doorway, and the walls glowed with a soft luminescence

so that our eyes adjusted and the flashlights were no longer necessary. The chamber had a high ceiling that was
still largely intact, and through the one collapsed point, I
saw at least one more story above. There was also a series
of side chambers, each reflecting its opposite like a mirror, all subdivided by lower partition walls that looked
like racks or shelves. The floors were scattered with broken stone and ash, but in places there were fragments of
other materials: twisted, blackened metal, melted glass,
scorched pieces of wood and marble.

"What happened here?" asked Teada, gazing at the
place.

No one had any answer to make, and in the silence
that followed she came to the same realization that I had.
For whatever reason, the walls of these ancient buildings
screened our thoughts from each other.

She gave me a questioning look, and, when I just nodded slowly, she said simply, "Huh. I guess we're back to
words."

The frankness of the statement, spoken with a hint of
relief, struck me as funny, but it was Muce who laughed
loudest. Even Yasmine smiled broadly, and only Sevin
looked a little put out, like he was missing the joke and
resented us for it.

They set Yasmine down, and then Teada started looking for "stuff to burn." I gave her a quick look that was
intended to be supportive, and she smiled, though it was a
wan, hollow smile.

"Can you roll me over?" asked Yasmine.

"I don't think we want you putting your weight on those stitches," said Bryce, kindly.

"I can't see," she answered. "I want to see."

Bryce looked at me, and I gestured vaguely: *I don't know.*

"Just for a little while," she said. "I'll roll back onto my belly to sleep."

Bryce hesitated, then did as she asked, taking her shoulders while Sevin lifted her about the knees.

"I feel like a princess," she mused, dreamily, then adjusted and looked about her. "Pretty," she said. "Like a painting."

I was reminded of what Bryce had said, about wishing he could paint the landscape. Now he'd probably prefer to paint her portrait, I thought, and the burden of all that had happened, all that had changed since we first landed here, suddenly weighed heavily on me. I looked at Yasmine, who was still gazing about her as if entranced.

"A library," she said. "A real, ancient library, like they used to have for books."

I looked about the room, guessing she was right.

"You think there's anything still here to read?" she asked.

"I doubt it," I answered, sadder than I would have expected. "Looks like it burned."

"That's too bad," said Yasmine. "I like reading. Not that I would be able to read anything here anyway. I don't speak alien."

CATHEDRALS OF GLASS

She chuckled softly, till something in her back made her wince and she stopped.

"Maybe not all burned," said Muce. She was standing behind what once had been a stone desk or counter built into the very architecture of the structure, a great sweeping arc that spanned half the room. "There's a basement. See? Steps. Cooler down here, and there are doors. They're closed."

Sevin and Teada both drifted over to her and looked down. Moments later, they were descending the steps. I checked that Bryce was okay alone with Yasmine and, on his nod, went after them.

The steps were undamaged, and the doors at the bottom were made of some smooth metal, its finish satin and gray, a little scorched but apparently still quite functional. They were each adorned by a familiar emblem at head height: a single crimson triangle. Together they made a kind of face, as if whatever was beyond the doors was the mind of the city itself, a mind that—somehow—had also touched everyone here but Sevin. The tattoos on our heads were part of this place, even if I did not know how that could be possible.

Despite the unusual materials, the doors felt perfectly ordinary. Not alien at all. Regular steps and regular doors, as if made by and for regular people. The thought was unsettling, though I didn't know why. I had seen nothing to suggest that the city had been the home of tentacle monsters. So why did the idea that it had been the home of people not so unlike ourselves trigger alarms in the deep part of my brain?

264

Sevin and Teada had their shoulders to the doors, but Muce just took the handle and twisted it. Even at a distance, I could see that that had done the trick. Both doors seemed to become weightless, and it took no effort at all for Sevin to push them open.

As they opened, there was an audible sigh, and a puff of dust rushed out into the little stairwell and drifted away.

A vault, then, sealed tight but left unlocked, which was curious.

"What's inside?" I asked, as Sevin snapped on his flashlight.

He gave a low, astonished whistle, and I found myself annoyed that I could not sense anything from him. I guess I had been getting used to it after all, even if I was glad to have my privacy back.

"Books," he said. "Actual books like you see in the fliks. Paper and card or something bound together."

I came rushing down after him as he drew a book out from one of the shelves that filled the sealed chamber. He turned to me, his face a mask of amazement, and then lowered his eyes to the volume in his hands. It was large—at least two feet long—and rectangular, and instead of disintegrating in his hands as I expected, it looked quite solid, even when he opened the stiffened cover and began to turn its pages.

Pages.

I had seen images of books but had never seen one for real. Didn't know anyone who had. But then Sevin became quite still, and his amazement turned to something else, something that blended confusion and panic.

"What?" I demanded, leaning in to see.

He looked up, pale with shock.

"I can read it," he said. "It's in our language."

CHAPTER **23**

T HE BOOKS SEEMED TO GIVE YASMINE THE ENERGY she had lacked. We brought them out in stacks, handling them carefully as if they were sacred relics, and she called for what interested her. There were myths and legends told in all manner of forms and styles. There were treatises on law and religion, books of recipes, maps, journals, and, most numerous of all, histories.

Every book in the vault had the same binding, the same triangle branded into the cover and spine, uniting them, I surmised, as the records of a single culture, the archive of a people who had lived and died on this very spot.

"Sola. Can I have a word?"

It was Bryce, who had left Yasmine to read. I said "sure" but felt a swelling weariness that was more than all the walking. I didn't want to talk.

He led me out into another smaller chamber, round and open to the cavern above, with what looked to be an ancient fountain in the center. The fountain was made up of stylized figures—human figures—twined together and holding a single torch aloft that, I imagined, once sparkled with cascading water.

"I didn't cheat on a school exam," he said, the moment we were away from the others.

"What do you mean?" I said.

"The reason I was put on the *Phetteron*. It wasn't cheating. I lied."

I braced myself.

"So what was it?"

"You have to understand something, Sola," he said, leaning in but not raising his eyes. "That version of Home as shiny and perfect, the place where everyone is middle class? That's a lie, too. You might not read about it on the tech grid or see it on the updates, but there are poor people on Home. Homeless people. Everywhere. Especially in Sindrone. From time to time the government rounds them up and ships them out, like they do us, but they don't just go to reeducation facilities. They get put in work camps."

"I've never heard of them," I said.

"Of course you haven't," he snapped back. "Because your information comes from government-monitored sources. The camps are remote, usually on other moons. If you prove to be a good worker, learn usable skills, and swear not to talk about the camps, you might get brought

A PLANET OF BLOOD AND ICE

back to Home and given some kind of menial job. You think everything's automated, but it's not. Sure, there are lots of computers and mechanical devices involved in collecting your trash, but even now there are still people up to their necks in stink, pushing buttons and working shovels. My father is one of them."

I stared at him. I could sense nothing that wasn't in his face, his voice, but I had no doubt that he was telling the truth.

"The man with no luggage," I said, remembering how he alone had no care package from his family when he boarded the *Phetteron.*

"What?"

"You didn't bring anything with you," I said. "Struck me as strange."

His face darkened.

"Yeah," he snarled. "That's the extent of my hardship: not having candy or fancy clothes to wear during my reeducation."

"I didn't mean—"

"And no, guys who have to scrub the oil and filth off their hands before they come home are not paid a middle-class wage. So you learn to supplement. Like you, I go out at night, but not just to wander around and feel alive. I go out to take the stuff rich people don't need and I do."

"You're a thief."

"I consider myself a redistributor of wealth," he said, permitting himself a bleak smile, "but yeah, I'm a thief."

"Does Yasmine know?"

That surprised him. Of all the things I might have said, I don't think that had occurred to him. He considered me with something like tenderness and regret, then shook his head.

"The time hasn't been right," he said. "I will. Not sure how she'll . . . Anyway. Thanks."

"Why did you want to tell me?" I asked.

It was a loaded question, pregnant with possibilities, and I almost wished I hadn't asked it. Almost.

He frowned, considering, then sat up straight, all business.

"The night I was arrested," he said, "I met Dren. They brought him into the holding center while I was waiting for my father to pick me up. I didn't speak to him, and we only saw each other by accident. Prisoners are not supposed to interact. But he was covered in blood. One custodian picked me up. They sent five to get Dren."

"You think he killed someone?" I asked.

"Someone died that night. The custodian said as much to my father, trying to convince me of just how dangerous it was to break curfew. Sevin knew about it, too. You remember him making some crack about how someone had been killed in Sindrone that first day?"

I did. It had struck me even then as oddly out of character.

"I think he was letting Dren know that he was watching him or something," said Bryce.

"Why would they put a killer on the same ship as a bunch of minor deviants?" I asked.

"Maybe they decided that deviance was more than unattractive," he said. "But I don't know whether he was convicted. I don't even know what they do with killers these days. There aren't supposed to be any, remember?"

More lies, I thought. They built up on top of me like old-fashioned blankets, heavy and muffling till I could feel nothing but the desire for sleep.

"I don't know for sure what Dren did," Bryce concluded, "or what might have driven him to it. There are crazy people in Sindrone at night. Maybe it was self-defense. Maybe he just found the body and wasn't guilty of anything. But be careful of him. I think he was dangerous before we ever came here, and now . . . who knows what he's capable of?"

●

WE RETURNED TO THE OTHERS, WHO WERE ALL READING IN silence. Yasmine didn't seem to notice that Bryce and I had been missing, and when he went to her side, I tried to ignore them and found a spot by myself. I picked up a book, but was too tired to really read it.

Muce sat beside me, but before long she laid her head in my lap and, as I quietly turned the pages, fell asleep. I couldn't blame her. The silence of the place and the stillness in my mind was strangely soporific. My muscles ached from the activity of the last few days, and as the stress fell away and the exhaustion registered, I found that I craved sleep more than anything else. I checked my comm pad—nothing—ate a little of the protein bar in my pocket, drank some water, and spent a moment watching the others silently reading these ancient artifacts, as if I were seeing through a window into the past. I watched them for perhaps half an hour before drifting off.

I dreamed of my mother. Not the benign, angelically protective mother of the letter, but the mother I had known during her sickness, hawkish and distant, snapping at me when I went into her room and demanding I turn my back till she had put on that ridiculous hat she wore to hide her baldness.

●

I woke with a start. Teada was tugging at my arm. There was no sign of Muce.

"Sevin's gone," she said.

"What?" I demanded, bleary eyed. "What do you mean, Sevin's gone? Gone where?"

"He was reading and talking to Yasmine," said Teada, "but eventually she fell asleep. We all did. When she woke, he was gone."

I got creakily to my feet and looked around. Muce was still asleep, curled up like an animal at the foot of Yasmine's bed. Yasmine was sitting up against a pillow made of bundled blankets, talking earnestly to Bryce.

"He just left in the night, alone?" I said, striding over to them.

"I was so tired," said Bryce. "I'd been keeping an eye on Yasmine, but I was just exhausted, and—"

"It's not your fault," she said, smiling at him.

"It's no one's fault," I cut in, confusion making me irritable. "No one saw him go? He said nothing about where he might head?"

The others shook their heads.

"He was upset," said Yasmine. Her voice was weaker than it had been before the accident, but she seemed more together than she had been the night before. "We were reading, comparing notes, but after a while he started to get really quiet. I thought he was angry at me, though I didn't know why, so I stopped talking to him, and I guess eventually I dropped off. When I woke—"

"What did you talk about before he went quiet?" I asked. My voice was fast, urgent to the point of rudeness, but I had to know, and quickly.

"This place," she said. "What we found in the books. Anywhere else on the planet I'd have been able to sense his thoughts, but in here . . . I just couldn't gauge him at all. He was angry, I'd swear to it. Furious even. But he didn't lash out or yell. It was like his feelings pushed him deeper and deeper inside himself."

"What was the last thing you remember talking about before he got mad?" I tried.

She looked around the floor by her bed, and frowned.

"A book is gone," she said.

"You're sure? Which one?"

"It was newer than the others, or seemed to be," she said. "A history of Valkrys. That's all I remember."

"You read it together?" I pressed.

"I only read the introduction," she said. "Speed-read it, really. Sevin had a copy, too. I'm sorry. I'm really tired . . ."

"We should let her rest," said Bryce.

"In a minute," I snapped. "What can you remember from the introduction? What is the history of Valkrys?"

"I was pretty out of it," said Yasmine. "I don't know. It was about a war, or how a war started. Something. Two different peoples living in the same place. Different cultures. Different ways of communicating, I think. I'm not sure."

"Ways of communicating?" I repeated. "What do you mean?"

Yasmine shook her head wearily, and Bryce shot me a warning look.

"I'm sorry. I was really tired," she said.

"And this upset Sevin?" I asked.

"He was angry," she said.

"Yeah," I said. "He would be. He must have gone back to the ship."

"Which one?" asked Teada.

"He never made it onto the flight deck of the *Hynderon*, right?" I said.

"They couldn't crack the code to the cabin doors," said Teada. "Why?"

"Then he's gone to the *Phetteron*," I said. "I'm going after him."

"I'll come with you," said Teada.

"I should probably—" Bryce began.

"Stay here," I concluded for him. "Yes. You'll be okay?"

"I still have Sevin's gun," said Bryce.

"He went unarmed?" I said.

"Left it beside me," Bryce answered.

"Okay," I said, picking up my makeshift spear. "Keep an eye on Muce. Can I have the other copy of the book Sevin took with him?"

"Here," said Yasmine, offering it to me with a frail hand, which fell exhausted to her side the moment I took the book from her.

I nodded at Teada, and we left.

●

I WAS STARTING TO FEEL LIKE I COULD MAKE THIS HIKE IN my sleep: across the cavern floor, up the basin, through the passage and out, around the singing columns, and across the snowfield to the *Phetteron*. It was just as well. The sun was not properly up, and the landscape was drained of all color but the soft pearl and opalescent glow reflected off the snow and pulsing in the exposed stone. My mind and legs felt sluggish, and I tried to focus on what Sevin was doing. As we left the city behind, my sense of Teada's presence gradually bloomed in my mind, and despite the tension between us yesterday, it was comforting, made me feel less alone. When she took my hand, I did not shrink away.

"Think you could read aloud as we walk?" I said, offering Teada the book. "I'll keep my eyes open, and in a few minutes we can trade off."

She gave me a puzzled look, then reached for the book with one hand, leaving the other in mine.

●

THE *PHETTERON* WAS UTTERLY SILENT AND DARK. WE boarded warily, and I did not lower the spear I had kept at the ready during our hike. Something felt wrong.

The only light came from the dim glow of the stasis pod controls. At least they were still running. Four showed the light that indicated they were occupied. Dren, Carlann, Trest, and Sevin would be inside, though they had chosen to rest at the back of the ship, not in the pods originally assigned to them. I pulled a face at Teada. Why would Sevin leave the cavern in the middle of the night and risk the journey back to the ship just to sleep in a stasis pod?

I moved quietly down the gangway and paused at the first occupied pod. As I peered in, the internal light snapped on. Trest's terrified face gazed up at me. I motioned for him to open up; with a flurry of clumsy fiddling, he did so.

"Sola?" he said. "Is that really you?"

"Of course it's me," I said. "And Teada. What's wrong?"

"What's wrong?" he echoed, his voice unsteady and barely more than a whisper. "You've got to get me out of here."

"What's keeping you here?" I asked. "What's going on?"

Trest got quickly out of the stasis pod and moved away from it like it might contaminate him. We followed him as he hurried to the flight deck doors.

"It's Dren," he said at last. "He's . . . I don't know. Changed."

"Changed?" I repeated. "Changed how?"

But as I spoke, I heard the soft hiss of one of the stasis pods opening. Dren's. He sat up, his eyes finding us with uncanny speed. He was the same blond boy he had always been, and, for a split second, I thought Trest was losing it, imagining the whole thing. But then Dren cocked his head slowly onto his left shoulder, and I saw that his eyes were glowing with a soft, amber light.

CHAPTER 24

As Dren climbed slowly out of the pod, Trest shrank away. His mind was shrieking like a siren, and I had to fight not to be overcome by it. Dren took a step toward me, his head still in that ungainly position, and then the mouth opened. The lips did not move, but the words appeared in my head.

Hello, Sola. I hoped you would come back.

"What happened to you?" I asked.

I chose to live, said the voice. It was and was not Dren's voice, just as the boy in front of me was and was not Dren. He sounded like the girl.

"You chose to live as what?" I asked.

That doesn't matter. I will survive. You should join me.

The boy's body took another step towards me, and I aimed the spear at his chest with both hands.

"No closer," I said.

The energy coming from the boy who had been Dren almost knocked me back. It was pure and cold, and it felt like appetite, like hunger. The minds of everyone else had been complicated and muddied with competing feelings and ideas, but this was raw and undiluted. I knew it gave Dren—or the thing which looked like him—power, and the will to use it.

Another of the stasis pods was opening. Carlann. She peered out, still herself, I thought with relief, but not as scared as she should be. I felt for her mind and sensed only a kind of mild curiosity, even a little pleasure.

"Come over here, Carlann," I said.

She looked at me, and something like disdain flashed through her eyes. She climbed out but just sat on the edge of her stasis pod, looking at us as if waiting for something to happen, something interesting or amusing.

If you don't join us by choice, said the voice in my head, *we can make you.*

"We have to get out of here," Trest said. It wasn't directed at anyone. He was just thinking aloud. Teada was up against the exit hatch, ready to run back out into the snow.

"What about Sevin?" I said, eying the remaining occupied pod. "We can't leave him here."

I forced myself to move toward Dren. The first step was faltering, but the second was long and confident as my body took over, pushing through the horror of the moment as I made for the last stasis pod that was still closed and powered up.

"What are you doing?" shouted Trest.

I ignored him, taking three more strides to where Dren stood, eyes blazing, head now tipped to the right, mouth still empty and lifeless. I elbowed him out of the way, and he staggered slightly. Carlann's brow clouded, and she retreated into the luggage racks as if afraid I would touch her.

I dropped into a squat beside the last stasis pod and, just as Trest yelled out, pushed the release button on the control pad. I heard the distinctive clank of the mechanism that unlocked the flight deck at the other end of the ship. I turned to the sound, bewildered, and saw the twin doors ease open.

Sevin emerged, looking hunted in spite of the uniform he was still wearing. He stared the length of the hold down at me, his expression quizzical, and only then did I turn back to the stasis pod I had opened.

The girl from the *Hynderon* lay there, eyes glowing, her hunger spiking as she reached up and seized me around the throat with a strong, cold hand.

I fought. Of course I fought. But the struggle was less in my body than my mind. The girl's presence was smothering, stifling, but it also promised rest. Her mouth fell open, and her voice curled through my brain like smoke.

Relax and live. Relax and survive.

The hand at my throat was a distraction. The real attack was in my head. But as I fought for breath and felt other hands seize my arms—Dren, maybe Carlann, too—I didn't think I could withstand either one.

280

The hands had a single purpose. They turned me around, and as the girl in the pod climbed out, one hand still gripping my throat, I found myself staring into Dren's amber eyes. His hands were around the back of my head, drawing my face to his and twisting it to mirror the awful angle of his own. Then, even as I tried to escape, to get one wholesome gasp of cold air, he was kissing me, his lips clamped to mine. Revolted, outraged, I jerked my knee into his groin, but it made no difference, and his hunger seemed to swell. Carlann and the girl held me tight, and then, without any sense of how it might be possible, it wasn't Dren, the snide and hateful Dren, who was kissing me. It was Bryce.

I felt his arms around me, his warm, soft lips against mine, the throbbing of his heart, and I gave myself to the bliss of it all. I reveled in it, and now it was like sliding into sleep. Not sleep in a stasis pod or on the hard ground of a ruined city, but a bed like they used to make them, all downy softness and silken sheets, and Bryce there with me, and everything else was fading . . .

The impact was like a bomb going off in my head. There was a flare of sound and light in my head, and I knew I was falling, though I was powerless to stop it. I landed hard on my side on the metal gantry, and my wrist shrieked.

The pain brought a kind of focus, and I rolled over, trying to see what had happened. Sevin and Trest and Teada. They had charged Dren and the others, hitting them bullishly, breaking the link and stopping whatever it was they had been doing to me. All three of my attackers had been scattered by the collision, but they were recovering fast.

Sevin and Trest snatched at my hands, dragging me to my feet and pulling me along with them. I cried out at the pain in my wrist, and the sound was shocking in my own ears. It rang not just with physical agony, but also with despair and loss. It was a horrible sound, and I clamped my mouth shut to prevent it from coming out again.

Teada was working the door latch desperately as Sevin and Trest pulled me towards her. Dren was on his feet, head cocked, the hunger radiating off him though I couldn't tell what it was he wanted. Carlann, still herself but thrilled and self-satisfied, was watching again, and beside her the pallid girl with the terrible stare rose to her feet and raised an arm slowly. There was something in her hand, something black and small and terrible.

I saw the flash before I heard the shot, and then I felt myself shrink from the report as it echoed around the ship. I saw the smoke, and moments later I smelled it, peppery and sour. Only then, as we were blundering out of the door and into the frigid wind, did I feel the pain in my gut. It was hot and cold at the same time, and I felt my legs start to buckle. I shrugged out of Sevin's grasp and clutched at my stomach, feeling for the blood, the hole.

But there was nothing.

For a moment I stood there in the snow, unable to process what had happened, what was still happening, and then I saw Trest stumble and collapse, a spatter of red spraying the pale ground. We had been so close, our minds so intertwined, that I had felt it, thought that I had been shot. But I hadn't. He had.

DREN APPEARED IN THE DOORWAY, LOOKING OUT AT us, face void of feeling, head cocked.

"Keep moving," snarled Sevin, hoisting Trest back upright. "Get under his arm."

I shouldered as much of his weight as I could, but Trest just gasped with pain and shock as we adjusted him. We turned our backs on the ship, and I waited for the agony of a bullet in my spine, but there was no more shooting.

"Are they coming?" Sevin asked, as we started our blundering retreat.

Teada looked back.

"Just watching," she said. "Carlann, too."

"Should we go back for her?" asked Sevin. It was the first time I had heard him sound so unsure.

"She's made her choice," I said. "Keep walking."

I knew it was the right thing to do: to try and save Trest rather than risk losing everything for Carlann, who was probably beyond saving. But it was still hard, and I injected certainty in my voice to reassure the others. Sevin blinked and nodded, but Teada looked at me, knowing, and her agreement was softer, sadder. I told myself that Carlann had always been a narcissist, and that the decision to save herself—in whatever form, even if that meant destroying her friends—was one she would always make. Still, striding away from the ship was hard and burned like failure.

For a moment, I just wanted to lie down in the snow and wrap my arms around Trest as if he were an infant, tell him I was sorry. I knew that they would come after us, but the prospect of lugging Trest all the way to the city, through who knew what other perils, seemed impossible. But even as I staggered under the burden of my friend—trying to keep the phrase "dead weight" out of my head—even as I stumbled in the snow, sweat running from under my hair down the back of my neck, even as a part of me wanted to scream that I was done, that I couldn't take any more of this, I reminded myself of one thing: Trest had been hurt—perhaps fatally—coming to my aid. I would not give up on him, however bleak things looked.

"We have to get him to the city," said Sevin.

The remark jarred me out of my own thoughts.

"Why there?" I asked. "The *Hynderon* is easier to defend."

Sevin said nothing. I looked at him, laboring on the other side of Trest, our faces inches from his, but Trest's

285

agony and fear drowned out anything I might feel from the others. Did Sevin really sense none of it, or was he just more skilled at keeping his thoughts to himself?

We kept going. Dren and the others did not seem to be following, and I found myself wondering what they were doing. Perhaps they were doing to Carlann what they had tried to do to me. The thought revolted me.

"Let me take him for a bit," said Teada.

She had been bringing up the rear, watching the ship for signs of pursuit. I had almost forgotten she was there.

"It's fine," I said. "I've got him."

"Take a break," said Teada. "Get your breath back."

"I said I've got him," I snapped back.

She blinked as if I'd slapped her.

"Teada's right," murmured Trest, his words slightly slurred. "I'm a pretty heavy guy. Didn't realize just how heavy till about five minutes ago, but then—"

"You got shot," I said, smiling at him, trying to make light of it. He grinned back, a broad grin that showed his even, white teeth and the blood in his mouth.

"A little bit," he conceded. "Just a flesh wound, right? Though," he added, determined to keep talking though his breath was raspy and erratic, "I never really got why that was supposed to make it sound better. I mean, most of me is flesh, right? However much we wish we weren't, especially when there's a hole in you, that's pretty much what we are. The bits that keep us walking and talking and stuff. So wounding my flesh doesn't sound that great. You see what I'm saying?"

Sevin just stared ahead and kept walking.

"Yep," I said, eyes on the ground, "I see."

"Sweating," said Trest. "Weird, huh? You guys are doing all the work, but I'm sweating up a storm. I can feel it running down my back and my legs."

I shouldn't have looked. It was just a reflex, a way to keep the conversation going. But I did glance at his back, and I saw what was running down his back and legs. It wasn't sweat.

Teada caught my eye, and I saw the anguished look on her face before she glanced away. In that moment, and in spite of all the mental noise I had shut out, I caught the certainty of her despair. He wasn't going to make it.

"Don't talk," I said to Trest. "Save your energy."

"Don't talk?" he echoed vaguely. "Have we met? Hi, my name is Trest, and I talk."

I laughed, or I tried to, though it was almost a sob. He didn't notice.

"You know what else is weird?" he said. "I keep thinking about my mom. I kind of thought I hated her, you know? For years." He said it with wonder. "But now—and I mean *just* now, you know—I feel like if I could just see her one more time . . ."

He gasped, a strange, earthy sound like a grunt or a stifled sob that came from somewhere low in his belly. Or his heart. A horrible sound. But then he took a breath and shook his head.

"That chain on my ear," he said. "Take it off, will you?"

I did, unhooking it and holding it out to him, my hands trembling. He shook his head.

"It never suited me," he said. "You keep it."

I closed my freezing fingers around it, avoiding his eyes.

"Tell me about this cave with the fruit," he wheezed, trying to sound bright. "That sounded cool."

I did, but as my breath got increasingly ragged, Sevin said I should let Teada carry him for a while.

"I told you," I said. "I've got it."

"You're tired."

"I *said*—"

"You're slowing us down," Sevin barked.

That shut me up. I said nothing as Teada hoisted Trest onto her shoulder and I wriggled free. It was only when I had fully separated myself from him, when I felt the cold wind chilling the sweat on my face and the curious weight-less quality of my own unencumbered legs, that I realized that my left arm, the one I had laced around Trest's waist, was drenched in his blood.

When we reached the singing columns, Trest hummed comically and made ghost noises, and as we began the long descent through the blue tunnel, he grunted with interest and surprise, but after that, nothing. He had been moving his legs, not walking exactly because we were bearing most of his weight, but mirroring our steps like a child trying to help, but halfway down the passage that stopped, too. He was unconscious, and we were half dragging, half carrying him. The prospect of trying to navigate that treacherous chute, where Yasmine had fallen, terrified me.

"Set him down for a moment," Sevin gasped. "I can't go any further."

I had taken over from Teada, but the freshness had gone from my legs much faster this time, and I was relieved to take a break, relieved also—petty though it was—that I was not the one who had asked for it.

We sat against the smooth stone, panting, and Trest lay between us. Because I was so used to seeing him grinning and talking a mile a minute, making jokes, usually about himself, the sight of him lying there so still and quiet was doubly upsetting. It seemed profoundly wrong. I thought of the angel in the picture, of being her, of furling my wings around him or lifting him effortlessly up, out and into the sky; but it was too painful to imagine, and I shut the image off like I was powering down my comm pad.

"Don't worry," I whispered into his ear, smoothing his hair around his temples. "Field Marshal Sevin will get us Home. In time for tea," I added, remembering something he had once said to me. "And I'm sorry about before, Trest. I didn't know you felt . . . I mean, it never occurred to me that . . ." I stopped, reaching for his mind with mine, but unable to sense anything. "Anyway," I concluded lamely, "I'm sorry."

I closed my eyes, inhaled the air of the passage, which had already developed something of the muggy sweetness of the cavern, and pocketed Trest's chain, which I had kept tight in my fist. The last leg of the journey would be the hardest, but then we would have access to water and the medkit Sevin had brought down for Yasmine. If

Trest was bleeding from his back, that meant the bullet had gone right through, which had to be good, right? Nothing inside to cause infection, nothing that would necessitate real surgery. Muce and I were getting pretty good at closing wounds. Keep the wounds clean, and he would be back to his garrulous self in a matter of days.

"Ready?" Sevin asked.

I got to my feet.

"Okay, Trest," I said, trying to sound upbeat. "One last hike. If you could help us get you up, that would be good. Trest?" I scowled at Teada, who had crouched beside him. "Out cold. Guess we'll have to do it the hard way."

Teada just shook her head.

"Come on," I said. "Give us a hand."

Teada looked up, her face startled as if someone had just slapped her.

"He's not out cold," she said, and now the tears flowed so freely down her face that she became like someone I had never seen before. "He's gone, Sola. He's dead."

W E CARRIED HIM ANYWAY. SEVIN CONSIDERED arguing, but I wasn't about to leave Trest as a meal for the great cat. It seemed to take hours, but there was no longer any great hurry. The last part of the journey, across the cavern floor and into the stone city, I carried him by myself, bearing his weight across my shoulders in some version of the fireman's lift. I stumbled three times but kept going, and Teada mopped my face with her shirt.

Bryce and Muce got to their feet as we entered the ancient library, and even Yasmine sat up, but no one said anything. They read our faces. Yasmine put her hands over her mouth and began to weep, eyes squeezed shut, her body rent with sobs that rocked her back and forth. Bryce took her hand and buried his face in her neck.

Teada helped me lay Trest on the ground, cradling his head as if afraid of hurting him. For a long moment, I just stood there looking down at him, and then I walked quickly to Yasmine's bed, picked up the gun that Bryce had laid down, and turned it on Sevin.

I pointed it into his face, and a new hush fell on the group.

"What are you doing?" Sevin asked. "It wasn't my fault he died. You know that!"

I did not move or speak.

"Sola," said Teada. "It wasn't down to him."

"No," I agreed, without lowering the gun. "Not directly."

"Not indirectly either!" said Sevin, with a little more bluster this time, as if he might just dismiss me and walk away. If he thought that—and in this place I had no way of knowing what he was thinking—he was wrong.

I stared him down, and he gave an exasperated look at the others.

"Why are we here, Sevin?" I asked.

"I don't understand the question," he said.

"Sure you do," I replied, the gun still and level in my hand. "I'll tell you what I'll do. I'll tell the story as I understand it, and you can fill in the blanks."

"I really have no idea—"

I cocked the pistol, and he fell silent, scared now, and not only because he knew I had no experience with firearms, that I might just kill him by accident.

"Okay." Sevin opened his hands in a gesture of surrender. "But if this is going to take a long time," he said, one last attempt at ridicule, "I'd rather sit—"

"Move and I'll shoot you," I said, quietly and undramatically. It was true, and he knew it. They all did.

"Okay," he said again.

"Delinquents like me, like everyone who boarded the *Phetteron* except you, Sevin, we're somehow connected to this place. We sense things. On Home, I think that ability was suppressed somehow—our meds, probably—but here, here it all comes back because we are somehow part of this place. Valkrys isn't the hostile world we were told it was, or at least it wasn't always, not to us. Maybe that's why we're troublemakers on Home, because we don't belong there and never did."

I thought of my mother and her absurd knitted hat, the way she hid her head after the cancer treatment cost her the thick hair she had worn long and flowing when I was little. I had thought it was vanity, but it was more than that. She was hiding, I was almost sure, the mark of her shame, a tattooed triangle on the back of her scalp, the mark—ironically—that bound us together.

There is much I have to tell you, said the letter. *Even things—or at least one thing—to show you that will, I hope, demonstrate the connection between us, a connection that goes beyond the parent-child bond as Home understands it.*

She was one of us, a delinquent, or—as I now saw it—gifted, and with one foot on an entirely different world that Home had been taught to forget. She was right. My mother and I were more alike than I could have ever guessed, and the fact that this had become clear only now, when she was impossibly far away, when I needed her more than I ever had before, was like a white-hot lance thrust into my heart.

"Wait," said Yasmine, "are you saying we came from here?"

"Not us," I said, not taking my eyes off Sevin, who had grown very pale. "Our great-grandparents, perhaps. I don't know, and no one remembers because Home decided to forget. When things are wiped from the only places we know to look—the fliks, the net archives, all of it—they really do vanish like they never existed. There will be hackers, like Trest, who start digging around and asking questions, but no one trusts degenerates like him, do they, Sevin?"

"I'm one, too," he said. "Remember?"

My trigger finger tightened involuntarily, and it took an effort not to shoot him where he stood.

"No," I said. "You're not. Never were. You are a military cadet, a pilot, and you were placed on this mission—yes, mission—deliberately and with one purpose in mind."

He was staring now. Bryce got to his feet and stepped a little closer.

"Is this true?" he demanded.

For a long moment, Sevin said nothing. Then he nodded.

"Yes," he said.

"Twelve years ago," I said, "a ship full of kids like us left Home bound for a reeducation facility on Jerem. I don't know what happened, how much of it was accident and how much was deliberate, but the ship landed in the wastes of Valkrys. They sent messages back, but they did not survive, though I'm still not sure what killed them. Twelve years later, the government sent another mission to the same spot, disguising it as a navigational error."

"It's not the government," said Sevin. "Not really. It's not that simple. There are corporations, companies that supply the security services and the government but have interests of their own. Maybe it amounts to the same thing. I don't really know, and I'm not paid to ask."

"Paid," I said, the word sticking in my throat. "And what are you paid to do, Sevin?"

He looked away, then turned back to me and shrugged.

"I'm good at what I do," he said. "I'm an excellent pilot, the youngest of my grade. I was ordered—paid, if you prefer—to land a damaged ship on a hostile planet, to report back what happened, and then to return with the survivors."

"If there were any," I said.

"There would be," Sevin replied. "Me and one other, though that other would not be the same person they had been when we landed."

I stared at him, processing the enormity of what he had just said.

"And the rest?" I managed.

"The rest were to be considered casualties of war."

"Expendable then," I pressed.

He looked away, his jaw set.

"Yes?" I demanded.

"Okay," he said. "If that satisfies your sense of moral outrage, sure. You were all expendable except for whoever lasted longest."

"Home looks after its own," said Yasmine. She said it wonderingly, without bitterness, as if recalling something from long ago, something she now understood differently. Teada glanced at her, then returned her gaze to Sevin.

"And you would be bringing back what, exactly?" Teada asked, her face flushed. Her shocked disbelief had quickly turned to anger. "One of those things that killed Trest?"

Sevin pursed his lips, and there was none of the defiant smugness that had been there moments before.

"Yes," he said. "The people on the *Hynderon* called it 'the Presence.' It's a bodiless alien life form that feeds on psychic energy. If I had to guess, I'd say it evolved alongside whoever used to live here as a kind of mental parasite. I didn't know that when I took the mission. Didn't even know the planet had ever been inhabited. I guess they were more like you."

"A civilization of deviants?" Teada mused. There was wonder in her voice, something wistful in spite of everything.

"But they knew how to keep some things private," added Bryce. "I think it's the stone, the rock they used to build the city. It acts as a kind of shield, so we're not always in each other's heads."

I had thought the same thing, but I said nothing and kept my eyes on Sevin.

"Most people," he said, "people like me—regulars, I mean—are immune to the parasite because we don't generate the energy it feeds on. In deviants like you—what we call LPAs, people with latent psychic abilities—your gift increases when you are co-opted by the Presence. Instead of just being vaguely aware of people's feelings, you come close to truly reading minds."

There was a light in his eyes now, not the unearthly strangeness I had seen in Dren and the others, but the light of excitement.

"Imagine if we could control it," he said, earnestly wanting us to understand. "Imagine specially trained operatives possessed by the Presence who could reach into the mind of a criminal or a terrorist and know exactly what they were planning, what they knew, when they were lying."

"So, you were looking to turn us into spies?" asked Teada.

"One of us," I said.

As the implication of what I had said landed, the others stared at him, their faces mingling shock and a dull horror. Struck by it, made hesitant, Sevin lowered his eyes.

"I didn't know what the Presence would do to the host," he said. "I didn't know that the host would try to create more of itself, or what it would do to us if we—if you—resisted."

"The host?" I said through gritted teeth. "That's all we were to you? Receptacles?"

He needed no special sense to feel my anger.

"I thought the Presence and the host would live together harmoniously," he said, trying to explain. "That's what I was told. I didn't know it would be like a life form, trying to survive and propagate, that it would kill to do so. I thought it would be like having a spirit in your head that

297

would do your bidding and tell you what other people were thinking. I thought it would be . . . I don't know. Cool."

He trailed off, shaking his head. I gazed at him, suddenly aware that for all his commanding manner, his increasingly ragged uniform, and cadet training, he was no older or wiser than any of us. In spite of everything, I felt a little sorry for him.

"It's not just you who were misled," he said. "We were all raised, taught, trained inside a lie."

"Jeopardizing all we hold dear," said Yasmine, vaguely. Bryce looked at her.

"Sola, I think you should put the gun down," he said.

I ignored him, glaring down the barrel at Sevin.

"It's still his fault we're here," I said. I didn't really believe it, but I was sad and angry. "His fault Yasmine is hurt. Herse. Trest. Hell, even Dren—"

"Dren was lost long before he came to Valkrys," said Sevin. "You know that."

I didn't say anything.

"No need to take my word for it," said Sevin, something of his defiance returning. "Ask Bryce."

This time my eye flicked to where Bryce sat.

For a moment, the ancient city was so silent you could almost hear it breathing.

"I don't know how the Presence selects which people will be its hosts," said Sevin, "but I think it was attracted to Dren from the moment we landed. I thought it was his LPA ability, but now I wonder if it wasn't also something about who he was, you know? His willingness to spy on others, to do whatever it would take to keep himself alive, even if that meant hurting or killing the rest of you. You know I'm right, Sola. You all make fun of my cadet training, but there's value in discipline and order, in putting selfish concerns aside for a common good. Dren doesn't have any of that. Doesn't believe in it. He might not have meant to, not consciously, but he invited the Presence in, promised it whatever it wanted. Including you."

"Guys," said Teada.

I stared Sevin down, daring him to move, then turned to look at her. She was watching the great door into the library. Standing there, pale and ghostly in the blue light emanating from the rock, was Carlann. She faced us in her beaded choker, standing quite still, head cocked onto her left shoulder and her eyes aglow.

CHAPTER  27

"**N**o," Yasmine gasped.

I took a hurried step toward Sevin, then turned to face the girl in the doorway. As I did, without even thinking about it, I raised the gun and leveled it at her.

Carlann just stared for a moment, expressionless, then her mouth opened, wide and slack as Dren's had been. I braced myself for the voice in my head, but it did not come.

"Can anyone hear her?" I asked. "Her voice in your head. Anyone?"

They shook their heads.

"It's the walls," said Bryce. "The stone. Maybe it does more than shield our own thoughts."

"So we're safe?" said Muce.

"They killed Trest when he resisted," I said, my eyes fixed on the girl—or whatever it was now—that had been Carlann.

"So shoot her," said Sevin.

I blinked. He sounded so sane, so rational, and a part of me thought he was right.

Kill her now, and we walk free. Kill them all. It's not like they're people anymore.

They were just aliens who meant to smother us slowly till there was nothing else and then walk around in our skins.

I tightened my grip on the pistol.

"Sola," said Bryce. He had taken a step closer. His voice was low.

I stared at the girl, feeling the chill weight of the gun, the curve of the trigger.

How much pressure, I wondered, *before it goes off?*

And then? The girl with the strange eyes dropping, crying, bleeding. I did not like Carlann. She was self-involved, whiny, and ungrateful. She would sacrifice the rest of us to save her own neck: I knew it. But the thought of her crumpled on the ground and me standing over her with the smoking pistol . . .

I relaxed my grip on the weapon and lowered my arm.

"Just as well," said Bryce at my elbow.

I half turned to give him a quizzical look.

"It's empty," he said. "There were only four shots left. The sabertoothed cat came into the city while you were away. I tried to scare it off. Don't think I hit it, but—"

"You used all the ammunition?" Sevin said, staring at him in disbelief.

"I guess."

301

"All of it?" Sevin pressed. "You shot off every round and didn't think to tell anyone?"

"I thought there would be more," said Bryce, embarrassed.

"Where?" snapped Sevin.

The motionless girl in the doorway had suddenly acquired an altogether new kind of menace.

"Okay," I said, getting a grip on myself. "They don't know the gun is empty, and so long as we are in here, they can't read our thoughts." I gave Bryce the gun. "Keep it trained on her while we figure out what to do."

"What is there to do?" asked Teada. "We're safe in here, right?"

"For now," I said. "Until they decide to come in and drag us out. So far as we know, their gun still has bullets in it."

"And we don't have much food," said Sevin. "Eventually we'll need to go out for more fruit or something."

I avoided his eyes.

"That will have to be me," he said.

"Why?" I demanded, instantly suspicious again.

"Because they aren't interested in me," Sevin replied. "The Presence can't co-opt me. It, they—whatever—barely know I'm here. They can see me, I think, and hear me, but it's vague. Your psychic abilities . . . those are what they want. And how they get in. Me, they can't touch."

Teada reached down for something beside Yasmine's bed and came up with the homemade spear. Bryce put a steadying hand on her shoulder before she could thrust the weapon at Sevin, but she broke free of him. I stepped between them.

They both looked at me in amazement.

"You'd protect him after everything he's done?" Teada gasped.

"We may need him," I said, grudgingly, "and he's done his best to keep us alive so far."

"For them!" Teada protested. "For this *Presence*, and for the people on Home who are pulling his strings and filling his bank account."

"That's not true," said Sevin. "I *was* helping them. I admit it. I was following my orders to the letter. Not anymore."

For a second Teada stared at him balefully, and I really didn't know if she would try to stab him or not. But finally she shrugged furiously and turned away.

"What are we going to do?" said Muce. "Sola?"

She gazed up at me, utterly trusting, sure that I would come up with something. I took a breath. Maybe I just didn't want to let her down. Maybe it was something about her faith in me. In any case, I nodded.

"Okay," I said. "Let me think."

"It's them," said Teada, glowering at the figure we had once called Carlann, which stood eerily silent and watchful in the doorway. From time to time, the angle of the girl's head would shift from one shoulder to the other, but otherwise she remained motionless, a broken, malevolent statue. "We blame ourselves," Teada continued, "but it's them."

In the immediate aftermath of Trest's death, Teada had seemed crushed with sadness, as if a great weight had broken the person she had been. The person who had emerged since was harder, angrier. I was relieved that I couldn't sense her feelings. I wanted to stay clearheaded.

I turned to Sevin, who had started to say something, and as my eyes left her, Teada moved, snatching up the spear and running at the doorway with a long shriek of fury and despair.

I went after her, but that momentary head start was all she needed. She raised the spear over her head, shouting curses and accusations, but Carlann did not react, standing impassive, eyes glowing, as Teada charged. For a second I almost had her, snatching at her clothes as I leapt headlong after her, but she slipped through my grasp and, a moment later, was on top of the other girl, lunging, stabbing.

Except that the spear never made contact.

At the last possible second, the thing that had been Carlann stepped back, a tiny gesture made somehow enormous by her previous stillness, and as Teada lurched into the space where she had been, Dren and the nameless girl from the *Hynderon* came from either side and seized her.

I got to my feet screaming, and Sevin came blundering over, but as Dren clamped his face to Teada's, his lips on hers—less a kiss than a terrible, vengeful devouring—the nameless girl's arm came up, gun in hand. I saw its black eye searching for me, and rolled aside looking for cover.

Teada fought back, elbows and knees jerking, looking for vulnerable spots, but Dren and Carlann had her gripped tight. They dragged her away down the elegant glass street toward the door into the cavern. The girl with the gun waited, head cocking onto the other shoulder like a clockwork toy, holding us in her blank, unearthly gaze till the others were gone, then quietly withdrawing.

"**W**E HAVE TO GO AFTER HER!" BRYCE SAID.

"And be shot down as soon as we step out there?" Sevin shot back.

"If we can hit them before they get her out of the city, they won't have time to . . . *change* her."

"Hit them?" Sevin roared back at him. "With what? Your broken arm? Your crippled girlfriend's sickbed? The empty gun or the infant Muce's sewing kit?"

"I'm not an infant," Muce snapped.

"They are strong," Sevin said, ignoring us. "They are fast. I don't know why, but they are. Single-minded. Calculated. Instinctive. They haven't had bodies to walk around in for a long time, but they know how to make them work. Maybe better than we do. They also have a pistol with actual bullets in it," he added, with a pointed look at Bryce, "and the ability to get inside your heads and paralyze you if you let your guard drop for even a second. Still think we should go after them?"

I lay on the hard, cool floor where I had sprawled to get away from the gun. My hands and knees stung, and the blood was pounding in my chest, my throat. I was sweating. I was furious. I was doing all I could to hold back a grief and hopelessness I knew would be paralyzing. But I knew he was right.

"Let's think for a moment," I said, deliberately, unnervingly calm. "What will they do? The conversion—or co-option, or whatever you want to call it—takes time, right? How long?"

Sevin shook his head.

"It took days with Dren, I think," he said. "Started almost as soon as we got here, but it was gradual."

"Yes," I agreed. "His behavior was erratic, like sometimes he was still himself, and sometimes it was the Presence inside him. But it was different with Carlann. She was still herself but knew what had happened to Dren. When she was ready—or when they decided she was ready—the change was almost instantaneous."

"So we don't know how long Teada has," said Bryce.

"She'll fight it as long as she can," I said. It was a terrible thought, and I had to push it away so that it did not overwhelm me.

"They'll need to get her out into the cavern," said Sevin, "away from these walls. Maybe they'll take her all the way back to the ship."

"If they did," I said, "do you think we could trap them in it?"

"Not on the main level with that great hole in the roof," said Sevin. "Maybe below decks in the storage area and engine room. Some of the systems are still online, and the internal bulkhead doors are designed to contain fires in an emergency. I could activate them from the flight deck."

I swallowed and looked away.

The underdeck.

"Could anyone do it, or does it have to be you?" I asked.

He bristled at the question, as if it meant I didn't trust him, but he answered it.

"I guess anyone could use my codes," he said. "But how does that help? Yes, I could seal them in if we caught them below decks, but there's no reason for them to go down there."

I closed my eyes for a moment, unwilling to say it, knowing that the plan forming in my head would inevitably lead to something terrible.

"We could give them a reason," I said.

●

Yasmine, as Sevin had bluntly reminded us, could barely move. Bryce only had one good arm, even if he could be coaxed from her side, and Muce was half Dren's body weight. So it fell to Sevin and me.

First we had to get out of the library unseen. Muce, who was determined to help, dashed around the fractured remains of the building looking for other doors into the street, but in the end she pronounced that there was no need. She had managed to climb onto an overhang of the building I had thought of as the cathedral that gave her a good vantage on the city.

"They're gone," she said.

"I don't think they like it in here," I said, slipping my arm around her. "They probably can't communicate effectively inside the city. Good job, Muce."

The little girl gave me a serious look.

"You sure I can't come with you?" she said.

"I'm sure," I said. "Keep watch for Bryce. And Yasmine."

She nodded thoughtfully.

"Don't do anything dumb," she said. "We need you back here."

I forced a smile, then turned to the others. Yasmine had lain down again, eyes half closed. Bryce was watching me, and when our eyes met he blinked and opened his mouth to speak, though the words wouldn't come. I smiled and shook my head, as if to say there was nothing to say, nothing to apologize for. I raised my hand in a kind of wave. It was as heart-breakingly inadequate a farewell as I could have imagined.

"Ready?" asked Sevin, oblivious as ever.

"Ready," I said.

We had left the empty gun with Bryce, figuring there was no point trying to use it anywhere the Presence might be able to sense our thoughts. They couldn't take over Sevin's mind, but they still might be able to read it. Even so, Sevin left the gun behind reluctantly, scowling at it. I carried the homemade spear with the knife bound to the tip. I doubted it would be that effective and still wasn't sure I could plunge it into human tissue, but I took it anyway.

We moved out into the street in a haze of nervous apprehension, but there was no sign of Carlann and the others. Now that Sevin and I were alone, I took the opportunity to settle something that had been smoldering in my head for a long time.

"So tell me about the ship that's in orbit around the planet," I said.

There, I thought. *It's out at last.*

"What ship?" said Sevin, but the hesitation in his voice, the shock spoke volumes.

"The one you've been talking to every night after the rest of us have gone to bed," I said. "The one I had to look for on the *Hynderon's* radar because the *Phetteron's* communication system is so conveniently disabled. It's just us now, Sevin. No more lies."

He stood quite still for a moment, seeming somehow smaller, and then he nodded.

"I never lied about it," he said. "I just didn't—"

"Just tell me," I said. It was too late for explanations.

"Okay," he said, taking a breath and holding my eyes for as long as he could. "My handlers knew the *Phetteron* was unlikely to be airworthy after our forced landing, so they've been shadowing us. They set off a week after we left Home, but their vessel is faster than ours and has been orbiting Valkrys ever since we got here. Yes, I've been talking to them. Those were my orders: to keep them apprised of the status of the mission."

"So all the time we've been talking about rescue," I said with a grim smile, "they were already here, waiting for word from you?"

"When I learned of the city," he said, his eyes on the ground, "when I saw exactly what the Presence did to Dren, what it made him into, I told them to abort the mission."

"You did what?" I said, aghast.

"I told them to prepare for immediate extraction of all survivors," Sevin said. "I'm going to get you all Home. I swear. All we have to do is get back to the ship and radio them, and they'll come."

I stared at him. For a long moment I said nothing, but I needed to be absolutely sure.

"You told them you'd seen the city," I said, suddenly very tired. "You told them that the Presence destroyed the people it possessed, and that the mission was blown."

"Yes," said Sevin, "and that they should fly us out of here. So?"

"Nothing," I said, shrugging my mood off like a heavy coat. "Okay. Good."

I was thankful he couldn't read my thoughts. Sevin might have meant well. Relaying what he knew to the orbiting ship might have been intended to save our lives and get us Home, but I had my doubts. It seemed more likely, since it was clear they would not get what they wanted out of this *mission*, that they would simply leave us here. Surely that made more sense than bringing us Home and having the risk of us talking about what we had seen, what they had tried to do . . .

Muce had been right. Our enemies—if that's what they were now—were nowhere to be seen. I felt a rush of tenderness for the little girl who had put such faith in me from the start. It was almost unbearable that I might never see her again. Or Yasmine. Or, I thought with a dull pang, Bryce.

Because there was no real doubt in my mind about that. I might save the others, or buy them a little more time, but I was going to my death. I just didn't see how it could be otherwise. Sevin didn't agree, but Sevin was a cadet, trained to believe—in the cells of his blood and the marrow of his bones—that his superiors knew what they were doing, that they acted for the best, that they would do all they could to save us. Sevin still thought we were going Home.

Not me.

We left the city through the majestic gateway and entered the great bowl of the cavern, scanning for signs of life and moving cautiously from rock to rock with painful slowness. We knew that if any of the aliens were watching, they would be motionless and hard to see, but we had to keep going.

"If you wanted to keep watch on the cavern but stay a safe distance from the interference created by the city," I whispered to Sevin as we crouched together behind a heavy bush on the edge of a pool, "where would you go?"

He craned his neck a fraction, raking the pale hollow all around with his eyes. When he was satisfied, he dropped down again.

"The best vantage point is where the tunnel emerges onto the slope over there."

I followed his nod.

"Where Yasmine fell," I said. "Yes. So if we head out that way, there's a good chance we'll walk right into them."

"If they want to be closer to the ship, maybe they're in the tunnel itself, nearer the surface."

"Either way, we'd better take another route out of the cavern," I mused.

"Is there one?" asked Sevin.

"There is," I said. "But you aren't going to like it."

"Why is everything with you so difficult, Sola?" He said it wearily, but there was a smile in his voice, too. For the first time, I was reminded that we were outside the city and that I was able to sense something of his feelings again. I caught my breath and gave him a look.

He was immediately defensive.

"What?" he said. "Stay out of my head, Sola, okay?"

"I'll do my best," I said hurriedly. I felt flustered and uncertain. He had bottled it up as quickly and firmly as he could, but the emotions I had felt from him contained things I had not sensed in our conversations before: curiosity, interest, affection. More than that actually, something strained and a little painful, which—if I had to name it—was yearning. I avoided his eyes.

"You were saying?" he said. "This route I'm not going to like."

"Right," I replied. "It's on the other side of the cavern. You can barely see it from here, and they probably don't know it's there at all."

"So what's wrong with it?"

"It's where the sabertooth lives," I said.

"Of course it is," said Sevin, deadpan.

CHAPTER

I T WAS IMPOSSIBLE TO KNOW FOR SURE IF WE HAD BEEN seen or, for that matter, sensed by what we were now simply calling the Presence. It would have a harder time latching onto Sevin's mind than onto mine, but what kind of range it had, we had no idea. I imagined Dren tipping his head and considering, like an animal trying to identify a scent borne on the wind, but that only reminded me of more immediate perils.

We inched around the cavern floor, loping from one patch of cover to another, then began the steep climb to the lair of the sabertooth and the passage beyond. There had been no sign of the cat on the ground below, but halfway up toward the tunnel mouth we chanced on the rotten remains of what might have been a goat, all bones and matted fur, a pair of curling horns. There was also a shoe. It was gray and modern, marked with a familiar logo, and though I would not have been able to say what Herse had been wearing the day he died, I knew without a doubt that it was his.

My stomach lurched, and I felt a tide of sadness and rage unpleasantly mixed with nausea. I turned away and, for a moment, closed my eyes. When I opened them, I saw Sevin giving the shoe a long look. I felt his unease, though he was more concerned about the creature responsible. His lack of feeling for Herse bothered me, but I supposed I couldn't blame him. Prudence and self-preservation were more important right now than mourning those we had lost.

I thought of Teada and what might be happening to her, but pushed the images away. I had to stay functional.

The scent of the great cat met us as we reached the hole in the side of the basin, the tunnel mouth breathing foul air upon us with each draft from the surface. I readied the spear, though it felt pathetically small. Watching the ground for anything my feet might dislodge, I crept in, Sevin at my heels. He was still wearing his cadet uniform, but it was streaked with dirt and the sleeves were torn. One of the brass pips from the collar was missing. The stink of his fear came with us like a cloud, and I wondered for a wild and horrified moment if the sabertooth had any of the mind-sensing abilities possessed by the other residents of this world.

The tunnel reached back and up into the rock in a long, straight-edged shaft, which might have once been carved by hand. A few yards inside, it opened up to the right to the den that was the source of the smell. I kept very still, straining to hear, but there was nothing. No breathing or snoring. The beast was either not there at all, or it had gathered itself in silence to spring. I looked at Sevin, then flattened myself against the wall and, with infinite care, leaned fractionally around the corner.

There was the rounded alcove. It was dark inside, the gray rock lacking the undulating glow of the glassy blue stone, but I was as sure as I could be that there was nothing living within.

I released the breath I had not realized I was holding and turned to Sevin. He was watching me anxiously from where the tunnel opened up into the great cavern. And standing silently behind him, so massive that it filled the passage entirely, was the sabertooth.

Sevin saw it in my face, and bolted past me. How we had not seen the great cat in the cavern, how it had followed us quietly up to its very home, I had no idea, but I swung the spear up and around, pointing it into the beast's face with both hands.

Its mouth opened, the massive sweep of those yellowing fangs fully exposed, and it growled, a low, rolling, primeval sound. I took a step backwards, bumping into Sevin so that he did the same.

I flourished the spear and gave an angry shout, hoping that the creature would hear more menace than terror.

"Go!" I roared over my shoulder. "Get to the ship."

I jabbed with the spear, and the sabertooth feinted with its head, jaws lolling. It swatted at me with one massive paw, claws extended, and I dodged, stepping back, and lunged again with the spear. It shrank back, then surged forward, mouth gaping. I took another step backwards, but thrust the spear forward again, and this time it connected. The knifepoint caught the great cat's cheek, opening a deep gash that sent it flinching away, hissing and spitting.

Then it leapt forward, snapping at my arm. I flung myself aside, landing heavily against the stone wall. Dazed, I dropped the spear, which rolled away. The sabertooth pounced, slamming one paw into my stomach so hard that the air was driven right out of me and the world got a little darker. I was pinned, and Sevin was gone.

The monstrous creature loomed over me, mouth open, its fetid breath shocking me into a heightened sense of what was happening. I recoiled and flailed, jabbing my left fist at the beast's heavily furred throat as my right hand reached blindly for the fallen spear. The cat bared its teeth and snarled into my face, looking for the kill spot, and in that instant my right hand found the slim, round shaft of the spear. It rolled from my grasp, but I stretched hard enough that something in my shoulder popped, and got it.

I stabbed sideways, catching the sabertooth in its shoulder. It wasn't a mortal strike, but the cat was surprised and leapt back. I rolled to my feet and lunged again, this time finding the animal's forepaw as it reached for me. This time its wince of pain was touched with something other than fury. It was momentarily scared.

I took the opportunity to take two more steps back, and the cat hesitated before coming after me. I rounded the corner, turned, and ran headlong up the passage, almost careening into Sevin's back. I urged him on, faster, checking behind me whenever I dared, dreading the snap of that awful maw around the back of my neck.

But it did not come.

I doubted we had scared it off, but perhaps we'd made it think twice about pursuing a meal it hadn't been desperate for to begin with. In any case, we made it to the pale light of the surface and collapsed into a snow bank, breathing heavily, eyes on the entrance to the passage in case the cat followed us.

It was snowing again, a great, lashing storm that blew the flakes in horizontal swirls and reduced visibility to a few yards.

"You think you can find the ship in this?" Sevin shouted over the wind.

I nodded, knowing he wouldn't sense my doubt.

"Make it fast," he added. "The closer we get, the more likely they are to sense us. I don't want to be stuck out here when they do."

Under different circumstances, the unhelpful remark would have irritated me, but I had other things on my mind.

Twenty minutes later, the *Phetteron* loomed out of the white haze. One moment we were trekking, heads down, into the blizzard, and the next it was just there, dead ahead, jutting out of the snowdrifts as if frozen in the act of burrowing out of the ground. The main hatch was open, and the stairs that folded down with the door were thick with snow. Sevin gave me a look, then moved closer. I followed, cautiously, but there were no footprints to be seen.

We entered in total silence, the snow muting any noise our shoes might have made on the stairs, then stood in the cold body of the ship, tasting its metallic air and listening.

Nothing.

Outside, the wind howled, and the plastic panel we had lashed in place so very long ago flapped and rippled down at the tail of the ship, but there was no sign of life on board. Sevin tried the doors to the flight deck, and they opened as before—sticking and groaning—but revealing no one in the cabin. When we were satisfied on that score, we checked the stasis pods. All empty. Herse's pod was marked by grimy bare footprints. The girl from the *Hynderon* must have been using it from the day he was killed. That was why we hadn't been able to find her.

"We need to check the underdeck," said Sevin.

I nodded but said nothing. At least there were two of us, though now I knew there really was something to be afraid of beyond the darkness and the eerie, echoing groans of the vessel.

We descended together, picking our way by flashlight to the storage lockers where I had seen the girl. I shuddered at the thought.

"You okay?" Sevin whispered.

"Yes. But this is futile. If they are here, they are here. Let's go back up. At least we can see what we're doing there."

He didn't argue, and for once I sensed that he was as uncomfortable as I was down here.

We didn't speak again till we were up among the stasis pods.

"Where are the bulkhead doors?" I asked.

"Underdeck Two," he said, not happy about it.

"The Well," I confirmed, my voice flat with dread and resignation. "Tell me about them."

"There are two doors," he said. "When you go down into the Well and reach the foot of the ladder, you turn right into the stern, left into the bow."

"That's the front, right?"

"Right. The front and back sections of the Well can be sealed off to isolate an engine fire from the rest of the ship."

"Okay," I said, conscious that we were still speaking in hushed voices. "Let's just call the back 'green' and the front 'blue.' When I call the color, you shut the bulkhead doors to that section. Okay?"

"Sure," he said, "but how do we get all three of the Presences to go down there of their own free will?"

"They will."

"Why?"

"Because," I said. "Something they want will be there. Something they will sense from far away."

I thought of the girl standing out in the storm that first night. She—or some other form of the Presence—had already reached out to Dren with her mind, the golden light I had seen moving around the ship. He had resisted for a while, but eventually he had let her in. He knew what would happen, but he had chosen to do it anyway.

"Wait," said Sevin, piecing together what I had said. "You? You're going to be bait?"

"I think I became bait the moment I left the city," I said. "You should lock yourself onto the flight deck."

"The moment I do that, I'll get a message from the commander of the orbiting ship," said Sevin. "He'll want to know what's happening and when we'll be ready for extraction. I'll tell them to land so we can get Yasmine and the others, but they know about the Presence. They won't come down till they're sure we have Dren, Carlann, and the girl contained."

"Don't tell them about Yasmine," I said. "Tell them everyone is aboard and ready to go."

"Why?"

"Sevin," I said, standing very close to him. "You have to trust me on this. It's very important. For once, please forget you are a cadet. Forget your orders. I'm sure of this, okay? It's not just a hunch. You must not tell them that anyone still alive is not aboard. Do you understand?"

"Not really."

"Will you do it anyway?"

He looked at me for a long time, and I felt it again, those strange unruly feelings he did not know what to do with and could not quite suppress.

"Yes," he said.

"Thank you. Now seal yourself into the flight deck and wait. You can monitor communications all over the ship from there?"

"There are mikes and speakers in each quadrant of the craft," he said. "Just no working lights."

"Okay. Turn everything on and listen."

●

WHEN SEVIN HAD CLOSED THE DOORS BEHIND HIM, I pulled the outer hatch closed and took a moment to be alone in the ship one last time. I closed my eyes, listening to the sound of the weather and the occasional creak of the hull, and I was almost able to imagine that I had just woken—a little prematurely, thanks to my old instincts—on a ship bound for a tedious spell on a little moon called Jerem. I was a minor deviant who would sit through some lectures, watch a few fliks, and participate in a handful of stupid tests, games, and interviews before being packed back onto the same ship bound for Home. There, my parents—my sad, tired, hopeful parents—would be waiting. Then I would sit down with a mother who loved me and we would talk, really talk, for the first time in many years.

The ship's intercom crackled and sputtered into life.

"You ready, Sola?" said Sevin. "They are coming."

I didn't need them to see me, so I began to move before I heard the outer door start to open. They would sense my location wherever I was, and my real job—far more difficult than merely being found in the right place—would be concealing my intentions even from my own conscious mind.

I checked the knife I had unbound from the spear and replaced in my belt—a last and desperate resort if things got bad. I thought they probably would, but I felt not so much fear as resignation. One way or another, it would end today, and I was ready for that.

I took the front stairs down, nerves making my feet unreliable on the metal steps, clicking on the flashlight and swallowing back my apprehension. There was nothing in the darkness so scary as what was about to follow me down. Still, I forced myself to slow up, then moved through the tight gangway between the storage lockers and equipment racks.

I had only been down here twice, but the details of the layout had stayed with me, and I found my way to the central junction of passageways without a false turn. I could hear movement on the deck above me, then the distinctive ringing of footsteps on the stairs. They were coming.

I turned and stepped towards the end of the passage, the only place on the ship I had never been before, but stopped in my tracks. For a moment I thought the flashlight had gone out, but then I realized that, beyond a single rail, there was nothing ahead for it to illuminate. This was the edge of the Well, a cavernous, sucking void in the black heart of the ship. I swept the flashlight along the rail till I found the top of the ladder, then tucked it into my waistband and turned my back on the emptiness below. Gripping the rail with both hands, I lowered myself onto the first rung, then the second, and on, descending into blackness.

I could see nothing, hear nothing beyond my own echoing movements and the hammering of my heart. The rungs felt flaky and rusted under my palms, and I had no idea how deep I had to go to reach the bottom, but I kept moving, steadily, carefully.

At last I felt something like solid ground, turned till my back was against the ladder, then drew the flashlight from my belt and turned it on.

I had descended perhaps twenty feet and was at the lowest point in the ship. The floor bowed, and every few feet were great welded joints reinforced by massive bolts. The floor was scattered with discarded parts and lengths of steel cable. To my right was one great doorway, to my left another. The bulkheads.

"In position," I said into the silence.

Sevin said nothing, but I knew why. They were already in the underdeck and would hear any message he gave me. I kept still and listened. There was movement close by and above. Someone had started working their way down the ladder.

I turned left into the bow and played my flashlight over the room. The massive and incomprehensible engine dominated it, but there was no way out the other side. If I was trapped with anyone in here, I would have to find a way past them to escape.

I concentrated on the engine, trying to pretend to myself that I was looking to fix it, to get the *Phetteron* airworthy again. I knew nothing of engines, but I reached in, touched the cold steel and fiddled until I found pieces that moved. One was stiff, a wheel whose axle was twisted out of alignment so that it couldn't turn. I focused on it, flexing my arms as I tried to force it into motion. It gave a little, then stopped, so I pushed harder, and my mind was full of the effort of the thing, so that I barely noticed the Presence till I felt its voice in my mind.

Come with us, it said.

It was the girl's voice. She had entered the engine room with Carlann behind her. I turned my light upon them. Their appearance was familiar to me now, the strange eyes, the slack, open mouths, the heads cocked to the side, but up close like this, the disjunction between their soulless manner and their children's bodies was especially awful.

"Why should I come with you?" I said, trying to drown out the true thought in my head.

Where is Dren? Why isn't he with them?

And then I heard him standing in the central well beyond them, not in the rear section where I could trap him, but waiting in the middle. Even if I could get past the two girls, he would be waiting for me.

"We can make the engine work again," I said to the girl. "See? We can get it running and we can leave this place."

They came a little closer, and in that moment I made my move, killing the flashlight beam, sidestepping them both, and breaking for the door. I shouted "Green!" before I was fully out, and the door scissored shut with a great screeching clank.

I barely had the flashlight back on, had just made sure that the girls—or what had been the girls—were still in the engine room, when Dren caught me by the shoulders.

I seized the boy with the blond hair and dragged him through the doorway into the stern. He came with me, clumsily off balance, surprised by my not trying to get away from him.

I tried to remember him as he had been but could not.

"Dren," I said, urgent with fear. "Are you still in there somewhere? You don't have to do this."

He tipped his head onto the other shoulder but showed no other response. In one hand, he held a long and ragged splinter of the blue, glass-like rock. It came to a point like a needle, and its edges sparkled. His mouth was already open, and his voice sounded in my mind.

Come with us, Sola. We can save you.

"Like you saved Carlann?" I demanded. "Where is she now? Where are you, Dren?"

I am still here, said the voice.

A lie, or almost. But for a moment he let me go, and I took a hurried step away. He stood between me and the bulkhead doors, so there was nowhere to run, but it felt better to be out from under his hands.

"Let me see him," I said. "Show me Dren, and I'll come with you."

There was a strange stillness. I felt the girls beyond the green bulkhead door, their consciousnesses reaching through the steel for mine. And then he was there in my mind, Dren, a shrunken, seething ball of jealousy and hatred. My head was full of the squirming rage of him, like hot black smoke that could not escape, could only writhe like snakes biting themselves in their fury and bitterness.

The body lunged at me, one hand clawing for my throat, the other raising the spike of blue rock in case I resisted.

I reached for his weapon hand—ignoring the one that had closed about my windpipe—dropped the flashlight, and used my free hand to pluck the knife from my belt. His glowing, empty eyes bored into me, but I felt the torrid and murderous storm still churning in Dren's mind. He was wrestling as much with the Presence as he was with me. The Presence wanted me alive—my body at least. Dren wanted me dead.

The flashlight was on the ground and pointing at the machinery, which meant I was fighting a shadow. I struggled to keep the blue spike over my head, but he was too strong for me, and even in the low light I could see its lethal, splintered tip descending steadily toward my face.

He did not sense the knife till I had swept it up, and his attempt to block it was clumsy. He knocked it from my hand, but not till it had opened a long slash along his forearm. I heard the knife fall, skittering and clanging on the metal hull, out of reach.

Dren considered the wound on his arm, and though it didn't seem possible, his rage was building, darkening like a thundercloud.

I kicked at his weapon hand, stepped past him, and turned, elbowing him hard in the face. I felt his nose break, and blood spattered my shirt. I seized his wrist just below where he was holding his stone dagger and twisted till he released it, then kicked again, hard and high this time. My foot made contact with his chest, and he stumbled back against the machinery. I snatched up the spike, and in an instant I was halfway to the bulkhead door.

"Blue!" I screamed into the empty ship, praying Sevin was listening and ready. "Do it now!"

I had to hurl myself through before the doors could shear me in two. I did not have time to stoop for the flashlight, and the closing of the bulkhead plunged me into total blackness.

I felt the rage of those trapped in the Well drowning out their savage hunger. I turned, groping till I found the ladder, then began the long, slow climb up.

Even at the top, I could make out nothing in the darkness, and now I was acting on memory alone. Hands outstretched, I inched my way along the first corridor, then made a left and reached what I took to be the storage lockers where we had all stowed our personal effects so very long ago. It was hard to judge distance, but I traced the doglegged passage, made two turns, and then caught the graying of the blackness that meant I had reached the rear stairs. I clambered up, laughing with relief, and ran down the gangway to the flight deck doors.

"Sevin!" I shouted. "Let me in. We have them."

Sola.

I knew the voice before I turned round, before I realized that the sound was not in my ears but in my mind. Teada.

No, I thought. *Please no.*

I revolved very slowly. She had been, I guessed, in the front stairwell, though whether she had hung back on purpose or by accident I couldn't say. In either case, she had still been on the stairs when the bulkhead doors had closed. She looked as I had feared she would: both like herself and not.

You forgot about me, said the voice.

328

"I'm so sorry, Teada," I said. "I really am."

The mechanism of the door onto the flight deck disengaged with a hollow thunk.

"Wait!" I shouted at Sevin. "Don't open it yet."

You don't trust me, said the voice in my head. Teada's voice. She took a step closer. Her skin, usually a warm, tan color, had an icy pallor almost as unsettling as the slack mouth and smoldering eyes.

"I did trust you," I said. "But it's not really you anymore, is it, Teada?"

Of course it's still me, she answered in my mind. *I remember everything we went through together. The walking, the conversation, the moment I let you into my head—*

"You remember," I cut in, keen to head off the memory, "because you—whatever you are—have access to the mind of the girl who was once my friend. But you have stifled her, killed her or are in the process of killing her, so if you think that pretending to be her will make me trust you, you are making a serious mistake."

For a moment there was silence, on the ship and in my head, and then I felt a surge of hunger and rage so powerful that it was like being back in the tunnel with the sabertooth. In the same instant, she snatched for my throat and pinned me against the flight deck door. My head clanged against it as she drove her face towards mine.

Bits of memories of our time together swum into view, and for all the violence of the moment, there was a beguiling intimacy that was strangely seductive. For a moment I considered—really considered—giving in, letting go of my strange, misfit self and sliding into whatever kind of survival I would have as the Presence.

But only for a moment.

I felt sorry for Teada even as her body forced itself upon me, but no amount of pity would make me give in. I fought her with my mind and with my body, trying to raise the crystalline spike I had taken from Dren, but she was too quick for me. She seized my wrist with one hand and my throat with the other.

I was already tired, and Teada, driven by the thing inside her, was more powerful than I could ever have imagined. I realized with sudden and absolute certainty that I could not beat her. I was going to die.

Or worse.

Yes, said the voice in my head. *You cannot resist us.*

And because I knew it was true, I did the only thing I could think of. My mind focused, tightened like I was trying to get a grip on something slippery, and I spoke her name in my mind.

Teada, I thought. *If you are still in there. Stop.*

At first it seemed to make no difference, but then something of the fight went out of her. The pressure on my throat lessened, and a change came over the girl's distorted features. The light in her eyes stalled, and the gaping mouth flexed slightly. Words came, slurred and clumsy so that I could not make them out, but they came not in my mind but in my ears. She was trying to speak.

I saw her tongue move and the mouth close a little. The lips flexed, and then she tried again.

"Sola?" she said. "I can't see you. Are you there?"

"Yes," I said. "It's me."

"I can't see you," she said again, and her voice sounded small and far away. "They are too strong for me. They say I have to tell you something."

She sounded so lost, so plaintive, so much younger than the girl I had known, and I felt my chest constrict with sorrow.

"What is it?" I asked.

We were still locked together, but she was quite still, and when I started to work my fingers under her grip around my neck, it slackened and released me. I twisted my other hand and that too—complete with the deadly splinter of blue rock in it—came free. I lowered it slowly.

"I have to tell you . . ." Teada began, but her voice faltered and trailed off. "I have to tell you," she began again, and this time she seemed to swell with conviction. The golden glow in her eyes died entirely, the head that had been cocked on one side straightened, and she was, for a moment, the Teada I had known.

"Run!" she said.

Then they were back. The effort to keep them at bay gave out, and they seized her once more, body and mind. And as they took her, they turned every ounce of her strength on me.

The grip on my throat tightened like a steel talon, threatening not just to stifle my breath but to break my neck.

Live with me, said the thing inside Teada. *Feed my hunger.*

I angled the blue spike between us, but the Presence sensed the thought before I could act, and Teada's other hand snatched and held on, squeezing so tight that I thought my wrist would snap.

"No."

It was a small voice, and for a moment I thought it was mine. But then I saw the fractional movement of her mouth and realized that Teada was still in there, still fighting. I felt her final surge of energy concentrated on the hand locked hard around my wrist. The force pushing my weapon hand back suddenly reversed, snapping it forward and up.

I could not have stopped it.

I felt the tip of the stone spike go in beneath the spot where the left side of her ribcage joined the sternum. It slid in easily, the dagger-like point spearing through muscle and lung before I could pull it back.

I felt the Presence's astonishment, its confusion. The hand at my throat released me as the link between us snapped, and I saw her face as she stared at the spike in her chest. I felt her shock, but the face was no longer capable of expressing such things. Teada, it seemed, was gone, lost in that final act of defiance.

I clapped a hand over my mouth, horrified at what I had done. Horrified, and relieved.

"Teada!" I gasped. "I'm so sorry. I . . ."

But I could think of nothing to say. I embraced her then, holding her tightly to my heart as if to stifle my own sobs. I clung to her until I felt her weight increase as her legs gave way, and then, reluctantly and with a welling sense of loss, I let her go.

CHAPTER 30

TEADA STAGGERED BACK, TURNING SLIGHTLY AS SHE crumpled, so that when the flight deck doors opened, Sevin saw her lying there, the blue spike still where I had put it, midway up her chest and angled into her heart and lungs.

He stared for a moment, horrified, then stepped aside as I pushed past him.

He closed the doors behind us and locked them.

"Is she dead?" he asked.

I shook my head.

"Not quite," I said. "If she were human, she would be, but the Presence seems to sustain them somehow. She will die, but I have no idea how long it will take or how much danger we are still in. They can exist outside a host body. Can communicate. I don't think they can get into our heads against our will in this form, but I really don't know."

I was talking as if I had not known her, as if the situation were merely a conundrum to be solved. The horror of what I had done was locked beyond the steel doors of the flight deck. I would keep it there. For now.

"You okay?" asked Sevin.

I nearly laughed. Of course not. I would never be okay again.

"Yes," I said.

"Good."

He indicated the copilot's seat, but before sitting down, he removed his cadet's jacket and hung it on the door handle. He did it slowly, thoughtfully, his eyes lingering on it, and I felt a confused rush of feeling, memories, and regret. He was making some kind of decision, though I could make little sense of it.

"Strap yourself in," he said.

"Why?"

"Just do it," he said.

I was, for once, too weary to argue. I had done my part. This next bit was his. I buckled the harness over my shoulders and across my lap as he flicked switches and brought the controls to life. He put on a headset and handed another to me, saying, "Keep the mike turned off. I don't want them to know you are up front with me."

I wanted to ask why, but he held up a warning finger and tapped a button.

"This is the *Phetteron* calling Home vessel *Dareth-Spur*," he said. "Come in."

The hesitation was momentary.

"Reading you, *Phetteron*," came a man's voice through the headset. "This is the *Dareth-Spur*. What is your status?"

"Ready for extraction, sir," said Sevin. He was staring straight ahead, eyes half closed with concentration.

"Can you confirm that all transportees are aboard?" said the man's voice.

Sevin took a breath, but when I looked at him, he raised the same warning finger. I kept silent, but I felt his doubt and anxiety.

"Yes, sir," said Sevin. And then he checked them off one by one. "Myself, and the deviants Sola, Dren, Carlann, Teada, Trest, Bryce, Yasmine, Muce." Each name was like the chiming of a distant bell. "Herse, as I told you, was lost, but his place has been taken by the sole survivor of the *Hynderon*."

●

"AND ALL ARE ABOARD THE *PHETTERON* AS WE SPEAK?"

Another fractional hesitation, then, "Yes, sir, they are."

I stared at him, but he kept his eyes forward.

"Very good, cadet," said the man. "Hold your position. Keep all doors sealed and await further orders."

"Are you still in orbit?"

"Broke atmo half an hour ago," said the voice in the headset. "Not easy navigating in this weather, but we'll be right there. Ninety seconds, tops. And cadet?"

"Sir?"

"Well done."

Sevin deflated a little. In spite of the praise, I felt a spike of emotion as pure as anything I had ever felt from him, and as simple. He was sad. Nothing more.

I reached across and took his hand, not wanting to say anything in case it was overheard on the comm system, and he gave me a fleeting look before reaching into his pocket and taking out two protein bars. He tucked them into a pocket of my jacket.

I gave him a quizzical frown, and he just smiled sadly, and then, hurriedly, he turned and kissed me softly on the cheek.

I opened my mouth to say something, then realized that as he had leaned across to kiss me, he had also dropped his hand to the side of my chair and shifted a lever. I was about to ask what he was doing when he reached for a button on the console. He slammed it with his palm, and the world exploded.

Or that was how it felt. There was a bang, a burst of smoke, and I was hurtling up and out through a blown hatch in the roof, shooting high into the storm. For a moment all was simply white and cold and swirling, and there was pain in my head, bright as the noise and light that overcame me. I was rocketing up into the freezing, airless sky. I gasped for breath but nothing came, and I felt the terror of falling and death.

And then the ejector seat reached its zenith, and I felt the pop behind me as the chute deployed. The seat I was strapped in turned slowly in the chill air, and for a moment I was plummeting face-first toward the ground, my eyes running and sightless. There were two, maybe three terrifying seconds of free fall through the snow, and then the chute caught and I swung beneath it.

As my momentum stalled and I seemed to just hang in the air, I became aware of two things. First I could see, dimly through the squall of white flakes, a great ship hovering directly ahead. The *Dareth-Spur*. It was long and sleek and menacing, and its downturned jets blew the snow in torrid, swirling wells. It was moving slowly through the air like some ancient ocean predator, swimming to where the crippled *Phetteron* lay half buried on the planet below.

The other thing was that I could still hear the chatter through the headset.

"Cadet Sevin," said the man's voice. "We're detecting deployment of the copilot's emergency extrication system. Please confirm."

"Yes, sir, sorry sir," said Sevin's voice, far away now. "That was my mistake, sir. Accidentally hit a button. Nerves, I guess. I apologize."

"The ejector seat was unoccupied?"

"Yes, sir. Certainly."

"And everyone is still aboard?"

"Absolutely."

"I'm going to need you to sit tight for one more moment," said the voice. Then, the volume slightly lower, he added, "We got a visual on that ejector seat?"

Another voice joined the conversation.

"Negative. Visibility is next to nothing. We're flying on instruments as it is."

"Understood," said the commander's voice. "We'll do a sweep when we're done here."

It was surreal. I shifted and swung in the wind, but my descent was strangely slow, so that I felt like the angel in the antique painting, high in the vaulted ceiling of a great cathedral, looking down on its people below. I was still suspended up there, riding the snow clouds like they were wings, when the *Dareth-Spur* opened fire.

It came as a single burst from what I took to be a pair of laser cannons in the ship's nose. Noiseless pulses of golden light emerged and slammed into the *Phetteron* below.

I cried out as the shots landed and our little broken ship exploded into a million fragments, and again as I felt the silence. Something snapped off, and I knew they were gone.

I drifted down, past the *Dareth-Spur*, picking up speed. Soon the storm smashed me into the snow, dragging me along the drifts and banks, till—weeping—I was able to free myself from the harness and slip out. The chute dragged the seat further, and I watched it blow away like angel wings, till it was lost in the storm.

The *Dareth-Spur* pivoted in the air, hovering, searching, but I buried my face in the snow and lay there, waiting to be covered by the freezing, white crystals of Valkrys's winter.

•

I don't know how long I was there. Hours, I think. The landing had been muffled by the snow, but I felt strangely broken. Gripped by a physical and emotional exhaustion I had never felt before, I slipped for a while into a deep sleep. I dreamed of Home, but a Home where I sat with Bryce and Yasmine and Trest, who wore the fashionable ear chain I now had in my pocket. I chatted with a version of Dren I had never really known, a Dren who was funny and clever. And Sevin, of course. I dreamed of him too, and when I woke I cried again for all that had happened. All that had been lost.

There was no sign of the *Dareth-Spur* and only a blackened crater scattered with debris where the *Phetteron* had been. I did not inspect it closely. There would be other days for that.

Weeks, even. Years, if we could survive them.

Because I knew for sure now what I had only suspected before. There would be no rescue from Home. Indeed, if anyone from the planet on which we had grown up guessed that we were still alive, they would come for us and kill us. That seemed clear. We had become . . . what? A danger? A nuisance? An embarrassment? All of those, I think, and something simpler: we were a mark of Home's failure, something they did not want to examine or admit. Ever.

I found my way back to the cavern and the city within it. Muce, Bryce, and Yasmine were exactly where I had left them, all watching and waiting anxiously. They cheered my return but read what had happened in my face. I said very little. Just enough that they knew what had happened, what Sevin had done to save us. I ate and drank and slept, glad that no one could hear the screaming and crying in my head, relishing the silence. The following day was no easier, nor was the one after that, but on the third I felt a little less dead inside.

We held a kind of service, like the one Sevin arranged for Herse. We made a fire, laid flowers from the cavern, and talked, not just about the people who had died, but also about those we had left behind, our families who thought us dead and whom we would never see again. It was hard, and I am still not sure if it helped. From time to time, I thought of Sevin talking over the headset to the commander of the *Dareth-Spur*, reciting the names of everyone on board, living, dead, or in the co-opted limbo of the Presence. It had struck me as odd at the time, unnecessary, but that was because I did not then know that he was saying goodbye, that—in what he knew were his final moments—he was honoring them. Every night since, just before I go to sleep, I repeat the list. It's not so much a prayer as an act of remembering. I don't really understand why I do it, but I think it is important.

It has been almost two weeks now since the *Phetteron* burned, and life, such as it is, has settled into a kind of rhythm. Yasmine is up and walking, albeit slowly, her wounds having healed remarkably well. Bryce stays close to her. He still can't use his right arm, but that too seems to be mending. Muce is content. Sometimes she cries at night, but her memories of Home and what happened here seem to be fading fast: a survival mechanism, no doubt. She has stopped checking her comm pad for signs of a signal. We all have. Such things are in the past, though—as Sevin once remarked—the past casts long shadows. I'm not sure when we will emerge from ours.

As for me, I keep to myself. Sometimes I roam the remains of the city, relishing its grace and beauty, and when I return to the surface I watch the skies, wary of anything that might come looking to take us back. I listen to the singing of the great blue columns, and it seems now that they are lamenting all our losses, their voices drifting through the great icy cathedrals of Valkrys like smoke. Perhaps they always were. One day, with luck, I may use the remains of those old books and fragments of monumental buildings to gain a sense of the people who once lived here, learning in the process how like me they might have been, and what happened to them. Till then, I walk. I hunt for food. I stay alive for the others—a wingless angel watching over them—and for myself, which, for the moment, seems just about good enough. In time, I plan to rebuild parts of the city structures that have collapsed. I'm not sure how we'll do it, but I'd like to try. It is, after all, home.

THE END